Mayhem on the Marzipan Express

Other Books by

REBECCA CONNOLLY

A Brilliant Night of Stars and Ice

Hidden Yellow Stars

Under the Cover of Mercy

A Carol for Mrs. Dickens

CLAIRE WALKER MYSTERIES

The Crime Brûlée Bake Off

A CLAIRE WALKER MYSTERY

MAYHEM ON THE MARZIPAN EXPRESS

REBECCA CONNOLLY

SHADOW MOUNTAIN PUBLISHING

Visit us at ShadowMountain.com

Library of Congress Cataloging-in-Publication Data

Names: Connolly, Rebecca, author. | Connolly, Rebecca. Claire Walker mystery.

Title: Mayhem on the Marzipan Express / Rebecca Connolly.

Description: Salt Lake City : Shadow Mountain, [2025] | Series: A Claire Walker mystery | Includes bibliographical references. | Summary: "A romantic getaway through the Scottish Highlands turns deadly when a passenger on the train is murdered—and a famous chef is the prime suspect. Claire Walker and her boyfriend Jonny are on the case again."—Provided by publisher.

Identifiers: LCCN 2025022229 (print) | LCCN 2025022230 (ebook) | ISBN 9781639935000 (trade paperback) | ISBN 9781649334732 (ebook)

Subjects: LCSH: Celebrity chefs—Fiction. | Railroad travel—Fiction. | Highlands (Scotland), setting. | BISAC: FICTION / Mystery & Detective / Women Sleuths | FICTION / Mystery & Detective / Amateur Sleuth | LCGFT: Detective and mystery fiction.

Classification: LCC PS3603.054728 M39 2025 (print) | LCC PS3603.054728 (ebook) | DDC 813/.6—dc23/eng/20250519

LC record available at https://lccn.loc.gov/2025022229

LC ebook record available at https://lccn.loc.gov/2025022230

Printed in the United States of America
Publishers Printing

10 9 8 7 6 5 4 3 2 1

To Julia Child, a pioneer of baking
and a champion of all things buttery.
Also a ridiculously amazing woman with
super secrets that are epic and which make her
pretty much the most awesome person ever,
but the butter and fats thing is really a plus
in my book. "Be fearless and have fun!"

And to David Tennant, who is the only
person who could ever be Alan Gables
in my head or in any adaptation.
You hear that, executives?
ONLY DAVID TENNANT.
David, are you listening?
DAVID! PLEASE DO THIS. DAVID!

CHAPTER 1

Scotland. The bold. The brave. The beautiful. Fresh air. Rolling brogues. Wild landscapes. Dashing Highlanders.

Tartan.

Lots and lots of tartan.

Like, crepes alive, all the tartan.

Claire Walker would have included kilts before she'd visited Scotland for the first time, but the truth was that kilts weren't as prevalent as she'd imagined they'd be. There were some, of course, but not nearly as many as she'd predicted.

Tartan, on the other hand, was everywhere. Coats, trousers, dresses, socks, shirts, curtains, hats—all available in tartan. She'd even seen a horse-drawn carriage yesterday, where both the horse and the carriage had been wreathed in tartan. And she herself was wearing a tartan scarf as well as tartan gloves.

Even the tops of some pies were decorated with tartan.

She would know. She'd seen them. And eaten them.

And tried to recreate them.

And, if the paper napkins she had seen earlier on the trolleys of the steam train on which she was currently baking were any indication, tartan was going to take over the food of this crazy venture as well.

What was Scotland without tartan, after all?

Which was why she was currently rolling out and cutting shortbread in the kitchen on the Marzipan Steam Express—formerly and usually known as the Mallaig Steam Express—alongside her mentor and former *Britain's Battle of the Bakers* judge, Alan Gables. The same man who had set this train venture in motion and could hold her career in the palm of his tartan-loving hands.

Back in the day, Alan had gotten his big break on a long-canceled show called *UK Bakes*, cementing his place in baking history by creating a model of Edinburgh Castle entirely out of marzipan and placing that model atop his traditional Scottish Christmas cake. He had been unofficially dubbed "The Marzipan King" ever since, so the organizers of this trip had temporarily renamed the train "The Marzipan Steam Express" in his honor.

Cute, right?

Fans of *Britain's Battle of the Bakers* had been given the opportunity to either pay an almost obscene amount for a guaranteed seat or enter a ticket lottery for a much more reasonable fee. All for the chance to ride on this train where Alan Gables would be baking and serving food to the passengers, mingling with them at times, and escorting them all to their final destination of Mallaig, where a ceremony honoring Alan's achievements would be held and a brass relief plaque would be hung on the wall of the bakery where he had spent summers as an apprentice.

Roughly sixty passengers had signed up for the exclusive event, and last week, Alan had called Claire to ask for her help with the food and to take part in an interview with a journalist who'd been hired to cover the story. Claire and her boyfriend,

Jonny Ainsley, Viscount Colburn, wouldn't have to pay a thing. He'd pitched it as a chance for the new couple to enjoy a getaway, as Mallaig was a gorgeous coastal town and had ferries to the Isle of Skye, which, according to Alan, Claire simply "had to see." And it only required her to bake on the train.

And have a chat with a journalist, but talking was easy enough for Claire.

As she removed another tray of shortbread from the ovens, Claire glanced over at her mentor, who was laying strips of rhubarb in a peculiar fashion on a counter. "What in the world are you making over there, Alan?"

He glanced up at her and grinned, which was a bizarre sight. Not in general, but in the kitchen. Alan's smiles were the coveted prize of every episode of *BBB*, simply because he only did so when something was extraordinary.

Never, in the history of the show, had he *grinned* on camera.

Then again, he was grinning over something he was making, not what someone else had made.

That was very Alan Gables of him.

"Tartan tarte tatin," he chirped in between syllables of rolling brogue.

Claire blinked at him. "Come again?"

He snorted a laugh and waved her over. "Get the next pan in and come see."

Curious and amused, Claire slid the next pan of shortbread into the oven and walked over to him. The smell alone told her what he was working with, but she still looked from the thin strips to his face in surprise. "Rhubarb?"

Alan nodded, still grinning. "Correct. This is a rhubarb

and blueberry tarte tatin, and in recent years, I've made it Scottish. Because I can."

His smile of pride made Claire laugh. "Of course. Why not?" She looked at his careful work, the latticed effect resembling a tartan pattern, and shook her head. "What do you want me to do?"

"Melt the butter in the pan," Alan advised, flicking his finger in the direction of the portioned ingredient. "Then add the sugar. I've got the puff pastry chilling, so we can roll that out in a bit."

"Yes, chef," Claire quipped with a quick grin that Alan caught.

"Watch the sass, lass," he warned, laughing a little. "I might make us do a cooking show together just so the viewers can hear you call me that."

Claire scoffed as she set the stove to the appropriate temperature and brought the pan and butter over. "Everyone knows we're inferior beings compared to you, Alan. No one would be surprised."

"Only in the kitchen," Alan reminded her with a warning finger. "Not inferior anywhere else."

"Except the real world," she retorted. "You're Mr. Famous Baker, and this entire train has been rented out and renamed in your honor, plus an elite magazine is here interviewing you. This entire trip is pretty much a tribute-slash-publicity stunt for you. I wouldn't be surprised if they bring your mother out from the conductor's station to surprise you."

Alan chortled at the idea, resuming the latticing of his rhubarb. "I certainly hope that doesn't happen. Mam is in a residential home and thinks I'm her neighbor boy these days."

Claire winced in sympathy and embarrassment, lifting the

pan to allow the melting butter to coat the surface before returning it to the heat. "I'm sorry."

"Don't be. She thinks it's funny too. She's had a good life, and since I'm not her son, in her memory, I get to hear far more juicy gossip about the place than I might otherwise."

Claire winced. "Do I want to know?"

"Let's just say romance is not dead in the elderly population," Alan replied, giving her a quick wink. "Nor are shenanigans."

Claire pretended to gag, focusing on carefully adding sugar to the melted butter. "Yep, didn't want to know."

The kitchen's off-white walls made the space bright and open, giving the illusion that it was larger than it really was, and the stainless steel appliances and sinks provided an air of professionalism, matched by the sleek, steel counter space. The floors were, delightfully, an old-school black-and-white tile that reminded Claire of American diners. The classic wood cabinets and pantries were painted a soft white. Over in a corner, a pair of empty trolleys sat, waiting to be filled.

It was a perfect small kitchen, sequestered as it was in this train, far away from the eager fans and secured by guards two cars up for their privacy. Only badged passengers could enter the private compartment car and the kitchen car beyond.

Given Alan's popularity with the fans of *BBB*, it was only right that he be protected from their antics. These moments of baking serenity might be the only moments of peace they'd have until they reached Mallaig.

The door to the kitchen opened, revealing Claire's dashing, charming, people-averse-but-sweet-as-custard boyfriend, whose smile took out her left kneecap in one heartbeat.

"Looking good, *ma crème*," Jonny praised, using her

absolute favorite pet name, which decimated her right kneecap.

Who needed kneecaps anyway?

"Hi," she replied breathlessly, even though they'd seen each other less than an hour ago in their compartment. Why was the attractiveness of this man still so startling after six months together?

Unsettling inconvenience, that.

"Am I not looking good, Viscount?" Alan asked with some indignation.

Jonny shrugged his broad shoulders. "Sure, Alan. Very Scottish."

Claire rolled her eyes, scoffing as she returned her attention to her melting sugar. "What does that even mean? What kind of compliment is that?"

"Take that off the heat now," Alan interrupted firmly, gesturing for her to bring the pan his way. "Heat the oven to two hundred Celsius. And it's the best compliment, Claire. Your man is very sensible and wise beyond his years."

"Thank you." Jonny held out his fist, and Alan bumped it without looking.

Claire shook her head at them. "I'm not sure I like this thing between you."

"Tough," they said together.

She shook her head again, this time in resignation as she carefully poured the pan of hot caramel sauce over the large baking sheet Alan had placed on the counter. Then she pulled the last tray of shortbread out of the oven before switching its temperature as Alan indicated.

The previous tray of shortbread hadn't been emptied, so she transferred the biscuits onto the cooling rack while also trying to watch Alan's work on the tarte tatin. He picked up one layer of his tartan creation and laid it carefully atop the hot caramel sauce, somehow without remotely inconveniencing his fingers. He even adjusted the structure a time or two, but never once did his fingers twitch or jerk away from the pan.

The man was a baking god and immune to such mortal things as burns.

Once he was satisfied with the rhubarb's placement, and had applied the other layers, he placed the pan in the oven. "Ten minutes in there, aye? I'm going to get the puff pastry set."

"Okay," Claire murmured as she stepped closer to the stove to keep an eye on the pan. "By the way, Alan, thanks for inviting me to do this. I know you had loads of other options, but I'm glad to be here."

Alan looked surprised by her words. "I should be thanking you, lass. Doing the interview and helping with the baking on this trip won't just help me out. It will also look very good for you when we release our cookbook."

"Our—I'm sorry, our what now?" Claire bleated without any grace or poise whatsoever.

Maybe it was the accent, or maybe something was clogging her ears, but there was no way he'd said what she thought he'd said. Alan Gables *never* partnered on a cookbook. Never. Not even once.

And he wanted to partner with her for one?

What the actual croissants?

"Our cookbook," Alan repeated, which was funny because it sounded exactly the same as before, and it still didn't make sense.

"Can you understand him?" Claire asked Jonny in confusion. "Should we find a Gaelic speaker to translate?"

Jonny's amusement increased, and he tilted his head, making it look like one eyebrow rose above another. "What do you think he's saying, Éclair?"

"Cookbook," Claire told him, beginning to laugh at the ridiculousness. "It sounds like *cookbook*."

"That's what I'm hearing too," Jonny whispered loudly.

Alan muttered incoherently before raising his voice. "That *is* what I'm saying, you—"

"Use baking swear words," Claire and Jonny said together.

"You . . . you underproved haggis," Alan grumbled as though he were cursing her entire bloodline.

"Do you prove haggis?" Jonny inquired with practiced innocence.

Claire smacked him across the chest, still struggling against her snorts of incredulous laughter.

She heard Alan's long-suffering sigh and tried to regain her composure. It seemed he was serious about the cookbook, and if she didn't straighten up, he might take it back.

Best to get things in motion before he changed his mind.

She coughed twice and took a deep breath, meeting Alan's less-than-entertained expression, her face still tingling from her laughter. "I would be happy to release a cookbook with you, but . . ." Her humor faded as she looked at him. "You are serious, aren't you, Alan? Don't tease me with a good time if you don't mean it. The cookbook, I mean." She bit down on her lip, nibbling gently. "I know you don't like partnering."

"How do you know that?" Alan inquired mildly, one side of his mouth curving.

Claire sputtered softly, shaking her head. "Everybody knows that."

"Do they? Interesting. I don't recall ever saying such a thing in my interviews." He lifted a shoulder in a hint of a shrug, now seeming to struggle with his smile.

What was his problem? Of course, he had said it. How else would everybody know?

She narrowed her eyes at him, a gnawing suspicion growing in her gut. "Explain."

"Certainly. It is true that I have never collaborated on a cookbook with anyone," he told her as though he hadn't been intentionally provoking her. "But only because I never wanted to. And now I want to do a cookbook with you because I think it will do well, it will help your career, and it makes me look good for partnering with a former contestant. Plus you're a good baker, so your recipes will be legit. I've been meaning to discuss this with you for months, but other things kept getting put at the forefront. I figure now is as good a time as any for you to accept the offer."

Claire creased her nose in distaste. "I don't think I like you saying 'legit.' Sounds like my uncle trying to be hip with the kids, and it's so wrong."

Alan gave Jonny another long-suffering look. "This is what I get for trying. A pity she's the only one I'd want to do a cookbook with right now, or I'd move on."

Jonny nodded sympathetically. "I understand."

"Still here, guys," Claire announced. "Back to the present, please. We still have baking to do. What's next, Alan?"

"Watch and wait," Alan answered as he returned to the pastry in front of him. "Once we add the puff pastry and get the tarte tatin back in the oven, we can whip up the custard and cream for the trifle."

Claire nodded. Alan's menu for the trip was ambitious: Scottish tablet, shortbread, and Dundee biscuits for teatime, followed later by a chocolate trifle and an unnamed surprise, which she now suspected was the tartan tarte tatin.

Say that ten times fast.

There was nothing about marzipan on the menu, but Claire suspected Alan had a plan to whip something up before they reached Mallaig just to appease the masses.

She wouldn't be touching that. Marzipan was not her friend, even if she had made a Nativity out of it for one of her bakes on the show. The result had been good enough, but she was happy to step aside for the Marzipan King.

Once Alan had his pastry the way he wanted, he pulled the sheet pan out of the oven and, to Claire's surprise, he began haphazardly sprinkling blueberries around. Except everything Alan Gables did was intentional, so even this had to be practiced and proven.

"Vanilla sugar, please," Alan instructed softly.

Claire reached for it and came to the stove. "How do you want it?"

He gestured aimlessly to the pan. "Just scatter it. No wrong way."

A knock at the kitchen door brought them all around in surprise.

"Come in," Alan called.

Two people entered the room, one a wiry, dark-haired young man and the other a slender but full-figured blonde woman encased in bright pink.

"Ah, Greg," Alan greeted, wiping his hands and coming over. "And Felicity Farrow, greetings."

Claire's eyes widened at the name. Felicity Farrow was a journalist for *Mode Magazine*, one of the most elite publications in the magazine world, and she was known for her exclusive access and piercing profiles of celebrities and the elite.

And she was the single most attractive woman Claire had ever seen in her entire life. She was in her mid- to late-twenties—tops—with long, perfectly curled blonde hair, a body wrapped in a bright-pink, tight skirt suit, and a face full of makeup, though it was professional and tasteful. Her legs were ridiculously long and perfectly toned, as her too-small skirt blatantly displayed, and her shoes . . .

Crepes alive, she had chosen to wear heels that skinny and that high on a train? The most impractical choice in footwear possible, but she rocked them, of course, and props for that, but she was asking for all kinds of trouble and injuries. Though if Model-slash-Journalist Barbie wanted to exude sex appeal for work, that was her prerogative.

But dang, those cheekbones of hers could have sliced bagels.

Claire tried her best not to look down at her cozy-chic outfit of jeans, a T-shirt, a jumper, and trainers, but she felt incredibly unfeminine. And frumpy.

A frumpy baker with a hot-as-flaming-pudding boyfriend wearing an actual Henley shirt that would make any warm-blooded female in the vicinity swoon.

Oh sugar.

"Get the tarte tatin back in the oven, please, Claire," Alan directed with a nod. "Twenty-five minutes."

Wordlessly, she picked up the now-pastry-topped tarte

tatin and tucked it into the oven, turning around just in time to see Felicity sidle up to Jonny with a perfectly predatory smile as she leaned closer.

"Hi," Felicity purred, popping her impractical heel off the ground. "Felicity Farrow, *Mode Magazine*. Who are you, handsome?"

Alan cleared his throat and gestured toward Claire. "Felicity, this is Claire Walker. From our last series."

Felicity's eyes never left Jonny, and she licked her perfectly full lips. "Charmed. And this is . . ."

"Her boyfriend," Alan said pointedly. "Jonathan Ainsley."

Claire held her breath, grateful Alan didn't expound on Jonny's title.

But Felicity gasped and dropped her heel back to the floor, twining her arms around Jonny's arm and linking their fingers. "Viscount Colburn! Oh, this is magical. I've wanted to meet you for ages and discuss your stunning estate at Blackfirth. You would not believe the praise we are hearing about it from fans of the recent series. You must let me talk to you. Drinks? Dinner? Dessert? Breakfast? All of the above?"

Claire gaped at the woman's audacity and complete dismissal of her claim on Jonny. This was the most outrageous thing she had ever seen, and Jonny—the poor dear—was practically a statue.

He really didn't like being around people all that much, and being touched without consent . . .

"We shall see, Miss Farrow," Jonny muttered, his cheeks pink.

Wait, what?

Felicity giggled and stepped back from Jonny, grinning at him.

Alan moved then, taking off his apron. "Shall we move to my compartment for the interview, Miss Farrow? The sooner we do, the sooner we can focus on other items. The passengers, for example. Or the bakes."

"Or my next conquest," Felicity quipped as she blatantly eyed Jonny from head to foot.

Oh sugar, she did not.

"Greg," Alan said on a sigh, "please have two sparkling waters brought to my compartment. And if Claire needs anything while I'm gone, please be available."

Skinny Greg nodded without smiling, his eyes darting rapidly between Felicity and Alan. "O-of course, Mr. Gables." He fumbled with the handle as he opened the kitchen door and held it for Alan, who led the way out.

Felicity followed but looked at Jonny as she left. "Until later, Viscount." She winked, her words heavy with meaning.

Claire was going to vomit.

Greg blushed as he closed the door behind them, and Claire stared at it for a long moment before looking at Jonny.

He was studying the floor, his hands clenched at his sides.

Silent.

"That was fun," Claire chirped.

"I hate people," Jonny mumbled as a full-bodied shudder rippled visibly through him.

Oddly enough, that was the most soothing thing Claire had ever seen or heard in her life.

Bless him.

"Do you need to take a walk, darling?" she asked with genuine concern, coming over to him. "Clear your head? I mean, it won't be a walk through the Highlands, given the speed of the train, but maybe you could find a quiet corner and watch the scenery."

His brilliant blue eyes met hers, and his entire expression softened as he reached out and touched her cheek. "I won't lie, that would be amazing. But do you need me here? I'm not a baker, but I can help."

Claire smiled and took his hand, kissing it quickly. "I'll be fine. Just finishing up a few things and waiting for the tarte tatin to bake. Then it's serving up the masses, and I am not about to throw you to the wolves. Go, and I'll join you as soon as I can."

Jonny leaned in and kissed her brow quickly. "Thank you, Éclair. I'd tell you to text me if you need me, but—"

"No phones," they said together, her with a laugh and him with a wince.

It was one of the conditions of the train trip—something about controlling the media around the extremely exclusive event—so all phones had been confiscated upon boarding and would be returned once the train reached Mallaig.

With one more tap to Claire's cheek, Jonny left the kitchen, turning in the opposite direction from where the others had gone.

Claire focused her efforts on preparing the chocolate custard and whipping the cream for the trifle. Once she finished those, she began assembling the dessert in two large trifle dishes, spreading a layer of chilled, set jelly in the bottom of each dish, followed by a layer of chocolate custard, another layer of jelly, and the rest of the custard. The freshly whipped cream was next, and, though Alan hadn't given her specific instructions, she arranged the cherries and raspberries on the top, followed by chocolate shortbread pieces and chocolate shavings. She covered each dish in plastic wrap and put them both in the fridge to chill.

No one would argue she had gone too far, would they? It was intended to be a chocolate trifle, after all.

When Alan still had not returned after she'd arranged all the teatime treats onto plates and had pulled the tarte tatin out of the oven, she began to worry.

What in the world had he gotten up to? How long could an interview take?

The mechanical pinging of the train Tannoy sounded, and Claire paused to listen.

"*If there is a doctor aboard the train, please report to Dining Car 3 for medical assistance. Again, if there is a doctor aboard the train, please report to Dining Car 3 for medical assistance. Thank you.*"

She caught her breath, and then she bolted out of the kitchen, racing up to Dining Car 3.

CHAPTER 2

The train wouldn't have been so bad apart from the people.

Then again, most things in Jonny Ainsley's life would be markedly improved if the people were removed from them.

He wasn't opposed to the opportunity this trip presented for Claire and her baking career. On the contrary, he wanted everything good and successful and fun to happen to her, and she deserved every bit of attention and praise she could get. The chance to be highlighted with Alan Gables, the Scottish baking legend, would be exactly the boost she needed after the fervor over her series of *Britian's Battle of the Bakers* faded. And Alan was talking a cookbook as well? Golden.

But Jonny also really wanted to enjoy this romantic getaway with his girlfriend.

Time together was rare for them, between his work schedule and trips and her substitute teaching in Blackfirth, not to mention the random opportunities she had to do press as a *BBB* contestant. It was, without a doubt, the slowest-moving relationship he had ever been in.

He didn't mind slow. Not when it was real.

And good heavens, was this ever real.

There was no one like Claire, and he constantly felt breathless and windswept that she was even in his life, let alone dating him. She was quirky and cute and warm and observant and snarky and genuine. She was the first breath of spring after an endless winter, the surprising laugh after an expanse of drudgery, the clear dawn after weeks of clouds, the sip of water after perishing of thirst . . .

She also made him a little bit dramatic and incredibly sappy.

It wasn't his fault. It was hers. And that soft smile she sent his way when he wasn't expecting it.

Those tender smiles unsettled him—not in a bad way—but they made him restless and embarrassed, as though he had done something without intending to and couldn't account for the reason behind her happy reaction. That strange vulnerability left him feeling exposed, and, of all things, ticklish. He wasn't exactly the soft and squishy sort, but when Claire looked at him that way, he felt as though he might actually melt.

Not sexy at all.

And he wanted to be sexy for her.

Which didn't explain why he'd completely shut down in the kitchen after the journalist had invaded his personal space like the Huns on roid rage. He'd needed to escape the perfume-drenched space before going completely catatonic in discomfort. Claire had seen his need to flee and wouldn't judge him for it. She knew him too well and cared about him even more.

He hoped she loved him actually.

They hadn't used the L-word yet, aside from the general term of endearment that could have meant your lover, your sister, your dog, your neighbor, or a cheeky stranger. There should be other words in English for *love* like there were in other languages, but until that happened, the all-powerful, all-elusive, L-word would remain the be-all and end-all for relationships.

And he really, really wanted the chance to tell Claire that he loved her on this trip. He only needed an opportune moment. Maybe she'd reciprocate, but he'd be happy to wait for her if she couldn't yet.

He wasn't entirely sure where she stood, though he hadn't felt the need to worry about it yet. His relationship with Claire had always felt natural and easy, like it had always been part of him, so, in his mind, there had never been an "if" to Claire loving him.

Only "when."

He had accepted that he would never really know everything with Claire, and that was a beautiful thing. Every surprise added a new layer to her depth and his fascination with her. The prospect of discovering the next detail about her was one of his favorite parts of their relationship. It was as tempting as the devil and as blissful as heaven.

But there would be a ridiculously primal sense of satisfaction in hearing those three important words from her the first time.

His alpha-male-esque revelation was interrupted by the mechanical dinging of the Tannoy through the overhead speakers.

"*If there is a doctor aboard the train, please report to Dining Car 3 for medical assistance. Again, if there is a doctor aboard the train, please report to Dining Car 3 for medical assistance. Thank you.*"

Huh. That was an interesting one. He'd taken trains thousands of times, and he couldn't remember ever—

His eyes widened as his entire body seemed to catch fire. Except for his throat. That clenched like someone had a hand around it, and sparks of ice began popping in the soles of his feet.

Claire.

Had she started her food delivery yet? Was she out and about yet, or . . . ?

Medical assistance.

He couldn't risk it. Would not.

He bolted from the back of the train in the next second and barreled down the aisles like he was hearing sirens.

He flew past the kitchen and into the VIP car without meeting any resistance. He walked as fast as his legs could manage. Long strides at a good clip. Olympic speed walkers should study him.

His chest tightened as adrenaline pounded through every muscle, vein, artery, nerve. He didn't even know if adrenaline worked like that, but it was fire, and it was everywhere. He could barely see straight; his mind was busy replaying the memories of Claire being forced to walk into the darkness of his estate grounds, knowing full well that a dangerous man would take the opportunity to grab her. And, in Jonny's mind, kill her. Intentionally letting Claire head toward that danger and not having any power to stop her had been the hardest thing he'd ever done.

It hadn't mattered that the police had her wired and protected every step of the way. It hadn't mattered that Claire had agreed to do it. It hadn't mattered that her actions would wrap up an entire murder investigation and bring justice to the victim.

It had only mattered that Claire would be in danger, and he had had to stand back and wait for danger to actually take her hand, cover her mouth, and make her beg for her life.

A cold shudder inched down his spine, and he trembled like a scared dog in the rain. That was what those memories did to him. That was what the prospect of Claire in danger made him become.

That was what could drive him to his knees in an outright panic attack if he didn't find her well and whole.

He forced his lungs to expand with a shaky inhale as he reached the gangway of the next car, the door of which clearly read Dining Car 3.

"Please, please, please," he whispered as his eyes landed on the handle, his knuckles white as he gripped it.

"Sir?"

Jonny ground his teeth and glanced over at the larger-than-average security guard who hadn't been there when they'd come on board. "Yes?"

"Pass?"

Jonny tugged at the lanyard around his neck, which had gotten twisted and turned around with his running. He jerked the badge up and held it out without a word, praying no actual steam was coming out of his ears.

The guard looked at it, then nodded and motioned for Jonny to go in. "Thank you, sir."

"No problem," Jonny grumbled, though he didn't mean it.

Then the door was open, and he was striding in, every heartbeat and movement of his lungs ticking against his chest like it was the only place he could feel anything.

To his immense relief, he quickly spotted Claire standing near the bar, her arms tightly folded against her.

"Claire," he all but gasped as he broke into a run again.

Her eyes snapped to him, and he saw the flash of confusion. "Jonny?"

"I thought . . . I thought . . ." he stammered as he reached her.

Understanding dawned, and she opened her arms immediately, holding him as tightly as he held her. "It's okay. I'm okay. I was worried it was Alan when I heard the call, so I came to see."

Jonny took a moment to breathe her in, his nose tucked in her hair as the tremors began to fade from his body. "Alan? Why?"

Claire bit her lip. "He never came back to the kitchen after he left with Zero-Boundaries Barbie. I was getting ready to load the trolleys, but this is *his* event, right? So he should be doing the 'among the people' stuff, and yet . . ." She shuddered and stepped away from Jonny, though she kept her hand pressed to his back. "I thought it might be him in here in need of help, but it's not. And no help is needed now." Her eyes flicked meaningfully to her right, and Jonny glanced over.

A man lay on the ground by the bar, his open eyes eerily fixed. Nothing about him moved, and while the rumpled creasing on the front of his blue dress shirt bore no bloodstains, a dark puddle stained the carpet around his head.

An older man in a tweed sports coat was kneeling beside him, scribbling on the clipboard in his hand. Beside him was a stout woman wearing the standard dark uniform of train service employees, her expression blank. Another figure in the same uniform was going through a nearby briefcase while wearing latex gloves.

"Dead?" Jonny murmured to Claire.

She nodded, her attention on the group. "Yeah. The doctor called the time of death once he realized resuscitation wouldn't be necessary. The woman is the conductor, and she's given him incident forms. The man going through the briefcase is Caleb, the lead service attendant. He's looking for an ID."

Jonny shook his head, looking back at the dead man on the floor. He couldn't have been more than fifty, and he seemed to be in decent shape. His clothing was high quality, and his shoes were immaculate. His facial scruff was grayer than his hair, and the carefully rolled back sleeves of his shirt revealed an expensive-looking watch with an intense set of buttons as its face.

Everything about him screamed money.

"What happened?" Jonny asked in an even lower voice.

Claire stepped closer to him. "From what I have picked up, the bartender came out from being in the back and found him like that. He called the conductor, who called the doctor, and there we are. The bartender says no one else was in the car when he found the body."

"So no one saw it happen."

"Nope."

"Where is the bartender, by the way?"

"The conductor sent him to the break room to compose himself, but not before entreating him to keep silent about the whole incident."

"Hmm. Any speculation?"

"Only mine."

Jonny slowly looked at her, his mouth curving. "Well, hello again, Sherlock."

Her cheeks immediately began to color, and she refused to look at him. "Looks like an accident. The conductor—I think her name is Lisa?—thinks he might have been drunk before he started drinking his whiskeys at the bar. And then, when the bartender was away, he fell and hit his head."

"You're not convinced, though." Jonny hadn't phrased it like a question because, honestly, Claire was still here and not asking to leave. She had questions, which meant she would be too curious for her own good until they were answered.

She hated questions and craved answers.

"No," she replied in a very low voice, her eyes flicking across various spots in the room.

"Tell me," Jonny urged as he rubbed his hand up and down her arm.

She bit her lip for a moment and stepped closer to him, tightening her hold around his waist. "Look at the state of him. He's not sloppy at all. His shirt still has crease lines on it from being pressed—his pants too. His eyes aren't bloodshot. He's not sweaty or flushed. His hair is tidy. Nothing in the room is overturned, not even the stools. There is no way he was drunk enough to fall and hit his head without something else being involved."

Jonny could see how her mind might go there, but without proof of what she was speculating, how could they know for sure?

"I don't know," he mused. "Not everybody that is drunk actually looks drunk."

She sputtered in derision. "I'm well aware of that, J. Family runs a pub, remember? I've seen the entire drunk spectrum and then some. I'm not talking about being able to walk a straight line. They're saying this man was so drunk he couldn't be upright. The train hasn't swayed or bumped enough to throw a wobbly person into anything, so I am telling you, from experience, that the victim could not have been so trashed that he hit something on his own badly enough to kill him. Not from force, not from alcohol, nothing. And certainly not the floor."

Okay, well, when she put it like *that* . . .

Jonny scanned the scene with a little more thought, his eyes narrowing. "You think he hit something else?"

"Or was hit *by* something else. Or someone."

He slowly nodded, his teeth gripping the inside of his lip a little.

Claire huffed and tucked a strand of hair behind her ear. "These aren't investigators, J. They'll have to wait for our next station stop to call anyone. And the trip might not even continue, if what I think happened is actually what happened."

Jonny was about to ask something else when the man going through the briefcase called out, "Got an ID, ma'am."

The conductor turned to face him, her expression taut. "Who is he?"

"Brian Donovan," came the terse reply. "There's some paperwork in here, and this book."

He held out a copy of *Bread Is Life* by Alan Gables for everyone to see.

"Oh, baguettes," Claire hissed beside Jonny. "Crumby, crusty, brick of baguettes."

"Everyone on the train is here for Alan," Jonny reminded her gently. "Doesn't have to mean anything."

"But it looks bad. A fan being killed on Alan Gables's tribute tour is . . ."

He couldn't really argue with her. It was bad optics.

"Do we know where Alan or Greg are?" Jonny murmured into her ear.

She shook her head. "Not since they left the kitchen." She was shaking a little in his hold, and he rubbed her arms gently.

"I think Greg might need to be named Flaky Pastry, just for us," he whispered.

She jerked and looked up at him, her shaking paused in the face of confused amusement. "What the actual tart, J?"

He shrugged, giving her a crooked smile. "What? It does the job it has to, but crumbles super easily. It fits."

Claire snorted before clamping a hand over her mouth. "Crepes alive, J. I'm rubbing off on you."

Jonny patted her shoulder soothingly. "There are worse things." He pulled her closer to him in a hug. "Feel better? You were shaking."

"I'm just so glad it isn't Alan," she muttered back. "My mind jumped to all sorts of conclusions when I heard the announcement, you know? Like it did in the whole 'tent of death' thing on the show."

"Yeah, that's not happening here," he assured her.

Then the train came to a horrible, screeching, and very sudden stop.

CHAPTER 3

The dining car erupted as the five people ricocheted into each other and the walls with the force of the train's braking. Faint screams wafted from the other cars, which made the doctor stand up, dropping his clipboard to the floor.

"What happened?" he demanded, looking around.

The conductor groaned and rubbed at her brow. "I don't know, but I'll go find out from the engineer. Can you have a look around and see if any passengers were hurt? Caleb, I need you to reassure everyone that things are fine, and we'll have answers shortly. Have your crew offer more tea or even something stronger, and maybe check in on the bartender. Miss Walker was just about to bring out the treats, I believe, so that should provide a nice distraction while we take care of things here and figure out why the train has stopped."

"Yes, ma'am," Caleb replied as he rose and stripped off his gloves.

The doctor picked up his bag and sighed. "I'll finish the incident report paperwork later. This one's not going anywhere, so I might as well tend to anyone else who might be injured. I'll be back when I can."

The conductor nodded as both men left the car, and then she looked at Jonny and Claire. "Miss Walker, thank you for your help. I don't know where Mr. Gables has gotten to, but if we're stuck for a while, would you be willing to help out later? We may need to provide some sort of dinner; I believe there were other menu items planned?"

Claire nodded, smiling sympathetically. "Yes, ma'am. Some things have already been prepared, and if I need to provide more, I am sure I can."

"Thank you. And please call me Lisa." Her eyes flicked down to the body for a moment before returning to Claire. "And perhaps don't speak of this? We'll have the car shut down and the body removed to the refrigeration car when the doctor is done. I'll assign security in front of this car instead of the VIP section. That way, only those with VIP access can get by. But even so, maybe we can put up barriers somehow to prevent others from seeing the blood?"

"I can figure something out," Jonny offered helpfully. "There should be enough tables and chairs to make some sort of barricade or wall."

Lisa nodded at him, a small smile briefly passing her lips. "Thank you. I'd appreciate that. I don't know when we'll be able to have authorities on board, but I know not to disturb the scene. It's best we protect it as much as we can, right?"

Claire didn't think the woman was actually looking for an answer, so she kept her mouth shut while trying to look helpful and sympathetic. Until Lisa left, Claire couldn't examine the crime scene or the victim.

If this *was* a crime scene.

It could just be a death scene. Was that a thing? It sounded like a thing. Maybe it should be a thing.

She shook her head to halt her mental rambling.

"Which compartment is yours, Miss Walker?" Lisa asked when she reached the door of the car. "So I can find you if we need dinner."

"We're in compartment 12," Claire told her. "If I'm not there, I'll be in the kitchen."

Lisa nodded and left the car without another word.

Claire released a breath and dug into the pockets of her apron. "Thank goodness. I thought she'd never leave." She pulled out a pair of clear, plastic gloves and put them on before grabbing another set tucked into the same pocket. "Come here, J."

Jonny reared back, his hands flying up in protest. "What are you doing?"

Claire gave him a look and waved the gloves at him impatiently. "What does it look like I'm doing? We're going to investigate."

Jonny immediately shook his head. "Not what it looks like at all, not even a little bit. You look like you're about to go back to the kitchen and get the treats to serve the passengers, and you want me to help."

She rolled her eyes and stalked over to him, shoving the gloves at him. "I do want your help, but not in the kitchen. Put these on."

"Not touching the body, Claire," he said firmly as he began to reach his fingers into the plastic.

"Is that an order for me or a statement about yourself?" she asked, folding her hands and lifting a brow at him.

He smirked. "Both. I will not be touching the body, and though I would never think to order you to do anything, you and I both know that touching a dead body is a big no-no.

So please don't commit that big no-no because I don't want to call my lawyer and explain why you've been arrested for tampering with a corpse."

Claire grimaced so intensely her neck ached from it. "Right. Not gonna go there. Promise. I am way too delicate for prison."

Jonny's bark of laughter didn't do much to reassure her, but she moved to the briefcase Caleb had been searching earlier.

She had already seen Alan's book in the briefcase, but everyone on this train was here for Alan Gables, unless they had missed the memo and bought an exceptionally expensive train ticket just to get to Mallaig. She set the book aside and pulled out a folder of papers, eyeing the information with a frown. Numbers and currencies and graphics galore, but what did any of it mean?

The header on the page said Dishable Inc., but that meant nothing to Claire. Well, maybe not nothing. There was a faint nagging sensation to one side of her brain, some inkling that said she ought to know the name, had seen it somewhere, but not a single possible connection came to mind.

"What's with the frown, Éclair?" Jonny asked as he came over.

She handed him the folder with a rough exhale. "This is your language, darling. Let me know if it's anything important."

He nodded and sat on the floor, looking at everything with far more interest than she could have managed.

Returning her attention to the briefcase, Claire pulled out a diary and opened it to the current calendar, scanning the neat, tiny scrawl for any clues.

Today's date only had Mallaig Express and its departure time listed. Not Marzipan Express, but Mallaig.

There was nothing for the entire month after that.

Bizarre.

There were plenty of abbreviations and times for earlier in the month. Never spelled out, and when she looked at the day-to-day format, the same abbreviations were used. No additional information.

She looked at the previous three months and found the same sort of thing.

Then she checked the previous six months.

Claire's brows pulled together, and she tilted her head as she looked at April and saw the following notation: AG BBB12.

Wait, had that been written on the other pages? She quickly flicked across the pages she'd just looked at, and, sure enough, it spanned the entire month. And the next. And some of the next. How had she missed it?

Then she spotted an additional entry in the day-to-day notes for April under the first instance of the notation.

Oxfordshire.

Chills raced across Claire's skin and up her spine, making her shiver dramatically. April in Oxfordshire. She had done that herself.

"Whoa!" Jonny said when he saw her, his eyes wide. "You okay?"

Swallowing, Claire shook her head and handed him the diary, pointing at the note.

Jonny's bright blue eyes somehow went even wider, and he stared at the page for a long moment before looking at her. "He knew when Alan would be filming in Oxfordshire?"

"I think so," Claire whispered hoarsely. "What else could it mean?"

Jonny's attention moved from her to the body, and he shook his head. "Who are you, Brian Donovan?"

"And where's Alan?" Claire added, feeling the chill settle into her stomach and kneecaps.

Jonny frowned as he rummaged through the briefcase and pulled out a wallet with a hiss of victory. "Can't believe Caleb put this back in here. Let's see if we can get an age and address for poor, dead Brian. Hmm . . . Okay. London address, randomly. Date of birth, August 24, 1973."

Claire made a face. "Not that old, really. Alan's age, I think."

"I don't want to know how you know that," Jonny admitted. He sputtered a long, low breath, his lips buzzing as he flicked his attention from the body to the papers and wallet in his hands to Claire. "Okay, what would Watson do in this situation?"

That was an excellent question.

Their friend and comrade, DS Watson, had been the whole reason they'd gotten into sleuthing in the first place. When a contestant had died on the set of *Britian's Battle of the Bakers*, Watson had secretly suspected foul play and brought Claire and Jonny in to help confirm his suspicions.

He'd probably regret that now.

Claire looked around the space with that thought in mind. "Examine the body first. Can you be my mental notetaker while I look?"

"Sure thing."

Claire moved over to the body. "Okay, he was found just like this. Hasn't been moved. Blood pooling from his head wound. No other injuries according to the doctor who declared him dead. The conductor speculated that Mr. Donovan fell from the barstool and hit his head on the ground and died."

"Which means we need to see the wound."

Ergh. Claire would rather not, but crepes alive, here she was . . .

She moved to look at the back of the victim's head and lowered herself to the ground to see it more clearly, holding her breath.

This much blood had a smell, and it was unpleasant to say the least.

"Okay," she said tightly, more for herself than anyone else. "We've got a shape. Pointy. Big ouch."

"Big ouch?" Jonny repeated from where he sat.

"Shut the piehole, J. You're not the one inches away from blood-borne pathogens, okay?" Claire snapped, not moving her eyes from the wound.

"Where did you learn that phrase?" her soon-to-be-pummeled boyfriend asked.

Claire huffed noisily. "Teacher safety training. Now hush!" She narrowed her vision to examine the wound more closely. "Right angle," she recited, tilting her head to look at it. "Not hit dead-on, no pun intended. One edge is longer than the other, so awkward hit. Inch and a half on the long side, maybe a third of that on the other. Blood has . . ." She paused to swallow her gag reflex. "Blood has run down the head to the ground. I can see some bruising beneath the wound, but it's following gravity. I think bruising means he didn't die on impact. I wish I had my phone to check this, but I think that's right."

"Those crime documentaries are paying off, *ma crème*," Jonny praised.

"I will attack you with a baster if you don't stop," Claire warned him, finally flicking her eyes to him.

He held up his hands in surrender or apology.

Sugar, the man was cute. Maddening, but cute.

That would save his life.

Claire looked at the wound again, then pushed herself back to sit on her heels. "But he'd have had to hit whatever it was with some serious force to die from it. And there's no way this dude just passed out at the bar without some underlying medical condition."

"Goodness, it's so hot when you pull out the big words," Jonny said on a sigh.

"Jonny!" Claire screeched, her face immediately flaming.

But was it a flame of embarrassment or a flame of delight?

A flame of delighted embarrassment?

That sounded good, because there was definitely both.

Jonny looked pretty pleased with himself for someone who was dangerously close to not getting the delicious desserts that had been promised to the whole train.

Claire narrowed her eyes at his completely unapologetic self, only to receive a cheeky grin in return.

"Sorry. Inappropriate humor is my coping mechanism." Jonny shrugged, his nose crinkling. "It's dark, but I'm working on it."

Shaking her head, Claire moved around to the front of Brian's body, smelling his mouth and nose. "No strong odors of alcohol. I really don't think he was drunk before he came in here. I mean, we can't exactly test his blood alcohol content, but I'm as sure as I can be."

"Good enough for me." Jonny exhaled in a rush and looked over the numbers on the sheets before him. "I'll need time to study these in depth. Have you ever heard of Dishable Inc.?'

"No," Claire said slowly, that odd nagging sensation returning to tug at her stomach. "Why?"

He hefted the papers for emphasis. "Donovan had some serious data on the company, and I'm thinking he was either in the company or trying to get in it. It does seem like something fishy might be going on with these numbers, though. Dunno what yet . . . Having Alan's book probably just means he was hoping to get it signed, like everyone else on the train. There's not much to go on here . . ."

Claire stared back at him in silence. What in the world were they dealing with here?

"So why is the guy dead?" Claire whispered.

"Hmm." Jonny's hesitation was palpable, and the longer he hesitated, the more Claire wanted to grimace.

It could still be an accident. A strange one, but an accident all the same. They couldn't say with any proof that a crime had actually been committed. But it certainly looked that way.

It wasn't like she *wanted* to be at another potential crime scene, but here she was.

This time without police to keep her safe.

No big deal, right?

"If this wasn't an accident," Jonny said slowly, "there has to be something that hit Brian's head—or that his head hit, as it were—to kill him. So let's find that thing. Look for anything that could be used as a weapon to make that mark, or any surface that might have done it. But it could all be nothing, you know. A true accident."

"I would love for this to be an accident," Claire assured him quickly. "Because the alternative is a killer on this train. I've read Agatha Christie, and I have no desire to deal with that."

"I very much doubt it will be the same thing, Éclair. That's way too complicated for this."

"Sure about that, are you?"

His silence wasn't at all reassuring.

Claire nodded for emphasis and began looking around the dining car for a possible murder weapon.

But also to look at it like an actual crime scene.

She wished she had her phone to get photos of everything. It was what Watson would have done, and it seemed like the most basic step to take. But there were no phones allowed on the trip, and she couldn't exactly tell Conductor Lisa that she needed to break that rule so she could secretly investigate a death without any sort of authority.

Mental pictures it was. She felt like a bad actor portraying someone with a photographic memory as she tried to notice absolutely everything and memorize it. The body and its position, the victim's face and clothing, the wound, the blood pooling, the distance to the bar, the bar itself . . .

She cocked her head as she looked at a corner of the bar. There was a break in it for a small half door, no doubt for the bartender to access the space behind the bar, but it was a particularly sharp corner. She wasn't an expert in geometry, nor did she have a ruler, so she couldn't be certain. Yet it *could* have been what caused the injury.

But neither corner bore any stains. The first one she saw, however, was chipped.

Was it chipped before the train had left Fort William? Was she seeing clues that didn't actually exist?

Glancing around the barstools, she noticed something small on the floor next to the nearest stool. She stooped for a closer look and smiled to herself.

Well, well, well, if it wasn't the exact chip from the counter's corner.

Right, so if that was a fresh mark of damage, what happened?

She looked from the body to the bar corner, from the bar corner to the barstool the man had supposedly been sitting on, from the barstool to the body, and between all three in random patterns, trying to find an answer. Or the equation. Or whatever connection might exist.

Recipes were far more her thing than exact depth perception, an understanding of physics, and the ability to play out scenarios like a film in her mind.

Alas for lacking particular skills.

"Hey, J?" Claire called over her shoulder. "Can you come here for a second?"

"Yep." He moved over to her and put his hands on his hips. "What's up?"

She looked down at the body. "How tall do you think he is?"

Jonny scanned him quickly, his mouth twisting in thought. "Six feet tops. Why?"

Claire sat down on the barstool and faced the bar. "I think he hit this corner." She pointed at it, and then to the debris on the floor. "Chips the corner when he hits it. But falls like that, which is weird."

"With you so far," Jonny told her. "But why weird?"

She shook her head. "First of all, he'd have to fall in a funny way to hit the corner at all. I'd never hit it sitting here, but I'm short. With him . . ." She imitated falling to the side, placing her hand against her head. "He couldn't have fallen to the side and had the wound he does. He'd have to fall this way." She turned on the barstool, looking behind her to try to match the wound.

Jonny cocked his head. "Even then, he wouldn't have hit it in the right place. It'd be too high on his head. Probably grazed it."

Claire nodded and hopped to her feet. "So he was standing."

"Facing away from the bar," Jonny continued, turning to act it out. "Which makes the force increase."

"So did he stagger back? Or was he pushed?"

They looked at each other without speaking, answers seeming to avoid them both.

"Murder or accident?" Jonny asked softly. "Completely sloshed or slightly inebriated?"

"What I wouldn't give for a coroner and a lab," Claire mumbled.

Jonny snorted. "Next time, Éclair. Right, why don't you take the briefcase to our compartment, and I'll finish up? Then we can put our brains to work."

"Ah, Viscount Brains," she mused fondly. "It'll be nice to work with him again."

Her boyfriend swatted her head with a half laugh, sending her scampering back to work while he stacked tables and chairs to block off the potential crime scene.

CHAPTER 4

Death was following him.

Well, not literally, but it certainly seemed to be hanging around Jonny more than he would like.

How else could he explain that he'd gotten close to Claire when there was a murder and now, when he was trying to take the next step in their relationship, there was another one?

Granted, it could just as easily have been a regular old death due to an unfortunate accident, but the nagging sensation in the pit of his stomach told him that wasn't very likely. There were too many unanswered questions for this to be a twist of fate.

Which would mean death was following him. Or Claire. Or their relationship.

Oh goodie.

And now, of all blessed things, they were out and about. Among the people.

If you could call agitated, stranded, passionate-to-the-extreme fans of Alan Gables who hadn't actually seen Alan Gables yet "people."

They were more like hyenas in clothing.

Frothing at the mouth included.

"Where. Is. Alan?" the dramatically dyed redhead standing in front of Jonny demanded, her heavily painted eyes wide and bulging. "I paid a fortune to meet him, and he has not been by yet and now we are stopped. The *very least* he could do is to be with us in our suffering."

The spittle flying from the woman's mouth had nowhere to go but on Jonny, as he was the one standing at that end of the trolley, and the misting of someone else's moisture upon his skin was not helping his present irritation.

"We don't know," Jonny ground out in as pleasant a tone as he could muster, which was somewhere above murderous but only just. "Would you like some biscuits?"

Red's nostrils flared in an abject sign of danger—if nature documentaries were to be believed—and she huffed. "You do not understand. I have devoted my life to Alan, and wherever he is hiding will not be enough to keep me from him. For eternity, he will be mine."

Wow. Okay, that was not on the bingo card.

Jonny cleared his throat. "Biscuits, ma'am?"

Finally, the woman snatched the plate from him and whirled to her seat, biting so harshly into the shortbread that Jonny felt something twinge in his left arm in fear.

He turned to face Claire, who stood behind the other trolley, her eyes wide and her face pale. The rest of the car was as irritable as Red, only less aggressive in their approach. The grumbling of their current crop of diners was harsh and their looks dark, as though Claire and Jonny had Alan hog-tied and gagged back in the kitchen.

The masses were rabid, and he and Claire had no protection against them except for the VIP lanyards around their necks, which seemed to suggest the two of them held some sort of authority, and thus were targets for pointless verbal assault.

He could also call it shameless, tactless, brainless, and tasteless, but excess had never been his way, so pointless would be the only word he used.

For now.

Thankfully, service for the rest of this particular car passed without further incident, and as Jonny moved into Dining Car 1, he fought to keep a grimace from crossing his features. Just as in Dining Car 2, several passengers were at the bar, making up for the lack of availability of Dining Car 3, which now required VIP access. The lack of motion of the train apparently drove passengers to drink, which would not bode well for later if there was really a problem.

"Hey!" a man at a nearby table called, looking directly at Jonny. "How come we aren't getting any answers?"

"Yeah!" another hollered. "We've been sitting here for ages!"

Jonny ground his teeth together. "I don't work for the train. Sorry."

"Come on, you've got a badge! You're in charge of something, so tell us what you know!" the first ordered.

Jonny raised a brow at him. "Sir, I do not work for the train, and I don't have answers for you. Sorry."

The passenger rolled his eyes like a teenager. "Yeah, you sound really sorry. We're never gonna make it on time to Mallaig, and we haven't even seen Alan Gables yet."

"Where is Alan?" a woman in the back asked, standing up and putting her hands on her hips. "We're getting these treats, but no Alan. I didn't pay this kind of money to see a mediocre contestant from *BBB*, you know. I came for Alan!"

Jonny heard Claire hiss at the comment fired right at her, and he wanted nothing more than to breathe fire at every single ungrateful passenger he saw.

He had not signed up for this.

Mediocre? He had once teased Claire about calling herself that, and it was still a joke between them, but only affectionately. Anyone else who used that word about his girl?

Dead. Freaking. Meat.

"Oh, Miss Walker is anything but mediocre," came a sultry voice from another table.

Dread clawed at Jonny's stomach as he caught sight of the woman wreathed in bright pink at one of the other tables, martini glass in hand.

"Of course, it's a martini," Claire muttered from behind him, clocking the same thing he was.

Felicity sipped from the glass pointedly, her eyes on Jonny alone. Then she set it aside and stood, but not before her fingers ran the length of her leg to her too-short skirt as she did so, indicating the path all eyes should take on her.

"Claire Walker is the daughter of a publican," Felicity announced, striding forward with leisurely grace, "which is a pub owner, if you didn't know. She would be right at home here, but she's a teacher. Or was. Then *Britain's Battle of the Bakers* called, and voilà! She's now a baker, and a finalist too. And, if rumors are to be believed, she is linked to this fascinating, sexy specimen of nobility right here. Anyone who can do that is not mediocre, and if Alan Gables wants her here to bake with him on his tour de force? Why, he must know more than the rest of us do." She stopped in front of Jonny, her gaze locked on him. "Why does Alan like Claire so much, Viscount Colburn? Care to share?"

It was astonishing how tone affected words, really. She had defended Claire with what she said, and yet, her utter disdain was clear, her words sharp with an almost predatory edge. And there was no missing her insinuation at the end, nor what she had chosen to say about Jonny in front of Claire.

Warning bells rang in his head, but what could he do?

He wanted to look back at Claire to see how she was taking it, but he was afraid the viper before him might strike somehow. If her attention remained on him, Claire might be spared.

He cleared his throat. "Biscuits, Miss Farrow?"

Her plump, painted lips spread in a smile, and she held out her hand for the plate, though he would have to reach to close the distance between them.

He wasn't used to anyone being this blatant around him, or about him, and the way it flustered him was the most uncomfortable feeling he'd ever known. Years of perfecting an expressionless and icy facade served him well, but the creeping chill in his veins and the rising nausea would wreak havoc beneath the shield.

Through sheer force of will, and impeccable molar strength, Jonny managed to speak through his clenched jaw. "Here you go." He set a plate of biscuits on her outstretched hand, careful not to touch her skin.

He was afraid the contact would burn him.

Wordlessly, he pulled the trolley around to other tables, not caring if Claire was lagging behind him. He needed to get this done and get away. Go somewhere else. Anywhere else.

The dead body would be a good place. No one would talk to him there.

Great. Now he would rather be with the dead than the living?

Charming.

No one else in Dining Car 1 had anything to say about Claire or anything else; they just moodily accepted the plate of teatime treats he and Claire offered.

The next compartment car was filled with grumblers, but they, at least, seemed to recognize that Claire and Jonny did not work for the train and kept their opinions and complaints about the trip to themselves.

As soon as they entered the foremost passenger car, however, another confrontation was waiting for them.

And since Jonny was in front, it was Jonny who had to face it.

Again.

A man immediately approached them when they entered, waving his hands in the air. "Finally! Someone had better give us some answers, and it had better be right now!" He was in his forties or fifties and stood a good six inches shorter than Jonny but outweighed him by at least fifty pounds.

"Erm, sir," Claire tried from behind Jonny, leaning around. "We have some food—"

"I don't care what you have!" the man bellowed, his throat tightening visibly against the collar of his button-down shirt. "Where is Alan? Why is the train stopped? We are never going to make it to Mallaig in time for the ceremony if we don't get going, and the whole point of this trip is for those of us who have spent good money to enjoy face-to-face time with Alan Gables! I want to see him now, or I will be demanding a refund."

Jonny's jaw clenched as his teeth ground together hard.

"We have nothing to do with the train service or Alan's ceremony. We are only distributing the food that Alan made, as requested."

The man did not settle a jot with that revelation. Folding his arms, he shifted his weight to his back foot. "And where exactly *is* Alan? I don't like to be kept waiting."

"Alan is preparing the next item on the menu," Claire announced, surprising Jonny and causing him to look at her in disbelief.

She let nothing slip in her expression. Her attention was wholly focused on this man and his ire. Her own concern about Alan wasn't apparent at all as she faced this man. For all anyone could tell, this was just part of the plan.

Ingenious.

"Is he?" the rabid fan queried, only slightly mollified.

Claire nodded eagerly. "I didn't even know what he had planned, and when I saw it . . . You won't be disappointed. It is a masterpiece, and you all will get to be the first to enjoy it. He has never done this before, I can promise you that."

Jonny blinked and glanced back at the fan, whose energy had completely shifted.

It was as though Claire had handed the man the softest puppy ever born. His eyes shone with moisture, his cheeks turned pink, and his smile looked like it might break his face.

Considering the raging bull he had been moments ago, there was only one conclusion that made any sense: This man was an actual psychopath.

Probably murdered that Brian guy too.

Jonny found himself looking at the man's hands, which were clenched together in front of his chest like a teenaged girl.

No bruising or scrapes on the knuckles, but that didn't mean anything.

He didn't look particularly rumpled either, and there was certainly a closer bar than Dining Car 3, but there was no accounting for impulses of the confined and crazy.

"Can we soothe your agitation with some of Alan's treats?" Claire offered sweetly.

"Please!" the man begged.

What the actual poppycock . . .

Barely hiding his irritation, Jonny handed over one of the plates without a word, not caring if he looked as murderous as he felt. What would one more dead body on this train be, really? Especially if he had good reasons . . .

Keeping his jaw tightly clenched and his teeth clamped together, Jonny did his part in dividing the rest of the prepared plates of treats to those in this section of the train. The promise of a brand-new treat from Alan in the future had soothed everyone else in the car, not just Mr. Crazy, and now the fervor was one of excitement and not complaint.

Jonny did not—and could not—care. He was done with this. The people, the questions, the anger, the lack of personal space. He was no runner, but he wanted nothing more than to open the train doors and go for a run out in the majestic Scottish Highlands.

A long, silent, people-less run.

"I can take the trolleys back," Claire murmured quietly. "The tarte tatin needs to be turned out and then put back in a warm oven, so I'm headed to the kitchen to check on it, and I can tell you need—"

Jonny shook his head before she finished. "I can manage them. You run ahead of me so you can do what you need to with the tatin thingy, then go to the compartment and relax. After I've cleaned up the trolleys, I'll join you and look over what we brought back from you-know-where. I need the distraction, and the menial work of putting this away might help."

Claire nodded, not meeting his eyes.

He bit back a sigh, knowing his brusque tone was not warranted with her; she'd always been able to read him like one of her favorite cookbooks. But he wasn't about to explain himself in front of others and air their personal business among those who were absolutely insane.

Together, they passed silently through Dining Car 1, Felicity still watching their every step, a notebook and pen on the tabletop in front of her, and a smirk on her lips.

Once they reached the gangway between the next two cars, Jonny cleared his throat. "Claire," he said as gently as he could. "Seriously, it's fine. Go. I'll be right behind you with the trolleys. You deserve a breather."

Her brilliant green eyes rose to his, searching for a moment.

He managed a smile, and received his favorite small one in return.

"You're a bit of a cinnamon roll, you know that, J?" Claire told him softly.

Jonny gaped for a moment. "I beg your pardon? A cinnamon roll?" His smile was much less forced now, even as irritated and disgruntled as he had been. "You take that back!"

"Abso-frosting-lutely not." She hummed a little, shaking her head. "Adorable, slightly crusty, gooey cinnamon roll of a man."

Okay, that was actually a decent compliment, especially considering the adoration in her tone, and the way her low hum had sent fire into the soles of his feet. Melting might be a good way to go, in this case.

Opinion revised.

Claire reached across his trolley to put her hand over his, her thumb brushing his skin back and forth for a moment as her smile lit up the rest of his body like a Christmas tree.

Then she was gone, down the corridor of the train, taking the light and warmth with her.

Jonny sighed and pushed-pulled the trolleys along into the next car. He wasn't about to give anyone else the chance to say something to him, so he did his best to maneuver quickly through the next few cars toward the kitchen, his eyes straight ahead and refusing to acknowledge anyone.

Until at the gangway that led into Dining Car 3, he was stopped by a security guard. The guard's eyes flicked to Jonny's badge, then nodded to the door with permission.

Once within the dining car, Jonny glanced beyond his makeshift barrier to find that Brian's body had been removed, leaving only the suspicious stain in its place.

Yeah, that would unnerve anyone, so hiding it had been a good call.

Jaw aching, Jonny moved through the dining car, past the private compartments in the VIP car, and into the kitchen, relieved to find all of it empty. He could use some peace and quiet. As he steered the trolleys back into the corner of the kitchen and then wiped them free of crumbs and spills, he felt grateful for the chance to work in silence and let his mind decompress.

Claire was sitting at the foldaway table in their compartment when he arrived, writing careful notes in the notebook she'd packed for new recipe ideas. She glanced at him with a slight smile as he entered, but that smile didn't reach her eyes.

Odd.

Then something else drew Jonny's attention.

Scratched into the table were two words: *Stay away.*

Jonny tilted his head. "What's that?"

Claire's eyes darted to it, exhaling a short, shaking breath. "Not sure. Table was down when I got here, but I know we put it away before we went to the kitchen. It's creepy, but probably nothing." Her tone wasn't convincing, but it was clear she'd hoped it would be, either for herself or for him.

Tension knit Jonny's brows together. "No, I don't think so, Éclair. We had that table down when you were telling me about where this train goes, and there was definitely no message on it then."

She shook her head. "We had so much stuff scattered around, J, we p-probably didn't notice it," Claire said, returning to her notebook, but her hands shook as she held her pen over it.

Was she *intentionally* trying to ignore this? Willing herself not to view it for what it was? With an actual dead body on the train, was she going to pretend this wasn't something to worry about?

"No!" Jonny yelled, surprising himself with his vehemence.

Claire stared at him with wide eyes, their emerald depths almost blinding with her constricted pupils. "What?"

Forcing himself to breathe, Jonny held out a reassuring hand, even if it shook. "No," he said again in a much calmer tone. "I'm sorry; I'm on edge. But that was not there before, Claire. You know it wasn't. Stop pretending, okay? I can see that you're spooked, and it's okay that you are. It was not there before. Which means not only is there a dead body on this train but someone is leaving messages in our compartment while we're out. I'm all for coincidences, but this isn't one of them. I can feel it."

She watched him for a long moment, her gaze darting between his eyes and various parts of his face, before she exhaled heavily. "You're right. Okay."

He released a sigh as relief punched him in the solar plexus. "Okay?"

She patted the seat next to her. "Okay, Cinnamon Roll. Come sit by me. Let's work this case and see what's happening on this train."

"I'm not a cinnamon roll," he grumbled, even as his mouth quirked. He moved to sit by her, almost collapsing onto the seat. "Unless I can be an intimidating one."

"An intimidating cinnamon roll?" Her brows rose again. "What is that supposed to mean? Or a fierce cinnamon roll?"

"You're the baker. You figure it out."

Claire heaved a sigh and patted his cheek with all the condescension in the world. "Very well, J. You're an adorable, fierce, handsome, grumpy, squishy, intimidating, half-baked—"

"Hey!" he protested loudly, flinging her hand from his face.

She snorted loudly and took his hand in hers, lacing their fingers and stopping the mischief. "But still pretty delicious cinnamon roll," she finished with her classic Claire grin. She brushed part of her hair from her face and touched his chin with her thumb. "But most importantly, you are *my* cinnamon roll."

Melting commenced.

Jonny took their entwined hands and kissed the back of hers quickly, ignoring the blatant threat on the table for now, but feeling an overwhelming dread that had him clutching her fingers a little more tightly than he would have done otherwise.

Just in case.

CHAPTER 5

"J, do you remember what you said about Brian's height and the distance to the bar?"

"No," Jonny answered without looking up at Claire. "I don't. Sorry."

Claire shrugged as she returned to her notes, forgoing any attempt at baking work and writing out her thoughts on the case instead. She adjusted her glasses that had started to slip down the bridge of her nose while she was hunched over her work. She wasn't bothered by Jonny's short answer, considering the mountain of paperwork he was currently reading through. He was only now getting a thorough look at the financial reports from Brian's briefcase, and from what she had glimpsed, they looked complicated.

He had been almost entirely silent since they had returned from serving treats to the passengers, and while she understood why, she was uneasy.

The confrontations with passengers they'd encountered would have been uncomfortable for anyone, but for Jonny—who avoided social situations wherever possible—having direct conflict thrust into his face was certainly going to send him into a tailspin. Or shut him down, in this case. He was like a hypersensitive introvert who had to completely power down in order to recharge after an uncomfortable social engagement, and he recuperated best when he could retreat into his perfect comfort zone bubble: Blackfirth Park, and, hopefully someday, with Claire.

She thought he was comfortable with her, even when he was overwhelmed. He was usually almost in constant contact with her physically when they were together, as though she helped to recharge his batteries. When he got back from business in London or trips elsewhere, it was even more prevalent. Holding her in his arms for long periods without words, linking their hands together whenever they walked, running his fingers up and down her arm or her back when they watched something on TV. He loved kissing her forehead, which always made her body ripple in warm shivers that edged her closer into his hold.

She didn't mind. She liked their natural and easy relationship, and even though she hadn't told him yet, she was certain she loved him. He felt like home to her, and what else could that mean? What else could explain the pull she'd felt with him from the first day they'd met until this very heartbeat? The connection only got stronger the more she was with him, and the idea of anybody else ever filling this role in her life made her feel sick.

But Jonny kept his cards close to his chest, and she was afraid of telling him any of this before she knew where his own heart sat. If this was a lopsided emotional connection, she didn't think she could bear it.

Which meant sitting and stewing over things entirely out of her control more often than not, but since her brain worked that way on almost every topic in existence, this was not a new trend.

For yeasted cake's sake, she was supposed to be working on the details of the late Brian Donovan right now, and she was worrying about her boyfriend's feelings!

Overthinking needed to stick to the topics at hand, not veer into other lanes and waste her productivity like this.

Her eyes flicked up to Jonny, and she felt her entire body soften at his look of frustration.

She knew it wasn't just about the material he was reviewing. He was certainly still bothered by the angry passengers who had taken out their frustration on him.

There were service agents on this train, all of them in uniform, and everyone should have known them by sight. Why would the passengers presume Jonny worked for the train company when he wasn't wearing anything official other than his lanyard and VIP badge? If he had been working in some official capacity, he'd have looked the part!

What was worse, it had been way too long since any of those official service agents had made any kind of announcement or update as to why the train was still stopped.

Slightly worrisome, that.

Poor Jonny. Nobody needed to face undeserved anger. But she knew him. He would rather face it than have her do it, and if they had come at her like that, he would have felt the need to defend her, and the situation would have gotten even more out of control.

But then he hadn't said anything when that Farrow woman had talked about her.

So maybe he would have frozen instead.

Or maybe—

"Well, blast," Jonny snapped as he set some of the papers down and pinched at his nose.

Claire jumped at the change in volume. "What? What's up?"

Jonny lifted the page before him. "He was skimming . . . Or someone was."

She did her best not to look as confused as she felt. "The only skim I know is of a pool and of milk. Care to explain?"

He turned the papers toward her, pointing at the lines he'd seen. "The financial reports are bogus. What is supposed to be showing investments is actually a bunch of garbage. You have to know what to look for, but as someone who has studied investment banking, it's plain as day. Someone wasn't being honest. I don't know who, or why Donovan had papers to prove it. And I certainly don't know where this apparently accounted-for money is now. But nothing is right about these numbers."

A knock sounded at their compartment, making Claire jump. The door slid open, revealing Conductor Lisa, looking apologetic.

"Sorry to bother you, Miss Walker, but I think we had better serve the next food item. I cannot find Mr. Gables or his assistant, and I've searched the entire train."

"Son of a biscuit," Claire whispered, giving Jonny a worried look before closing her notebook and tucking it into her bag on the floor. "I've got something ready and warming in the kitchen. Any word on whether we'll need to serve dinner?"

"It's becoming more and more likely." Lisa looked haggard as she answered. "The engineer still can't figure out the problem, and communication with the nearest stations is getting more troublesome."

"Why's that?" Jonny asked, standing up from the table.

Lisa glanced at him with tired eyes. "Storms, sir. They're rolling in as we speak, and they scramble the frequencies out here something terrible. We don't even know if our communication about the death has been heard, let alone our requests for help."

"You don't have a satellite or emergency phone?" Claire gasped, horror-struck by the idea.

"Not on this model of the train, no." Embarrassment added to the stress on Lisa's expression.

Crepes alive, was *anything* going to go right on this trip?

Jonny looked as though several non-baking swear words were circling his mind.

"I'll take care of the food," Claire said quickly, hoping to prevent her boyfriend's verbal explosion. "Don't worry. And let me know if there's anything else I can do to help."

Gratitude flashed in Lisa's eyes, and she managed a weak smile. "Ta, Miss Walker. And please don't say anything about this to Miss Farrow, if you see her. She's been sniffing around and asking questions I shouldn't answer."

"Of course she is," Claire grunted. "No worries, ma'am."

She nodded and left, striding back up toward the other cars.

"It's like being on the *Titanic*," Jonny growled as he held the door open for Claire to exit. "Stuck without answers and unable to communicate with anyone but hoping someone will come along and help."

Claire flicked her hand in his direction. "At least we're unlikely to drown in the Highlands. I'm more upset about Alan being missing and that Farrow cow sticking her nose where it doesn't belong. And if the train can't communicate with other stations, it means that word won't get to Mallaig that we're stuck. They're expecting Alan to arrive in a few hours, and he won't show up. Do you know how bad that'll look for him?"

Jonny tsked softly. "Don't call the Farrow woman a cow. You don't even know her."

Claire stopped and gave him an apprising look. "Did you hear how she talked about me earlier? And have you been present in your own body when she's around? She's as subtle as garlic breath, J. And if she says another thing about me in that snide voice of hers or comes onto you like that again, I'll have her kneecaps for knickknacks. Let's see how growing up in a pub works out for me then."

She whirled on her heel and marched toward the kitchen, shaking her head and muttering darkly.

"That's . . . actually quite terrifying," Jonny said as he hurried up to her. "I'm sorry, *ma crème.* I didn't mean . . . I'm on edge, and I don't like being here. Trust me, I want nothing to do with her."

"Just don't encourage her, okay?" Claire asked in a small voice, her anger turning to defensiveness. "I've got enough to be dealing with, and someone making moves on my boyfriend when I'm right here is unsettling enough."

"Plus the whole dead body thing?" Jonny suggested in a low voice.

Claire shuddered. "Yeah, there is that."

The moment the kitchen came into view, Claire felt herself go immediately into business mode.

"Alan didn't give me any indication of what we're supposed to do after the teatime stuff," Claire said briskly, taking the apron from the hook and tying it around her waist again. "I don't know what he was anticipating here, but I think the tarte tatin should go next. Small pieces, obviously. Smaller than we'd usually do. No slices, since we need to serve the whole train. Petit four size—yeah, that'll do it."

Jonny stood in the middle of the kitchen while she moved around it all. He was pretty good at figuring out what she needed in this state, usually waiting for her conversation with herself to stop and instructions to be heaped upon him. It was all part of her pattern; Claire would figure out what she had to do herself and what Jonny could assist with, and then make a plan. Only then would he take a step and begin helping.

He was such a good boyfriend that way. She had trained him well.

"J," Claire said with a quick turn that almost made him jump. "Plates. Small ones. I'll get to cutting. Then see if we have tartan napkins."

He made a face. "Tartan? Really, *ma crème*?"

She nodded once. "Really. This is Alan's creation: tartan tarte tatin."

"Please tell me that is all one word so I can use it in Scrabble."

She smiled, her eyes crinkling in delight. "Apologies, but three words. No bonuses for you. But take a look at the top and tell me it isn't dead on the money."

Crooking a finger at him, she pulled him to the oven, which had been set to warm, and revealed the creation within. She watched as his eyes widened and his lips parted. He blinked twice before shaking his head.

Yep. Tartan tarte tatin was impressive.

Because it worked.

Dratted Alan Gables and his talent.

"Always with the tartan," Jonny grumbled, shaking his head again.

"Okay, while I'm doing this, can I ask you something?" Claire bit her lip.

Jonny leaned against the counter and folded his arms. "Of course."

"Why me?" she blurted. "Out of all the bakers Alan knows—actual professionals!—why would he decide to collaborate with me?"

It was one of her biggest problems with this whole "partnering with Alan" thing. She was quite literally a no-name in the baking world, apart from the show. And even then, she hadn't done as many interviews as some of the others. She just couldn't see why Alan would pick her.

And Jonny wasn't the person to ask about this, but she didn't have any other options. He was too close to her, too biased, too everything, according to her. They'd had this argument about her insecurities before. Many times. Though it was mostly Claire arguing that he couldn't be relied upon for truth, and Jonny pressing his opinions anyway.

"How do you feel about what Alan said?" he asked in return.

Smart man.

Claire exhaled slowly, her eyes trained on her cutting work. "I honestly don't know," she admitted. "Don't get me wrong—I'm thrilled that he wants me to do the cookbook with him, but it's weird."

He frowned. "Why weird?"

She huffed. "J, there are plenty of other, more experienced bakers that are also fan favorites who would be amazing to work with. I'm worried that I won't have anything to offer. This could be my chance to actually become a baker professionally, and I don't want to mess this up."

"I don't think Alan would have brought you on board if he thought you would mess it up," Jonny assured her. "And he knows better than anyone what you have to offer, as well as who else is out there for potential partners. He chose you. Stop trying to make it complicated."

"But it's *weird*," she insisted with wide eyes. "I may not be the sharpest tack in the box, but I've got a good brain that works well. So when something doesn't make sense to me, I've got to know why."

He ruffled her hair, and she swatted his hand away. "Try not to stress so much about that stuff, okay? Alan is doing all this his way, for whatever reason, and he asked you to be his partner. That's got to tell you something."

"Like what?" she grumbled, his encouragement touching but also irritating with its perfection.

Jonny shook his head, smiling again. "Fishing, *ma crème*?"

She tilted her head back to give him a speculative look, her eyes twinkling. "Who isn't secretly fishing?"

"Me," he shot back.

Her eyes rolled dramatically. "If only we were all as secure as you, my crusty viscount. In the meantime, what do you think Alan is telling me?"

"That he thinks you can go toe-to-toe with him."

Claire snorted in derision, but Jonny went on.

"That he's comfortable with your name sharing space with his. That he sees more potential in you than just the show. That somehow you impressed him. Take your pick. It could be any or all of these things. Or none at all. Maybe he just likes you and he's not used to liking people."

Claire grinned up at him. "That seems to be the most likely scenario."

CHAPTER 6

The door to the kitchen opened, surprising them both. Greg entered, his expression frantic, his hair more unkempt than before. "Have you heard why we've stopped? We're going to be so late to Mallaig, and the unveiling will have to be pushed back. Why is Dining Car 3 closed? People are going to be so inconvenienced."

"Take a breath, Flaky Pastry," Jonny muttered in exasperation.

Greg looked like he might curl up in a corner in the fetal position in about five minutes.

"Greg," Claire said softly, as though fearing she would set him off. "It's good to see you again. We haven't heard anything, but maybe you can find out something by talking with the conductor? I am sure you can figure out how to adapt the schedule with this delay. Alan hasn't been here since he left for the interview, but I'm sure he'll be fine with whatever you come up with."

Greg began pulling at his hair, almost whimpering. "I need this to go well. Mr. Gables needs this event to be perfect so it honors him as it should."

"Just breathe, okay?" Jonny encouraged, though his tone left something to be desired. "Like Claire said, go fix the schedule. You can brainstorm how to adjust this to your advantage. That or you can help Claire with the tarte tatin thing."

Nodding slowly, then suddenly frantically, Greg turned toward the kitchen door. "Yes, yes, I'll go to the conductor. We'll make this work. We'll figure this out. Right."

And then he was gone, like an irritating muscle spasm that had no explanation.

"Well," Jonny finally said, looking at Claire, "that was random."

Claire shook her head, eyes widening. "He stresses me out, and that's saying something."

Jonny wisely said nothing on the subject, choosing instead to say, "I'll see what sort of napkins I can manage."

Claire returned to cutting the tarte tatin while Jonny hunted for plates and tartan napkins. He carefully situated each plate on the two trolleys they'd used before, then donned the spare apron himself.

He smiled at the sight of Claire in her own apron, quickly plaiting her hair, her glasses now safely in their case. Her eyes were tracking over the small squares she'd cut with swift analysis, and he wondered what her mind was spinning on, what her genius was up to.

She was a fascinating creature, and a steadying one for him. Even if they were about to go out among the passengers he'd just been cursing, her good nature was going to rub off on him.

At least enough to not have a second death on the train.

"What?" Claire asked, catching his smiling examination of her.

Jonny shook his head. "You're adorable. And I have no doubt the passengers will love your adorableness, too. Shall we deliver them their treats?"

She returned his smile with a curious look, her cheeks turning the slightest bit pink. "Probably should. I'll likely be figuring out sandwiches for everyone in a bit, and that's sure to be a stretch."

He tutted softly as they awkwardly maneuvered the trolleys out of the kitchen. "That bad?"

Claire shrugged. "I haven't gone through the kitchen thoroughly yet, but I know there's bread, and that's about it. Beggars can't be choosers, but I'm a baker. Surely I can do better than toast for everyone."

"I believe in your creativity and skills," Jonny assured her, gesturing for her to take her trolley ahead of him. "I just don't want you freaking out thinking this is some challenge on *BBB* that you might fail. Literally, this is feeding stranded people."

"You say potato, I say *pomme frittes*," she huffed. "Disappearing Alan or not, it's still his tribute train. This is happening." She pushed her trolley toward the next car, which housed compartments—including theirs—and paused a step. "Maybe we can use this to our advantage."

Jonny tried not to cough in surprise but failed miserably. "A disappearing Alan?"

She swatted half-heartedly in his direction. "No, you soft pretzel. Our investigation."

"Our what-igation?"

It was astonishing how blatant someone could be at rolling their eyes even from behind. She huffed loudly, her shoulders drooped, her neck craned, and her fingers splayed, all at the same time, right before her hands took the trolley handle in a vicelike grip.

"Are you really going to stand there and pretend we aren't investigating a potential murder, Jonathan?"

Jonny blanched at the use of his full name. His girlfriend had been hanging out with his sister too much. There was no other explanation for such extremes.

"Erm . . ." He tried to stall, like the raving idiot he was. "Not pretending as much as living in denial?"

"Why?"

"Because we can't possibly be that unlucky, can we?" He smiled with all the innocent hope in the world, though she had yet to turn around and look at him.

"Apparently, we can. Maybe I should title my first cookbook *Murder, She Poached*." She tossed a smile over her shoulder, her pert, full mouth curving up mischievously.

His grin could not be restrained. "How about *Dead Puddings*? *Battered Dishes*? *Croquette de Poison*?"

Claire tossed her head back on a laugh before turning around fully and meeting his gaze freely. "Why are you so quick with these? Have you been plotting since last time?"

"I have a sick sense of humor, remember?" he admitted without shame.

"Right." She cast a wink at him and turned back to her trolley, pushing again. "We should ask the other passengers some questions while we're handing these out. They might have seen Mr. Donovan around before, and he might have been acting strangely earlier. He might even have travel companions looking for him. Oooh, I wonder if we can ask the conductor about his reservation . . ."

Jonny shook his head as Claire continued to ramble,

amused at the way her mind worked and how her mouth seemed to be connected to the processing portion regardless of what else was going on.

He loved that about her.

Suddenly, Claire whirled back around to face him, making him stop in his tracks. "J!"

He took a step back, unsure if he was in trouble or if she had a horrible idea for him. "What?"

She smiled at him, which only half settled him. "Someone needs to talk to the bartender from Dining Car 3."

He blinked. How in the world had her train of thought taken her there with what she'd been saying before?

"Go find him," Claire encouraged with a wave, moving the trolley to the side. "I can handle both trolleys, and he could probably use a listening ear."

Jonny gave her a wry look. "Because I'm so good at that sort of thing."

She shrugged. "You listen to me."

He took a moment to wet his lips, then pointed a finger at her. "There are so many things I want to say to that statement, all of them true, and some of them not very nice."

"I'll be a good girl and listen to every single one of them," she assured him, her eyes sparkling with mischief. "*After* you talk to the bartender."

He looked at her for a long moment, then sighed, shaking his head.

He was hopeless at refusing her.

Grumbling good-naturedly, he passed her and went to the gangway connecting Dining Car 3 to the rest of the train, pausing to speak to the security guard.

"Do you know where the service attendants are at this time of day?" he asked on an already weary exhale.

The guard nodded. "Yep, in their break room just off Dining Car 2. You'll see it, no problem.

"Thanks," Jonny muttered, wishing the man hadn't had a clue and then Jonny wouldn't have had to speak with anyone at all.

Oh well.

The door to the break room was ajar, and only one person was inside. A large, burly man sat at a table, slowly drinking a coffee. He looked pretty shaken, and Jonny hoped it was the bartender trying to settle his nerves. That he was here alone was surprising, given what had happened. Was he not being watched by security? Or at least in the care of someone to make sure he didn't go into shock?

But no, he was just sitting here with his coffee.

The other service attendants were probably busy dealing with the understandably irritated passengers at the moment and might not even know the extent of what had happened yet.

All the better for Jonny.

"Hey," Jonny greeted as casually as he could, though it still sounded painfully forced.

The man looked up almost lazily, even with panicked, wide eyes. "H-hey."

"Are you one of the bartenders, by chance?"

He nodded, immediately wary.

"Dining Car 3?"

Again, just a nod.

Jonny held out a consoling hand. "It's okay. I'm supposed to come check on you, see what happened, that sort of thing."

Not entirely a lie, but . . .

"My name's Jonny," he went on. "What's yours?"

"Doug," came the grunted response. He ran a hand over his buzzed hair and pointed to the seat beside him. "You might as well sit, if you need to hear it all."

Jonny didn't say anything as he sat. He folded his hands in his lap and waited for Doug to speak.

After another long sip of coffee, Doug shook his head. "Mate . . . I don't even know what went down in there. The guy that . . . needed help . . ." He shifted his gaze around as though looking for anyone to call him out.

Jonny gestured for him to continue, trying for a reassuring smile.

Doug gripped the back of his neck. "He was nice enough. Didn't demand anything, unlike a lot of other customers you see. He came in completely sober, right? Stone-cold. He asked for whiskey neat, and that was it. Sat there quietly and minded his business." He took another swallow of his coffee. "I was in the back, prepping things for the evening rush. I can hear decently back there, and I leave a sign on the counter, so people know to ring the bell or call out." He shook his head. "I was gonna cut him off after the third was gone."

It was clear that Doug had been running this over in his mind like mad ever since it happened, coming up with defenses and excuses as well as reasoning everything out. No one expected a dead body at their place of work, certainly. And on a train, no less.

"So I hear some conversation, right? There had been a few others in the room when I'd gone to the back. But nobody was asking for me or yelling." Doug swallowed hastily, his eyes widening like he was reliving the situation. "And then I hear this crash, and I go out there . . . And the guy is on the floor, blood coming out of his head, and he ain't moving. Nobody else is there, everyone is gone but him. I come out and shake him, but there's nothing. He didn't even finish the third whiskey."

Jonny shook his head slowly. That was a tight timeline, and not a lot of time for anything nefarious to have happened. Not a lot of noise, not a lot of struggle, not a lot of alcohol. What in the world had happened in there?

"So he wasn't alone at the bar when you left?" Jonny asked, dropping his voice lower as if in simple curiosity. "When I was in there, it was just the doctor and the conductor and your boss. No witnesses or whatever."

Or whatever? Jonny didn't need to sound like an idiot to carry this conversation, but his word choices were certainly going to put him in that category.

Doug shook his head. "No, he wasn't alone. There were two others at the bar itself. I mean, the train hadn't been going that long, right? We just had the leg from Fort William to Glenfinnan, and the guy who . . . needed help . . ."

Apparently, Doug couldn't say the word *died*.

Interesting.

"Well, he came in just after we left Glenfinnan." Doug twisted his mouth in thought. "Red-haired lady came in shortly after, but she didn't stick around at the bar. Didn't see if she lingered in the car either. Apple martini for her, wanted an extra twist. Older guy came and stayed, just staring off at nothing. He was Jack and Coke. Young guy came in maybe ten minutes after him. Ordered a gin and tonic, which surprised me. I'd pegged him for craft beer or a Moscow mule.

Maybe a Firestarter or Corkscrew, possibly a sour of some kind, but he didn't seem *that* hipster, you know?"

Jonny's head was buzzing with the excessive details, but if Doug wanted to talk more than he should, Jonny wasn't going to stop him.

"Guys like him can be confusing," Doug went on. "I can usually read people well and start putting their drinks together in my head. I was pretty sure he'd like my vanilla whiskey mule, and I was gonna suggest it if he asked, but then, he might have been a Jack and Coke guy. Those come out of nowhere sometimes. Red, see, would have been a strawberry daiquiri for me, but an apple martini isn't too much of a stretch, so that's fine. Jack-and-Coke guy was totes Jack and Coke, trying to be all cool but he wasn't. One time, a guy just like him told me he wanted an Aperol Spritz, and I thought I'd lost my gift. Not that he couldn't enjoy that, of course, but drinks . . . drinks are like art."

"Uh-huh." Jonny could actually feel his eyes glazing over. Physically. It felt like tears, only much, much slower.

More painful.

Maybe Brian had hit his own head on the counter to stop Doug talking.

Rude, Claire's voice chided in his head.

"So young guy got a G and T," Jonny prodded when Doug took a breath.

Doug spasmed a little before nodding. "Yeah, he did. Just kinda sipped it and stared at nothing, just like Jack-and-Coke bloke. Whiskey dude, too. I don't think those three said three words to each other even though they all sat at the bar."

Except there had been some conversation when Doug

had gone to the back. Unless someone else had come in, they would be talking to each other.

And then one of them ended up dead.

"Any issues with anyone in the bar?" Jonny asked before he could stop himself. He winced and turned to look through the window in the door behind him. "I mean, I wonder if they saw what went down with the other one."

Doug hummed to himself. "Dunno. People usually stick to themselves, and it's a train, not a club. I wasn't really paying attention to the people. Dunno, man. My gift usually tells me what they'll drink, and I forget a lot of other stuff."

Ah, yes, his gift.

Jonny managed to refrain from rolling his eyes. "Wonder if there was a fight, you know? You heard something, didn't you?"

"There was a dark vibe, for sure," Doug told him eagerly. "Side-eye and such. Red was eyeing all of them like a cougar."

Well, that was as useful as useful could be, wasn't it?

Making a mental note to talk to Doug again when he wasn't potentially in shock, Jonny rose and patted him on the shoulder. "Alrighty, mate, if you need anything, let someone know, okay?"

"Thanks, will do."

Jonny moved into the next car as swiftly as he could, but swift was relative.

And the passengers were growing restless.

CHAPTER 7

It would have helped to have a picture of Brian Donovan to show people when trying to ask questions about him, but even if Claire had one, it would be of his dead body in Dining Car 3, and that would undoubtedly upset the passengers more than they already were about the delay and lack of Alan.

They were voicing those concerns at high volume, even as they thanked her for the treat.

And so far, she hadn't met a single person who had heard of Brian Donovan, let alone recognized her description of him. It was like he'd slipped onto the train right before it broke down and died the moment he'd come aboard.

That wasn't likely, she knew, but it was all the success she was having.

If Jonny was doing any better, he wasn't letting on.

In fact, he was as sour-faced as any of the passengers and saying nothing anymore. Whatever he'd learned from the bartender, he hadn't shared yet. If he'd learned anything.

Her stomach clenched every time she looked at him, and not in a way that was a testament to his attractiveness or her feelings for him.

She handed a plate to the next passenger to her right, a woman with two children beside her. "Would you kids like to try some tartan tarte tatin?"

Both began giggling at the rapid way she'd said the name. The boy might have been around ten, but the girl was certainly younger, maybe around seven. While neither had the gorgeous auburn hair of their mother, they looked just like her in every other respect.

"What kind of flavor is tartan?" the boy asked Claire with a wrinkle to his brow, his Scottish accent delightful to hear in his young voice.

"It's not a flavor at all," Claire admitted, crouching down beside his seat. "Alan said it was tartan because of the pattern on top. It's really just rhubarb. And there's some blueberry in there, too. I tried it earlier, and it's *so* good. But, I mean, Alan's the best, so . . ." She shrugged, not bothering to pretend like she wasn't a fan.

"Alan is my favorite," the girl admitted in much the same way, dragging out the A dramatically. "Dame Sophie always looks like someone has scared her, and she's trying not to be mad about it."

"Isla Grace Ferguson!" her mother scolded. "That is not a nice thing to say at all." She looked at Claire with concern in her eyes. "Sorry, Miss Walker. And we loved you on the show. You should have won."

"Definitely not Denis!" Isla chirped.

Her mother's eyes went wide, and her hand flew to her face in embarrassment. "Isla!"

"My sister doesn't like to use her filter," her brother confessed as he took a plate from Claire. "Drives Mam mental."

The mother now put her face in her hands. "Peter David . . ."

"What?" His bewildered look seemed as genuine as anything Claire had ever seen.

Claire chuckled and rose, reaching over to pat the mother's shoulder. "That's all right, ma'am. Kids say whatever they please."

She groaned and dropped her hands, revealing a crescent-shaped birthmark on her jaw and smiling kindly. "Mine especially. Hi, I'm Rose Ferguson, Miss Walker. And I promise, you really were our favorite."

"Thank you! And please, call me Claire." She winked. "I'll bring you a coffee later, Mrs. Ferguson, just for that."

Rose waved her hand. "Just Ms. Ferguson."

"Dad cheated," Peter offered helpfully. "He and his new wife moved to Majorca."

"Without inviting us," Isla added. "She doesn't like us, which is fine because her perfume is disgusting." She gagged before shuddering.

Rose sighed heavily, in that long-suffering way mothers often do, her smile going almost plastic. "Can you bring me two coffees? Especially if one of them has whiskey in it?"

Claire laughed and propped a hand on her hip. "I'll see what I can do." She looked at the two kids for a moment, her eyes narrowing. "Say, you kids seem to see and hear quite a lot."

"Understatement," Rose said with a nod as she cut into her dessert.

"Did you notice a guy in a blue dress shirt and dark pants earlier? Kinda blond hair with gray in it, clean-shaven, carried a briefcase?" She looked between the kids speculatively, banking on their lack of filters to help her out.

"There was that grumpy guy earlier," Isla mused, tapping her cheek. "He didn't talk to anybody at all, just sat over there in his seat and told the lady with the baby to keep it down. Didn't even say sorry for snapping at her."

Claire blinked in surprise. "Where was his seat?"

Isla pointed across and up the aisle a few rows. "Somewhere over there."

"Oh, him!" Peter nodded eagerly. "Yeah, he didn't have any headphones or anything. He just sat there. So weird."

"He could have been having a bad day," Rose murmured with encouragement. "Sometimes you just need to have quiet."

Peter rolled his eyes. "He could have read a book, Mam. But he didn't do that either."

Claire noted Jonny's trolley approaching, meaning he was almost done with his section, and she needed to move on to the rest of the car. "Thank you, Peter and Isla, for remembering that. And Rose . . ." She widened her eyes meaningfully. "I'll try to bring you something later."

"Thank you," Rose mouthed, her face bathed in gratitude.

With a nod, Claire pushed her trolley up toward the next row, handing out plates of tarte tatin and keeping her eyes alert for any passengers who might be able to help her.

It wasn't easy; most of the passengers were too irritated about the delay to want to talk about anything else. The ones who weren't complaining about that seemed to be determined to avoid conversation of any kind, apart from speaking to those they traveled with.

She couldn't blame them for that. She was the same way most of the time. When trapped in a confined space like a train—even one that was working properly—who wanted to talk to strangers? Privacy for the win, please and thank you.

Of course, there was always room for politeness toward those working in that confined space, and especially to those delivering food, drink, or safety information.

Not everyone seemed to have gotten the same memo that Claire had regarding that little detail.

The number of people who had completely ignored her except to take the offered plate and fork was astounding. No expression of gratitude, or even acknowledgment, and one gentleman had snapped at Claire that this was not what he had ordered and demanded to speak with her manager.

She'd never wondered what rhubarb tarte tatin would look like on green tweed, and she'd had to grind her teeth to avoid testing it by shoving the treat all over the man's ugly-as-aubergine jacket.

Not everyone was rude or dismissive, though. A few people had recognized her and accepted the treat for what it was. One had asked about the medical announcement from earlier, which Claire had been carefully vague about.

So far, however, the Ferguson family had been the only ones to give her any real information.

Those seated closest to Dining Car 3 had seen Brian Donovan head inside, of course, but no one had seen him come out.

No one had heard any problems from within, and no one had acted suspiciously in the vicinity of that car.

Which left randomly asking pleasant passengers for any information, just like she'd done.

And now, apparently, she'd found the seat where Brian Donovan had been sitting.

"Alan Gables's tartan tarte tatin?" Claire offered the beefy man with a bristle mustache sitting directly across from Brian Donovan's seat.

He grunted softly, nodding. "Why not? Boy's a Scot, seems to be doing well for himself. Must be doing something right, eh?"

"Must be," Claire echoed with a smile and a nod as she handed the plate over, biting back the flash of nerves about Alan's disappearance that lit up her body like lightning. She flicked her eyes across the space but saw nothing in the seats that might belong to Brian. There was, however, a small suitcase in the overhead.

She cleared her throat. "Any idea if your neighbor there would want one?"

The magnificent mustache swept brilliantly from one side to the other. "No idea, lass. Man's been gone since before the train stopped. Hasn't been back for his luggage either. Didn't seem to be traveling with anyone, so he might have settled in a dining car for the remainder. I have no doubt you'll find him somewhere."

Find him, yes.

Feed him, no.

Alas.

"*Pardon the interruption, ladies and gentlemen,*" came the clear voice of the conductor over the Tannoy. "*We have an update regarding the delay with our train.*"

The disgruntled murmuring sounds of the car stopped at once, many of the passengers looking toward the Tannoy as though it were a television.

"*Unfortunately, there has been some mechanical damage found in the wheels of one of the cars, and we are unable to safely move the train forward. We have been in touch with our nearest station, but the approaching storm has brought several delays in both the messaging and the resolution. We are working as quickly as possible on this issue and hope to have another update soon. Thank you for your patience."*

The clicking sound of the announcement ending was almost thunderous in the space, and, for a long moment, no other sounds were heard.

Then there came an almost collective groan, as if on a wave, and the gradual mumbling resumed.

Followed by an ominous flash of lightning and distant rumble of thunder.

"Strange," mused the mustached man beside Claire.

She blinked and looked at him with a polite smile. "What's strange, sir?"

The mustache twitched. "This is a steam train, restored etcetera from its days of regular use. As such, all of them are very carefully examined on the regular and pulled from service for repair and refurbishment the moment there is a hint of trouble. They take no shortcuts with these ones. No damage should be discovered during a trip with the steam trains. Just strange."

Considering the dead body that had been in Dining Car 3 as well, yes, that was incredibly strange.

And could not possibly be an accident, given that same dead body.

Coincidental accidents did not happen in quick succession like this.

A strange tingling started in the back of Claire's hands, but she did her best to ignore it as she continued along the train car, giving plates of tarte tatin to everyone. With the update from the conductor, no one was eager to engage with her, so she gave up asking about Brian Donovan. Why draw their attention to another strange thing when the broken train would clearly take precedence for them?

Besides, she'd have another chance when she delivered dinner.

Given the announcement they'd just made, it was fair to assume the train would continue to be delayed for even longer.

But how could she continue to investigate the death if she was in the kitchen again?

Could she and Jonny risk moving the investigation there? Really, all the information was back in their compartment, but it was portable, so all they needed was space to talk and go through the details.

Pushing her trolley into the final car in the line, she made quick work of handing out the last of her plates.

Then she pulled off to one side and waited for Jonny, who had only been slightly behind her.

He caught her look and came over at once. "What?"

Claire bit her lip, gnawing just a little. "I think I need to call a Chelsea Bun."

His eyes widened. "Oh, croquembouche!"

She snorted a laugh in surprise, covering her mouth.

Jonny's blue eyes sparkled with humor, his mouth curving crookedly. "I've been saving that one."

She nodded frantically, willing her impending hilarity to subside. Unsteady puffs of air exited her nostrils alone as she kept her hand in place, her chest tightening with the desire to throw her head back and roar out laughter.

But this was not the time nor the place.

Dead body. Confusing damage on a train. Public space.

Details.

Jonny chuckled at her attempted restraint and stood directly in front of her, blocking her face from anyone's view. "Doing okay there, *ma crème*?" He rubbed her arms a little. "Keep breathing, almost got it."

Her slow breaths were becoming less tinged with that tempting ridge of hilarity, and she lessened the pressure she'd placed on her face.

One more breath—no uptick in sound or giggles.

She dropped her hand to her throat, swallowing.

Still good.

She released a breath through gently parted lips, the final remnants of mirth dancing away on that same air.

How dramatic.

"Right," she sighed, patting herself at her pulse point. Then she pointed her index finger at Jonny. "Don't do that to me again. Rude."

He nodded obediently, his smile remaining perfectly in place.

"Also." She patted his cheek fondly. "Well done! That was good. I'll store it for later use."

"Glad I could help." He gripped her upper arms, finally sobering. "So, Chelsea Bun?"

Ah, yes, returning to the possible murder on the train where no one knew who the murderer was or if said murderer had also broken the train, thereby stranding them all in the Highlands.

"Yeah," Claire admitted roughly. "I found out some things, and the kitchen might be the only place we have where actual privacy can be assured. I don't know how much I trust our compartment, really. Creepy table scratching and all."

"And no one else has access to the kitchen without a badge," Jonny added with a nod. "Sounds good." He pointed toward the door behind them. "I see our friend the lead service attendant there. I'll ask him to arrange for the other attendants to collect the plates and leave my trolley here for them. Maybe they can field the incessant complaints about Alan not showing up and deal with the melee of stupid questions that have been shoved at me in the last few minutes."

Claire felt the sting in his words, the coldness of the previous version of himself returning. "You didn't have to do this."

"I couldn't leave you to do it alone," he retorted as though that had been obvious. "I can cope."

Except he wasn't coping, was he?

Jonny, like Alan, wasn't a people person. He'd been rude to the television team when *Britian's Battle of the Bakers* had first arrived at Blackfirth, hating the idea of people on his estate and those same people asking personal questions about his family and their history. And hating people he didn't know being in his general vicinity. But he had gotten so much better as the show went on, and as he'd gotten to know Claire. And she almost never saw the cool and detached viscount anymore.

But here he was, clearly hating anything to do with the other passengers and Claire's baking for them. He was fine when it was the two of them, for the most part, but the rest . . .

She was hoping to have a career like Alan Gables one day, which would mean occasionally doing things like this. Would Jonny hate that too? Would he be the aloof and distant

Viscount Colburn instead of her sweet and funny Jonny Ainsley?

Would he resent her for forcing him to do stuff like this?

"You head to the kitchen," Jonny said tersely. "I'll push your trolley back."

Swallowing the pain in her throat and the sudden desire to cry, Claire forced a smile and started back down the train. People didn't pay attention to her this time, and she didn't give them the chance to, tucking her badge into her shirt to keep anyone from thinking she was official.

Without a uniform or insignia to set her apart, she could return to being a regular passenger without responsibilities, inside information, or a nagging sense of inevitability and helplessness about the situation she was in.

For the next few minutes, she could just be Claire on a train.

Not Claire Walker, *BBB* contestant.

Not Claire Walker, Alan Gables's sorta friend.

Definitely not Claire Walker, amateur sleuth.

Just Claire.

But even then, Just Claire had loads of questions that her mind would not stop turning over, and she had to be all the other Claires for those questions to get answers.

A waft of tacky, suffocating perfume hit Claire's nostrils, and she twitched like a dog needing to sneeze.

"Miss Walker, have you seen Mr. Gables?" asked the perky, snide, nails-on-a-chalkboard voice.

Still reeling from the olfactory assault, Claire blinked dazedly and tried to smile at the all-angles and contoured face of Felicity Farrow as she stepped into the aisle. "Sorry, Miss

Farrow, I haven't seen him in some time. Not since he left with you, actually."

Felicity pouted, and her too-thin brows pulled against her Botoxed forehead. "Pity. That was *ages* ago. I wonder if something is wrong." The pout faded, and the painted lips curved into a smile that Claire knew shouldn't be trusted. "It would be dreadful if something else should come out on this little tribute tour of his, right when he is riding the high of his career. It would be a shame if something salacious ruined everything. Do you have *any* idea where he is? Or why he is hiding? What could be so secret about Dining Car 3? Do you know anything?"

"I know a lot of things," Claire admitted with a shrug. "Just not where Alan is or what's going on with him."

The muscle beneath Felicity's left eye ticked, but nothing else on her face changed. "Thank you, Miss Walker. You're still okay to talk to me later, right? Maybe once the train is moving again?"

"Of course. I'd be happy to." Lies, but she had promised Alan she would do it, so . . .

Felicity eyed Claire's apron for a moment, then made a faint humming sound and resumed her seat, crossing one of her exposed, trim legs over the other and letting the ridiculous heels bob in the air. "And do let me know when you see that dish of a viscount again. He and I are going to have a rather in-depth, rather *personal* conversation before we reach Mallaig." She inhaled through her teeth like she was slurping something delicious and made a point of shivering. "I am fascinated by his stoic manner, and I think I have just the thing to unleash the primal beast lurking hungrily beneath the surface. It's just there, you know. I can see it in his eyes. Something forgettable women haven't a hope of pulling out. Best to leave the real men to the real women."

Claire stared at the woman in horror, her face flushing with embarrassment, indignation, disgust, and shame.

The fact that shame was in the mix was mortifying.

Felicity waved her away like a gnat. "Ta-ta, Miss Walker."

Claire rolled her eyes and continued toward the kitchen, clenching her jaw tightly so she wouldn't say any of the things in her mind out loud. No need to look unhinged with everything else going on. And if Felicity could wield the power of the pen even half as well as her ego projected she could, Claire didn't need to give her fodder.

And she definitely didn't like the excitement and speculation she'd seen in Felicity's eyes or her creepy smile.

Sniffing out a story bigger than Alan's exclusive was definitely high on the woman's priority list, and, whoever Brian Donovan was, he did not deserve to have his death ratted out by Felicity Farrow.

Claire pushed into the kitchen at last, grumbling under her breath about heifers and rough puff and combinations that didn't even make sense to her.

"Something to share with the class?" a deep brogue asked.

Some blend of a shriek, a yelp, and a cough escaped Claire's lips as her eyes flew to the figure in the room she hadn't noticed before, currently sporting a bruise on his right temple and his usual glower.

"Alan?" Claire managed, once her heart sank back into its proper place in her chest. "What the puffed pastry happened to you and where have you been?"

CHAPTER 8

Jonny hadn't expected to find Alan Gables in the kitchen with Claire when he entered with Claire's empty trolley. Nor had he expected to find the man putting a bag of frozen peas on his head. Nor had he expected that frozen peas would be in stock on board a train, but that one was a little irrelevant at the moment.

What he was not expecting most of all was that Alan would be shaking and sitting on the floor of said kitchen, bag of peas on his head, and talking to Claire as if he hadn't been missing for hours.

Neither of them did more than look at Jonny as he entered the kitchen, returning to their conversation as he parked the trolley and removed his apron.

"I've gotta get a doctor to look at you, Alan," Claire said in a low, urgent voice. "You were unconscious, for heaven's sake!"

"I remember, Claire," Alan grumbled. "Well, I remember waking up, anyway." He shifted his weight and held out a visibly trembling hand. "What do I do about this?"

"That's what a doctor would be able to tell you, you stubborn apricot," Claire snapped.

"I don't trust anybody on this train except you two," Alan shot back. "Can you blame me? I was minding my own business after chatting with Felicity and got a forcible nap for my troubles, then woke up in the ruddy storage car."

Jonny took the liberty of moving to the kitchen door and leaning against it, just in case anyone else on the train decided to enter unexpectedly. "No warning at all? Nothing suspicious?"

Alan shook his head, exhaling roughly. "I had been in my compartment doing the interview with Felicity, and we had just finished up with some wildly inappropriate questions about my past. She left, and I was in a right state and fit to pound some bread dough to get it all out of my system before seeing passengers in an official capacity. I went to the dining car where I was waylaid by some busybodies. All I did was move toward the compartment car, and then it was, Good night, Alan."

Claire sat fully on the floor, shaking her head. "Crepes alive," she whispered. "What is going on here?" She looked at Jonny, her eyes wide.

He had no answers for her, so he shook his head, folding his arms.

"What?" Alan inquired as he looked between the two of them. "What did I miss?"

Claire groaned and got up from the floor, snatching some of the leftover shortbread from earlier. "What didn't you miss? J, can you fill him in? I gotta think about dinner."

"Train's damaged," Jonny told Alan while Claire puttered

around the kitchen, munching on shortbread. "No word on how long the delay will be."

"Which my mustached friend I met says is weird," Claire chimed in. "Told me they check these trains regularly for even baby damage since they're so special. If there was even a hint of trouble before leaving Fort William, this train would have been pulled from service and another brought in. So, you know, super weird."

So much for Jonny filling Alan in, but Claire's information was really good, so he'd give her that.

"But not the weirdest," Jonny told Alan with a tight smile. "There was a dead body in Dining Car 3."

Alan's eyes went round, and the bag of frozen peas dropped to his lap. "A what now?"

"Body," Jonny repeated. "A dead one."

"Blimey," Alan breathed.

"Yeah," Jonny said on a long exhale. "Train officers and doctor both think accident, but Claire's pretty sure it was foul play. We just don't know who or what or why."

"Oh, is that all?" Alan asked with mild politeness before scoffing and shaking his head. "How did you two get caught up in it again? Someone trying to kill you, Claire?"

"Probably, given the carved threats on tables and such, but this time, I was freaked the dead body might be *you*. Turns out, not you." Claire huffed and closed the fridge with a frown. "There's gotta be a decent pantry in here."

Alan pointed toward the far corner, saying nothing.

"Thanks, boss." Claire moved in that direction and started looking in the indicated cupboard from top to bottom. "Nothing like desperation to work up one's creativity."

"Are we more worried about the murder or the meal?" Alan barked with a surprisingly dramatic flourish of his hand.

"Both!" Claire shrieked. "I don't know about you, Alan Gables, but being trapped in the Highlands on a train where we are supposed to be feeding people *your* recipes while bodies drop like flies wasn't exactly on my particular bucket list. And I've specifically been asked to provide dinner, since we'll be here a while."

Alan glanced over at her. "They said that?"

"Not officially, but pretty much." She went on her tiptoes to look as high as she could. "I'm trying to be proactive. And since we did so well with baking during a murder investigation last time, why not?"

Alan shook his head in an almost pitying manner. "There is something very twisted about what you just said, Claire."

"Plaited, if you please, Mr. Gables," she shot back. "I'm a good loaf, perfectly proved."

Alan groaned, covering his face with one hand, then drawing it down slowly until he gripped his chin. "Look, I may be going into shock here, and I know why we're all on this train, but I don't think I can go out there. I've already been attacked once, and when you throw a murder into it? Just not a good idea until you figure this out."

Claire stopped at his words and whirled around, her eyes wide. "Frosting fudge cakes and tripe!"

Alan looked at her in horror. "That sounds as disgusting as actual vulgarities."

"You."

"Me what?"

"What if this is all about *you*?" She inhaled a sort of squeal and leaned against the wall. "The victim looks a little like you, except you're darker in the hair. This is your special train thing. Everybody here is pretty much obsessed with you. You were attacked. We're in your homeland. Crepes alive, this is an 'attack Alan Gables' mission. And you brought us in here, which means we're probably going to be targeted too. Maybe even that journalist because she's interviewing you, and cakes and a custard, this is bad. Huge. Massive conspiracy. This is a train of doom and destruction. And dessert, actually, but . . . never mind."

Alan blinked twice, then looked at Jonny. "I lost her at the fourth random roundabout. You?"

"About the same," Jonny confirmed with a nod. He held out a hand to Claire, which she clutched at once. "We're not going to play hopscotch with conclusions, okay? As of right now, we don't have proof of anything."

Claire looked up at him, her eyes wild and filled with panic, something he hadn't seen in her since she'd realized the danger in the baking pavilion earlier that year.

He didn't have any answers or consolation to give her, but at least he could try to keep her from that ledge of desperation. It was most of what he'd done last time, anyway.

Last time. It was ridiculous that they were back in this sort of world again.

"What did you learn from the passengers?" Jonny asked in as calm and soothing a tone as he could manage. "Anything?"

Claire swallowed slowly but nodded. "He was a loner. Didn't travel with anyone. Didn't talk to anyone. Left his luggage in the overhead and it's still there. I'd kill a certain someone to get a look through that, you know."

"Oh, I know," Jonny assured her with a small laugh.

"Let's not talk about killing anyone when someone is actually dead in the vicinity. How about that, hmm?" Alan quipped in a surprisingly comical voice.

Jonny looked over at him. "Still feeling off, Alan?"

"Cannae feel my feet and my hands willna stop shaking, but my heid feels the same. Knees have vanished, and I'm rambling like Claire, so I dinnae ken what that means . . ." Alan's breathing turned more frantic, and all the humor left Jonny's mind.

"He's gotten more Scottish too," Claire pointed out as they moved over to their friend on the floor.

Jonny reached for a bottle of water in the fridge and twisted off the cap. "He got *very* Scottish for a second there."

"Right here," Alan reminded them as he took the water. "Just as Scottish a' before."

"Biscotti," Jonny scoffed in complete and utter derision. "You went from regular old Scottish to *capital* Scottish with italics and a tartan font. 'Scotland the Brave' called and asked for you. *Braveheart* fell at your feet. I'm surprised a golden kilt didn't materialize out of thin air and wrap itself around you."

Alan guzzled the water for a few moments, then sighed loudly. "Dinnae need tae wear a kilt constantly when the kilt is on the heart."

Claire scrunched up her face in clear disgust. "That was cheesier than fondue, and I really don't like that it came out of his mouth, of all people. Can I please get a doctor now?"

"I'll just put my feet up and drink this," Alan offered as he turned and laid down on the floor, propping his feet up against the cabinets of the kitchen. "That's what they say to do for shock, right? Raise the feet and all that?"

Jonny shook his head. "You're asking the wrong people. I've never taken a first aid class beyond the basics."

"And medical shows make me queasy," Claire offered with a grimace. "So just lie there until you feel better. I'll find something for you to eat."

Alan snapped his fingers and pointed up at the counter. "Just bring a piece of the tarte tatin. That'll do well enough."

She did so, patting his head like a child before going back to the pantry. "J, what about the bartender? We never talked about that."

"Ah, Doug." Jonny shifted his weight to lean against the nearest counter. "Brian was on his third whiskey when Doug went into the back, but when he returned to the bar, the victim was on the ground, dead. Said he didn't say much to him at the bar, didn't seem drunk when he got there, was polite. No problem."

"So, square one?" Claire prompted as her brows knitted together.

Jonny smiled against his better judgment. "Not quite. Turns out, a few others were at the bar while Brian was."

Claire's mouth fell open with an appropriately audible gasp. "Seriously? Why didn't anybody tell us this before?"

"Either Doug didn't tell them, or they didn't ask." Jonny lifted a shoulder quickly. "Who knows? But Doug told me."

"Who was there?" Alan demanded, drawing his attention.

Jonny made a face. "That's where it gets stupid. Doug doesn't know who they were, can't remember much except that what they got to drink. And one of them was maybe a hipster because he got a gin and tonic."

"Why is that a problem?" Claire asked with a laugh. "That's a pretty standard order."

Jonny clicked his tongue in agreement before holding out his hand and shrugging. "Doug's gift says he should have had something else. I was afraid to ask what that meant my drink should have been."

"Yes, we all wonder that," Alan mused, stroking his facial hair slowly. "Did Doug say anything else about what happened?"

"He was apparently gone for only ten minutes or so, but he might have been in his own head, gifting or whatnot." Jonny widened his eyes meaningfully before rolling them. "He swears he can always hear someone yelling for him or ringing the bell, and none of that happened. He heard some talking, none of it clear, and then a crash. He rushed back to the bar when he heard that."

"But whoever was in there left the car before Doug came back, obviously," Claire said as she bit her lip. "No one else was there when we saw the body. So who knows what those people know? No one can tell who was there when the trouble went down, but someone in that group likely knows he's dead."

Jonny shook his head, scoffing to himself as he heard another crash of thunder outside. "I can't believe we're actually stuck here and they're struggling to get word to the nearest station. Why don't they just give us back our phones and let us connect with people, if they can't do it themselves?"

"Good luck with that," Alan griped. "The contract for this trip is tighter than anything you drew up at Blackfirth. And besides, this train's Wi-Fi doesn't work well even when we're not stuck in the middle of the Highlands in a storm."

"Ride it often, do you?" Jonny asked with only a passing interest.

"Used to," came the reply from the floor. "Still the best

way to get from Fort William to the coast if you're not in a hurry. And if you don't want to work or communicate via devices on the way. The stations are the only places for stable connections."

Jonny twisted his mouth as he considered that information. "So if someone wanted to keep the train from communicating, say, a death or something to the authorities, making the train stop in the middle of the Highlands would be a good way to do it?"

Alan nodded in firm, clipped motions. "Exactly the way to do it. Especially on the run through the nature preserve like we are now."

"Not doing much to calm my conspiracy theory over there, are you?" Claire mused as she started pulling things out of the pantry and putting them on the counter. "People seemed to think Brian was irritating and cranky, wished he would apologize."

"Maybe that's why he needed a strong drink," Alan suggested. "I don't apologize when I need one either."

"Do you apologize ever?" Claire asked with a pointed look that Alan completely missed.

He seemed to consider that. "If it's deserving."

"Crepes alive," Claire mumbled, sniffing dismissively. "Like making full puff pastry with completely frozen butter."

Jonny smirked at her back. "I'll take your word for it."

"It just has to thaw, Claire!" Alan protested as though she'd insulted him. "Come on, that's not a great analogy."

"*You* need to thaw, is what you're really saying," Claire retorted over her shoulder. "And I agree, so no fridge time for you. Ugh!" She slapped the counter and looked around at what she had gathered. "What am I going to make with this randomness? I can't feed people on this!"

Alan rolled his eyes and uttered a gravelly, growling sort of groan. "Claire! Stop faffing about and just make tattie scones!"

"Gesundheit," she replied. "Speak English now and I might reply more specifically."

"Potato scones," came the dry and very succinct response. "I see the bag of potatoes on the floor of the pantry. Potatoes, flour, butter, salt. The end. Serve with butter and jam or part of a full breakfast or make a basting sandwich out of them, it doesn't matter. Easy and filling."

Claire turned, leaning back against the counter and looking down at her mentor in surprise. "Why didn't you tell me that a long time ago? You saw me going crazy."

"Sure, ask the man who got walloped on the head why he's not thinking clearly, that's fair." He closed his eyes and fumbled his hand around the floor. "Where's the ruddy bag of peas?"

Sympathy flickered across Claire's face as she picked up the frozen food and brought it back over to Alan. "Sorry. Stress. Don't really like the idea of a killer running around the train, and all that."

"Not especially fond of it myself, but here we are." Alan put the bag on his forehead, mostly covering his eyes as well.

Claire made a disgruntled sound. "Considering it might be all your fault, I would think you'd be a little less carefree about it, haggis eater."

"Oh, cheeky," Alan chirped from the floor. "Murder makes the good girl snarky."

"You have no idea." Jonny flicked his eyes to the man

knowingly, his tight smile hiding his amusement. "Last time, she—"

"Can we stop saying 'last time' like this is going to become a thing?" Claire interrupted, throwing her hands in the air.

Jonny thought for a moment, then shook his head. "No. Not until we prove it isn't going to become a thing, and, at this point, we can't do that."

Claire gave him a hard look. "Jonny—"

"Potatoes, Claire!" Alan barked. "Boil and peel."

That caught her off guard, and she looked at Alan in confusion. "Don't you mean peel and boil?"

"If I *meant* peel and boil, I would have *said* peel and boil!" he snapped, gesturing toward the stove. "Boil and peel!"

Claire's jaw worked as she stared at her mentor in irritation, but then she marched over to the pantry and picked up the large bag of russet potatoes. "Okay, master chef, let's see your game," she mumbled darkly.

Jonny turned and raised a brow at Alan.

The other man shrugged. "She can't be fussing as much if she's working, aye?"

"I can still hear and respond," Claire called from her new position by the sink, where she was filling a large silver pot with water.

Alan chuckled as he adjusted the frozen peas on his head. "Greg's going to burst a gasket. A bruise on my head, a dead body on the train. And based on Felicity Farrow's tone during our interview, she's probably out for blood, searching the train to find me."

Claire whirled around, her green eyes wide. "She can't. If she sees the blood in Dining Car 3 or sees how you look—"

Jonny was already nodding. "I've got this. You two stay here and do your thing; I'll distract her. Alan . . . maybe don't leave?"

Alan held out a thumbs-up, cradling the frozen peas to his head.

Claire bit her lip as she looked at Jonny, her brows arching upward in a perfect display of concern.

"Don't worry, *ma crème*," Jonny said with a smirk. "I'll give her some interesting details about Blackfirth that didn't make it into the show. She'll be thrilled."

Claire didn't look convinced but nodded all the same.

Jonny slipped out of the kitchen and headed for the compartment car ahead of them, followed by the infamous Dining Car 3, wondering how far Felicity would go in her search for Alan. He wasn't sure where her seat was, but that wasn't really the point. Keeping her away from Alan and Claire was the point, and that was what he was going to focus on.

He had almost made it through the entire next car of passengers when he saw her entering, her carefully constructed face of makeup set in a stony glare that perfectly matched the angles she'd given herself.

Against his natural inclination, Jonny smiled broadly enough to hurt his face. "Miss Farrow! I was just looking for you."

Her features softened in surprise, and her eyes widened before a seductive smile curved her lips. "Were you, my lord?"

Jonny nodded and fought back the shudder threatening his spine. "You mentioned how you'd like to hear about some of the legends of Blackfirth Park. There's much more to my home than what the show portrayed, and no one else has written about it."

"Oh, I am certain there is more to it," Felicity purred as her eyes shamelessly raked him from head to toe, her tongue darting out to lick her bottom lip. She tilted her head back in the direction she'd come from. "This way, my lord. I know a quiet spot where you can tell me all about it."

"Sounds perfect," Jonny said with a smile, wondering if it was a lie if his definition of "perfect" did not match hers.

CHAPTER 9

"Ladies and gentlemen, pardon the interruption."

Claire winced at the voice through the Tannoy, pausing in her ricing of the potatoes.

Yes, the boiled-*then*-peeled potatoes.

Alan insisted. Three times.

"*We regret to inform you that, in part due to the storm, no resolution to our malfunction will be possible this evening. We will be providing everyone with a full reimbursement of their tickets as well as blankets and pillows for tonight's accommodation. A light meal will be provided this evening as well as breakfast in the morning, by which time we hope the team from Glenfinnan will have helped resolve our problems and get us moving again. On behalf of Scottish Rails and the Mallaig Steam Express team, we sincerely apologize for this disruption of your plans. Passenger service team members will be coming around shortly to assist with your immediate needs. Thank you.*"

Even in the small kitchen space, the Tannoy clicking off was thunderous.

All night trapped in the Highlands on a train that couldn't move.

With a murderer.

"It's fine," Claire whimpered to herself as she shifted her weight from side to side and resumed the ricing of her potatoes. "It's fine, it's fine, it's fine, it's absolutely fine—"

"Got a problem there, lass?"

"It's fine," she insisted more loudly. "We are perfectly fine. I am perfectly peachy and fine."

"Keep saying it and you might get an echo."

Claire closed her eyes and exhaled slowly, seeking for zen or whatever. "Shut up, Laird McChuckles."

"On behalf of my ancestors, I find that offensive."

"To quote mine, you don't have to go home but you can't stay here."

Alan chortled loudly, the sound mingling with assorted snorts and gasps.

She looked over at him. He was no longer sprawled on the floor but sitting against the wall like a drunk university student. "Someone's feeling better."

He shrugged. "Can't do anything about the situation, my head is feeling better, and I'm not working, you are. So I am actually fine."

"Murderer on a train." Claire shook her head and added another potato to the ricer. "Why would they want to kill someone? And stop the train?"

"Well, maybe the train got stopped to keep the murder a secret a little longer. Maybe the murderer isn't even on the train anymore and made a run for it."

Claire turned mid-ricing, staring at Alan in surprise. "You think?"

His lips twisted and his brows creased as he shrugged. "It's what I'd do. We're in the middle of a national preserve, and no one on the train is going to be running after him, are they? I mean, security guards are around, but are they the police? Are they really?"

He said it so calmly, so carelessly, it was almost eerie. "Did you kill him, Alan? And bump your head trying to run away?" She smiled as she asked, but there was a hint of a catch in her chest as she did so.

He gave her a wry grin. "No, Claire, I didn't. Who is this bloke anyway? The victim, I know—don't be smart. But do you know who he is?"

Only mildly appeased, Claire turned back around. "Not really. Just what we got from his ID, and some business papers in his bag. So we know who, technically, and that's about it."

"That won't help all that much, really." She heard the rustling of shifting weight against the floor, followed by a sigh. "Without phones, they'll have to wait to notify the victim's family."

Claire made a noncommittal sound as she continued working on the potato scones.

Family. What about Mr. Donovan's family? Did he have one? He was traveling alone, they were fairly certain, but was there someone waiting for him at Mallaig? Back in Fort William? Was someone expecting a call from him about his day?

He hadn't been wearing a wedding ring, but not every man did. And not every relationship was a marriage. Were there kids at home?

Tiramisu, what a depressing train of thought.

And Jonny wasn't here to discuss any of it with her.

He'd been gone for ages now, which wasn't doing anything for her nerves. The potatoes had all been boiled and peeled and almost all of them were riced, and still there hadn't been a word from him.

The idea of distracting the journalist was a good one, and she hadn't thought anything of it when he'd suggested it, but it wasn't supposed to take forever. He was supposed to just give Felicity something else to write about or think about, something to keep her away from the investigation and Alan, not spend the rest of the afternoon with her. What was he doing? Giving her a tour of the entire train like he somehow knew it that well?

Seriously, how long should it take to distract a journalist?

"Depends on the journalist."

Claire froze, her eyes widening until they burned like a griddle. "Did I say that out loud?"

"Sure did. Missing your boyfriend?"

She harrumphed and began ricing with more enthusiasm. "Not in the sappy 'I can't live without him breathing my same air' way. I just wish he was here to talk some things out with me, maybe look over the information while I'm working. Can't solve a crime without the other half of my brain."

Alan scoffed. "Solving a crime. Who asked you to, Claire? Besides, you've met Felicity Farrow. She's a bulldog dressed as a Barbie. She's not gonna let things go easily. If your boyfriend is trying to keep her off the scent, it's gonna take some hefty finessing."

"Maybe it's the finessing that has me worried," she grumbled.

The rustling from behind her increased, and she heard surprisingly heavy footsteps behind her. Then Alan was leaning against the counter and folding his arms, staring at her.

But she wasn't looking at him, so what exactly his eyes and his expression were doing was a little unclear.

"Are you out of your actual mind, Claire Walker?" he asked in an scolding tone that was somehow still soft and soothing enough to be comforting.

It was a confusing combo.

"No," she protested stubbornly as she began carefully and forcibly ricing the last of the potatoes.

"Viscount Hots-for-You—yes, we all call him that—isn't about to elope from this train with some tart from Tottenham or wherever she's from. All that folderol and fashion and foundation she's got doesn't amount to half of the actual attractiveness that you've got in spades. And I'm saying this as a man who has exactly zero interest in you."

"Gee, thanks, boss," Claire managed, her face flaming. "Way to make a girl feel special."

He coughed in disgust. "Don't be petulant, Claire. It's beneath you. I've no interest in you, but that doesn't mean I'm blind. You're worth at least twelve of the Felicity Farrows of the world, and likely thirteen because a baker's dozen is better. And that's not me speaking as a friend. That is just God's honest truth from a red-blooded member of the male species. I may not be part of your boyfriend's fan club, but I ken well enough that he's got a good head on his shoulders and eyes enough to see what's real. He went up about forty points in my book just for being with you. So whatever nonsense you think he's up to with that woman, just don't. Don't."

Somewhere in the middle of Alan's speech, Claire's eyes began to burn with unshed tears. She could not—would not—cry in front of her mentor. Not about a boy, not about a bake, not about a murder. Someone needed to tell her eyes that, but if tears could fade by willpower alone, hers would vanish at any moment.

Any time now.

She managed a tough and watery swallow, which only made her eyes worse.

Where was that willpower again?

"Claire . . ."

She exhaled shortly and did her best to avoid blinking. "Stop being nice, Alan, or these tears I'm fighting are going to leak, and I'll never be able to look at you again."

"I'm not being nice, you daft woman. I'm trying to scold you."

"Then hit me on the back of my head because right now you sound like my dad or my uncle, and that's not helping my tears."

A friendly swat to the back of her head caught her off guard, then the tension in her chest burst into peals of laughter that pushed her tears out of her eyes and down her cheeks, but without any of the emotion behind them she had feared. Nothing but hilarity and relief remained in their wake—the perfect antidote to the pity party she had been hosting.

"That's more like it," Alan muttered. "Tears are terrifying, especially in a woman. Never ken what's behind them or what to do about them."

"Eh," Claire said with a half shrug and a sniffle as her laughter began to fade. "Most of the time, a hug and some chocolate will help. Arm around the shoulders will do if you're not the hugging type. Sitting next to her if you're not the touching type. Don't try to fix whatever it is unless she asks, but if you're there with her and waiting, she'll probably tell you why and what and all that."

Alan wiped away a tear on her cheek. "Thank you, Dr. Claire. Next on this episode of *Help Me Understand Women*, we have—"

She swatted at his hand with a playful scowl, which made him smile.

"Right, let's add some butter and salt to this riced potato blend of yours," Alan told her, rolling back his sleeves and rubbing his hands together.

For the next few minutes, the two of them worked in almost near silence on their potato creations. Alan never gave her any specific measurements for the ingredients, just kept adding butter and salt until it looked and tasted right. Since only he knew when that was, Claire was just going along with his instructions. Then he started adding the sifted flour while she mixed, and she was pretty sure he was doing that as a punishment.

Adding flour to what was basically mashed potatoes was rude.

A good workout, but ultimately rude.

Thankfully, the mixture became dough faster than Claire had expected, and soon they were dividing it into portions and forming balls. Alan dusted the counter with flour and started rolling each of the balls out with smooth, perfectly practiced motions. It was almost like a dance, how he moved with whatever dough was to hand. Some unique blend of composing, choreography, and painting with the dough as his partner as well as his medium.

Claire felt like a Neanderthal by comparison as she came in with a fork to prick the dough and a knife to divide it into shapes.

Still, if her brutish ways did what the maestro asked, perhaps she was just another tool in his collection.

"Alan," she finally said, her brain still trying to tumble over the events of the day without tripping. "In all honesty, why did you ask me to do the cookbook with you?"

He paused in his work, glancing at her with a furrowed brow. Whatever he saw in her expression cleared his own, and he exhaled shortly. "You're an enigma, Claire. Even on the show, I didn't know what you were going to present from challenge to challenge. You didn't follow any specific rhythm or pattern, barely even a theme, apart from what we gave you. You showed versatility and creativity, which we don't always find. And that fascinates me."

"Okay," Claire said slowly, trying not to burst from the praise given by the man who was allergic to praise.

"I wanted to see what you could do with a cookbook by my side," Alan went on, eyeing the scone dough carefully. "And I wanted to work with someone who could expand my vision beyond what I may be known for and what is expected of me. To be perfectly frank, Claire, you remind me of me."

Claire gasped, both in shock and in playful dismay. "You take that back! I do not! I could not!"

Alan barked a laugh and straightened to look at her. "Not personally, lass. Professionally. You remind me of me when I was getting started, and that made me want to work with you even more than what you showed on *BBB*. Fair enough?"

She couldn't answer that question. He'd gone from deflecting to blowing her away with compliments and honoring her with the distinction of being how he had once been. Was that a fair enough reason to work with her? Certainly.

Did it make sense?

Not a teaspoon.

"Besides," Alan continued, "this trip is supposed to improve my likability, which the show casts into some doubt with a percentage of the viewers. People need to see me as a whole at this point in my career."

Claire's frown deepened as her mind marinated on that. "What point—?" she began slowly.

"Watch that one, don't stab it," Alan sniped before she could finish.

Ducking her head, Claire did so, understanding all too well that her question would remain unanswered for now.

"So I remind you of yourself," she said after a moment, "which made you want to work with me."

He raised a brow, waiting for her to finish.

Claire grinned, feeling more like herself now that he had returned to himself. "Is that a way of saying you wanted to release a cookbook with yourself in a new way?"

"I've had enough of just myself, lass. Time to let someone else in."

The finality in his voice told Claire he was done with the conversation, so she returned to her dough with a small smile.

When all the dough had been rolled, portioned, and pricked, Alan swiped at his brow. "Any sign of a griddle, lass?"

She frowned in thought. "I haven't noticed one, but I'll check."

They dug through the cabinets, found two griddles, and then began working in tandem to cook each scone to the perfect brown warmth that Alan required.

"I didn't expect this to work," Claire admitted after she'd lost count of the number of scones she'd browned. "It's just mashed potatoes."

"What's wrong with that?" Alan flicked her a bright grin, surprising her. "These are a staple of a classic Scottish breakfast. My gran used to fry them in leftover bacon grease, and to this day, I can't make them better than she did. I don't know what magic she used, but I've had years and years of practice, and I still fail."

Claire returned his smile with one of her own. "How did you eat them?"

"I went through a few years of cinnamon sugar when I was really young," he told her, a distant light in his eyes. "My Aunt Darci made an apple butter that was ruddy brilliant on them." He chuckled, a surprisingly light, airy sound. "In culinary school, they became the vehicle for my breakfast sandwiches. Now it's pretty much whatever preserves I have to hand. But I haven't had them all that recently. You forget the little bakes that you grew up with once you take on a different place in the world. When you become something."

Nodding, Claire flipped her current scone over. "My great-granny made this ginger cake with cream cheese icing. It's the simplest thing, and she used to just bake it in a sheet pan and coat it in the icing, enough to probably make the adults sick, looking back on it. But as a kid, it was the best thing I'd ever eaten each and every time. She's been gone almost twenty years now, and I've never even tried to make it because I can't . . ." She shook her head quickly, not wanting to cry again.

"Yeah," Alan murmured as he flipped his scone. "I understand."

The kitchen door opened and a frazzled-looking Jonny swept in, followed by a timid-looking Greg. Jonny leaned hard against the door behind him while Greg just gaped at Alan.

"What are the odds that there are hard drinks in here?" Jonny asked.

"Slim to none," Alan told him with a sympathetic smile. "I've looked. But there is the bar car."

Jonny hissed, shaking his head quickly. "Not going back out there. And Dining Car 3 has—" He glanced at Greg, then cleared his throat. "Complications. And the rest of the train has the people thing."

"The people thing?" Alan repeated.

Claire scoffed. "Don't pretend you don't feel the same way, Alan." She looked at a pale and shaking Greg with some sympathy. "Greg? You okay?"

"Are you all right, Mr. Gables?" he asked weakly. "Your . . . your head . . ."

"Fine," Alan said with a wave. "Nothing compared to the dead body that was in Dining Car 3, right?"

"Crepes alive, Alan," Claire grumbled as she rubbed a hand over her face. "Discretion."

"D-dead body?" Greg stammered, trembling like a rabbit. "There w-was a . . ."

"Dead body. Yes. These two saw it. So I'm staying here for now." Alan looked at Claire with a raised brow. "Concerns with my assistant, lass?"

"I don't think it's the person so much as the situation," Jonny offered. "Plus Greg is Flaky Pastry. No offense, Greg. And being careless about the late Brian Donovan is not going to get rid of my currently brewing headache."

Alan dropped the tongs he had been holding. They clattered onto the stove and down to the floor, making Claire and Jonny jump.

"What the custard?" Claire yelped, her hand going to her chest.

But Alan was wholly focused on Jonny. "Brian Donovan? That's the victim's name?"

Jonny nodded, his brow creasing with his frown. "Yeah. And I think I figured out who Dishable Inc. might belong to, Claire. I was going over the numbers again after distracting Felicity, and then I was looking through Brian's briefcase again, and I have a good lead on the other party involved."

"What the what?" Claire chirped as she flipped another scone. "Who is it?"

"Me," Alan said bluntly, not bothering to wait for Jonny to deliver the news. "Brian Donovan is partners with me. Dishable Inc. is my company."

Claire slowly turned from the stove and stared at her mentor in horror. "Holy fondue, Alan. What have you done?"

CHAPTER 10

Jonny had never seen Alan Gables look more unnerved. He probably needed a stiff drink or a long walk, but there were a number of potato scones that still needed to be cooked, so the Scot remained by the stove and dutifully turned scones while looking as though someone had stolen his kilt and murdered his alpaca.

After dropping the bombshell that he owned and was a partner in Dishable Inc., Alan had stopped talking while the air filled with silent tension and the scent of frying potato scones.

Claire did her best to stare at Alan while she cooked her own scones, but Jonny had nothing to obstruct or distract from his staring. With their powers combined, they ought to be able to get some answers out of him.

There was no way Alan would have shared that bit of information without intending to follow through on context.

Greg, on the other hand, had sunk to the floor in what appeared to be shock and had said nothing since the revelation came out.

Flaky Pastry at its finest.

"Mind your scone, lass," Alan murmured, his eyes flicking toward Claire without actually raising his head.

Claire quicky turned her scone and removed it from the griddle before replacing it with another piece.

Jonny folded his arms and leaned against the door, frowning at the back of the scrawny Scotsman. Claire's conspiracy theory might have been far-fetched when she'd spouted it earlier, but it would appear now that she wasn't entirely wrong. What were the odds that Alan Gables's business partner would wind up dead while Alan was knocked out and dragged to a supply car?

If that's actually where Alan had been.

Jonny didn't want to think the man was lying or hiding something, but things were certainly lining up in a way that put Alan in the middle of a big mess. Especially if those financial numbers Jonny had been studying earlier were as skewed as they appeared. Someone was skimming from Dishable Inc., and now one of the two partners was dead.

That, coupled with the way the numbers were presenting, meant fingers ought to be pointing at *Alan* for the money skimming, not Brian. The account details were clear to anyone who had the understanding to read them. But why Alan would need to steal money from his own company was another question entirely, and Jonny was looking forward to an explanation he could accept. Provided Alan would tell them the truth.

Then again, Alan was a terrible actor.

Years of being on *Britain's Battle of the Bakers* had cemented the fact that Alan was never going to be known for his acting skills, let alone his people ones, and the ham-fisted skits the showrunners tried to put him in to open each series of the show had proven that again and again. Leave the man to his baking and his judging of the baking, and he would be perfectly in his lane.

Force him to stray out of that lane and into the world of television for television's sake, and you had a car crash.

Literally, in the series seven opener.

Audi still refused to sponsor the show after that.

Since Alan was incapable of acting, his shock at Brian Donovan being the victim had to be genuine.

But that didn't negate the fact that the papers in Brian's possession could be interpreted to make Alan look like the embezzler.

And, to be frank, Alan could have attacked Brian and left him in Dining Car 3, not thinking he would die. Just because his shock was genuine did not mean Alan was completely innocent in all of this.

So what had happened? Why was Brian dead? What was the story behind this doomed partnership?

And what happened to the money?

Questions upon questions assaulted Jonny's mind as he stared at Alan, willing him to give them something—anything—to shed light on what could be happening here. This silent mulling over details wasn't helping anyone except Alan, if it was even doing that, and it was making Claire an ever-increasing tangle of knots that would explode in an anxiety-tinted tear fest in a few hours if clarity wasn't given soon. And if Alan let it get to that point, Claire might never forgive him for it.

Jonny could tell him all of this if the man would open up even a little. If he would give them an inch.

Alan exhaled loudly, and Jonny's chest tightened in expectation.

"What I am about to say," Alan rumbled darkly, his brogue like the cursive penmanship tying each word to the next, "cannot—and will not—leave this room. I must have your word on that."

"But—" Claire protested in an almost tearful voice.

"It might all come out eventually," Alan insisted before she could finish. "The pertinent information, at any rate. But if the story breaks, I beg you to keep everything else to yourselves."

Claire looked at Jonny, her green eyes almost glowing with the tears filling them.

He tried to give her a comforting smile, but he was fairly certain all he managed was the weak curving of his mouth and zero consolation behind it.

But Jonny found himself nodding anyway. "I promise."

"I promise, Alan," Claire whispered, keeping her gaze on Jonny.

He managed a nod of reassurance, if that was worth anything.

They would be in on this secret together, whatever it was.

Wherever it led.

"Promise!" Greg chirped in a small voice.

Nobody paid him attention.

Alan kept his head lowered and worked at his potato scones with the sort of single-minded focus Jonny had only seen bakers use for decorating the most delicate of creations.

"Brian Donovan was an old school friend of mine," Alan began, his voice so low that Jonny had to strain to make out his words. "From primary school through university. We went into business together after I finished culinary school and it was clear I had a future there. As my career began to take off, so did the business. I became the face of business, but Brian managed the details of it."

There wasn't a scintilla of emotion in the words thus far; it was almost eerie. It could have been a disembodied voice speaking over the Tannoy, it was that detached, that lifeless, and that devoid of humanity.

Chilling.

Alan cleared his throat. "Had I paid more attention to those details, I might have caught on years ago to what Brian was doing. But he seemed so efficient at his job, and my role got so busy, that we barely communicated after a while. We became more like silent partners than true partners. He has been using Dishable as his own personal cash cow, pouring profits into his own coffers through less than sanitary means, and using me as a front for legitimacy. I never questioned his extravagant lifestyle or trips or cars because business was good, and we'd been working hard. He always made it look as though everything was on the up and up, and my own finances were always in check."

The slowest grimace known to man began to make its way across Jonny's features. Every word seemed to activate a new nerve or muscle, drew another branch of sympathy into the expression, sank a deeper rock into the pit of his stomach. It was an entire body experience, this grimace, and the story wasn't over yet.

"Today," Alan went on, "I became aware of the truth of the situation. Remember when I said I had an annoying discussion in the dining car? Brian showed up on the train and met me at the bar after I was done talking with Felicity. It was a true shock to see him. And the shocks just kept coming after that. He told me that he had been patiently embezzling for almost the entire time we'd been in business together. It seems the business is riddled with corruption, but because Brian hid his tracks so well, and because my name, my face, *is* the business, it will all blow back on me. The house of cards is going to crumble, and there will be nothing left but destruction. What's worse is that Brian has arranged a set of documents to make it appear as though I was the one who has been embezzling, and *he* was the victim. He was going to announce all of this to the world with his 'proof' when the train reached Mallaig. Just in time for the presentation of my plaque."

"How could he ever think to do that to you?" Claire gasped, her voice wavering dangerously.

"Scone," Alan instructed with the sort of calm one might apply to a newborn baby.

Claire blindly flipped it, her attention not wavering.

"Greed," Alan told her. "And jealousy for the success I was having. My tribute act, as he called it, was the last straw for him, and he claimed he just 'had to take advantage of it.' He wanted to use everything we had built to twist a knife in my back."

"And the train ride and the interview presented the perfect opportunity," Jonny said as understanding sank in.

Alan nodded, but his throat tightened. "I may play the villain as a judge, but now, I could be seen as a villain in life too. And I'm not. I'm really not."

"What else did he say?" Claire whispered.

"A lot of shocking things, actually," Alan admitted on a rough exhale. "I learned that he had not been my friend for many, many years. In our twenties, Brian and I had big dreams for ourselves, and mine also hinged in, on, and around a young woman we'd grown up with. She'd been one of our schoolmates almost from the beginning, and I'd loved her for years. We were on and off all through school, but always friends, and after school, we became serious. As my career progressed, my focus shifted."

"Oh, no," Claire murmured as one hand went to her mouth and one went to Alan's arm.

He didn't seem to feel her at all. "I wasn't prepared to split my time between her and my career. Didn't want anything to hold me back or down or whatever idiocy I thought marrying her would do to my career. And I wanted to be successful before I settled down. I wanted to make sure I was the very best, and I had to reach that next level, that next goal, whatever it was. I didn't want any distractions, and I didn't love her enough to—"

Alan's throat moved with another hard swallow before he continued.

"Well, anyway, I broke her heart. It seems Brian went after her—not that he told me any of this at the time. I'd known he'd always had a thing for her, but I had no idea until today that he thought he could sweep her off her feet after I'd broken up with her. I could have saved him the trouble if he'd mentioned it. She always thought he was a stuck-up little idiot, despite being his friend. Turns out, she refused to rebound from me with him, and that infuriated him."

"And that's why he ruined your business?" Jonny asked dubiously. It was the stupidest thing he had ever heard of, and if that was all this was . . .

"What would you do for love?" Alan glanced over his shoulder with a hint of a rueful smile. "Brian loved her. Blindly. And he thought it was his chance. When she said no, and emphatically no, he began to hate me—because he couldn't bring himself to hate her. He continued to pursue her for the next few years, but she always said no. When she blocked all communication with him, it became less about her and more about me. Eventually, he decided to make me pay for him missing out on the chance at a life he thought he deserved."

Claire was gaping by now, her head wavering from side to side as though the motion of a full head shake was too much. "That's delusional."

"To you and me, yes," Alan agreed. "To Brian? Righteous vengeance." He scoffed softly. "Thirty years of friendship dissolved in a twenty-minute meeting. At least for me. Brian's obviously been dissolving it for years."

Jonny clicked his tongue, as much in sympathy as disbelief. It explained a lot, but he wasn't sold on everything Alan was telling them.

This was a crushing blow. A blow that would incite anger—and perhaps violence?—in any recipient. And it still felt somewhat unbelievable that Alan hadn't discovered at least part of Brian's plot years ago. Jonny wanted to sympathize with Alan, but he wasn't ready to do so fully yet.

"Alan . . ." Claire murmured.

"I didn't kill him."

Claire snorted so loudly it thundered in the room. "We know that, you plaited pastry."

Jonny looked at her in surprise. "We do?" he asked at the same time Alan did.

Claire's attention shot to Jonny first, then to Alan, then between the two of them like a tennis match. "Of course, we do."

Her certainty was cute, but surely she could see the dangers of blind belief. The dead man was someone who planned on ruining Alan's career and his life, someone that Alan had every reason in the world to despise. It would solve at least a few of Alan's problems if Donovan turned up dead, so why shouldn't Alan be a suspect? Especially if Alan knew that Brian had doctored a set of books to implicate Alan as the embezzler.

"Why do we know that?" Jonny felt the need to ask, even if it was through gritted teeth. If his girlfriend was determined about this, he deserved to know what he was being looped into believing and why. He did not have the same loyalty to Alan that she held, and he wasn't about to pretend otherwise. He didn't *like* the idea of Alan being the murderer, but the man had motive and opportunity. Someone had to think like an actual investigator here.

Viscount Brains, not heart.

Why did that sound so icy?

"Alan couldn't fake the head injury," Claire pointed out, jabbing her finger toward the lump on her friend's head. "I saw what his eyes were doing and his trouble balancing."

"Could be faked."

She rolled her eyes. "Alan doesn't fake anything. He's lousy at it."

"That is actually true," Alan agreed without shame.

"It is painfully true," Greg announced, piping up needlessly.

Jonny gave him a look before focusing on Alan. "No offense, Alan, but you wouldn't exactly tell us if you had killed Brian, would you? Or if you'd faked all of this? So, lousy at acting or not, there's still an issue."

Alan looked at Claire. "He's right, you know."

"Not helping!" she shrieked at him. She returned her attention to Jonny, her green eyes severe. "He didn't do it, J. Why would he?"

"Because either his partner was going to frame him for embezzlement and bring down Alan's baking empire," Johnny explained patiently, "or because Alan is lying and he really *did* embezzle money from his company and he needed to keep Brian quiet."

"That is a good point," Alan praised, nodding his head in thought.

"Shut up, Alan," Jonny snapped.

Claire folded her arms in a defiant move. "Go on, Viscount. If you think Alan killed Brian, how did he do it?"

Jonny shrugged. "Easy. Accident. They have that nasty confrontation in the bar car, and Alan shoves Brian. Brian hits his head and dies. Alan goes into the supply car and hits himself to create a feasible alibi."

Again, Alan was nodding. "I'd buy that, yeah."

"Shut up, Alan," Claire ordered.

Alan threw his hands in the air and leaned back against the counter, glowering.

"Does Alan look like someone who panics?" Claire asked Jonny. "Or would fight someone? All Alan would have to do is walk away from a confrontation and call his lawyer or the authorities once we got to the next station. Wouldn't that be easier than shoving someone?"

"It doesn't matter what would be easier, Claire," Jonny reminded her. "It matters what happened."

"Alan didn't do it," Claire ground out.

Alan looked up at the ceiling of the kitchen, shaking his head. "You're not going to win this argument, Claire. And don't be angry with him either. He's making all the right arguments, and anyone else would see it the same way. Even if I hadn't seen Brian on the train earlier, with all this stacking up, the best anyone could argue is self-defense."

"Shut up, Alan," Greg announced.

Everyone in the kitchen looked at the scrawny, dark-haired man, who gulped at being the sudden center of attention.

"I very much beg your pardon?" Alan demanded in a dangerous voice, one brow quirking rather like Claire's did, impressively enough.

"Sorry, sir. Mr. Gables. Sir. I got . . . carried away in the moment. I'll . . . go get some work done . . . and be back soon? Ish?" He was shaking with fear and growing paler by the moment as Alan stared at him.

Alan nodded very slowly as though his assistant had said something wise.

Greg scrambled out of the kitchen, practically flinging Jonny aside as he did so.

"Flaky Pastry is going to become Soggy Pastry for the next twenty minutes," Jonny commented, jerking his thumb toward the door.

Alan sniffed and shrugged. "He'll be fine. Now, Claire, what's your problem?"

Claire looked at him helplessly, biting her lip. "If you didn't touch Brian, didn't kill him, if that's all the truth—"

"Doesn't matter what the truth is. What matters is what you can prove." Alan scrubbed at his face and looked at Jonny. "If I promise not to leave the train, will you hold off on telling anyone where I am until we get to the next station tomorrow? I'll face this head-on, I swear."

"The papers!" Claire blurted.

"What papers?" Jonny and Alan asked in unison.

"The fake papers Brian created to frame Alan. We have them in our compartment."

"Assuming they're fake," Jonny muttered, his irritation rising.

"If we can prove they're fake," Claire said, "then that would at least prove part of Alan's story, and it would prove Brian was the bad guy here."

Jonny nodded reluctantly. "It would certainly help."

Claire turned to Alan, waiting expectantly, as if Alan would whip out a financial spreadsheet as easily as he could whip up a dessert.

Alan's brow wrinkled in thought. "I do have the original documents. But I'd need my phone to get to them. Or a computer. Anything that could access my business accounts." He cursed loudly and slammed his fist into the cabinets behind him, letting his head fall.

Claire jumped at the sound, whimpering slightly and rubbing her arms like she was cold.

Jonny kept his attention on Alan, though. This sudden outburst certainly wasn't doing the famed baker any favors.

"Idiot," Alan hissed, the word a harsh whisper all its own. "Even dead, Brian could ruin me. Especially dead. He might actually be more trouble dead than alive."

"And *that*," Claire said with an emphatic jab of a finger in Alan's direction, "is why I think he's innocent."

Yeah, that pointing was for Jonny, and he felt a little heat on his neck from it.

"I promise not to leave the kitchen," Alan muttered, raking a hand through his hair. "Not until you're back. I won't go to your compartment and look at anything, I swear. You're just . . . you're just going to have to trust me on that. Can you, Viscount?"

A full-body spasm of surprise threatened to dislodge Jonny from his position at the door as he regarded the wiry Scotsman.

"Yeah," he managed after a moment. "For now. I'm meeting Felicity for dinner, so I'll keep her off your scent. Whatever the truth is, she doesn't need to know it. She shouldn't be able to get by the security guards into this part of the train, but just in case, you can hide on the floor of our compartment tonight. If we keep the lights low and the table down, you shouldn't be seen from the door."

"Aiding and abetting, my lord?" Alan suggested with a bitter smile.

Jonny returned it. "Doesn't count until there's a crime, and even the security guards think Brian's death was accidental for now. And, for the record, I'm just the devil's advocate, Alan. Not the enemy."

Even if he was leveling cold accusations, Jonny didn't hate Alan.

He just didn't want Claire mixed up in his mess.

"I know." Alan nodded once and gestured to the stove with a snap of his fingers. "Claire, finish up those scones. Gotta get these out for dinner before the masses revolt."

Claire was still staring at Jonny, any trace of emotion wiped from her face.

Jonny blinked at her. "What?"

Her slender throat worked on a swallow. "Why . . . why are you meeting Felicity for dinner?"

"She loved the Blackfirth stuff I teased earlier," Jonny said easily, shoving his hands into his pockets. "Wants to do a behind-the-scenes feature on your season of *Battle*."

"Can you even do that?" Claire asked him, her voice small. "Those contracts are so tight . . ."

Jonny offered her a reassuring smile. "I know, which is why I told her I needed to check the contracts before I said anything else to make sure everything was aboveboard. Which is a lie, of course." He chortled and looked at Alan, who was gawking at him. "I've got those contracts practically memorized, so I know exactly what I can and cannot say. No one will get a hint about that case from me. Just about the ghost and all of that."

Claire didn't look remotely settled or reassured. "And you're willing to do that? Broadcast your family's secrets to a journalist you met a few hours ago who clearly doesn't care about anything except her own ambition? If I remember correctly, you raised some serious noise about the contestants even chatting about the Blackfirth Park legend and ghost—and that's when you were being paid for it."

Jonny clearly caught the definite bite in her tone. Whether Claire was still worked up over what he'd insinuated about Alan, or the entire situation was getting to her, he didn't know, but his girlfriend was certainly irked. And was making it known.

He didn't blame her. Was he happy about any of this? Nope. But it was either this or they let Felicity snoop around the train, and that wouldn't serve anyone or anything. Besides, all he would tell her could be compiled by a moderately intelligent internet historian. There was nothing groundbreaking or newsworthy in that.

Felicity Farrow wouldn't know that, of course.

"Do I have a choice?" Jonny pushed off from the door and walked over to Claire, who didn't uncoil her arms. "We need her distracted, and that's what I can do. If I had something else to talk about that would keep her entertained, I would. But this is my wild card, and it's time I play it. This way, you two can try to figure everything else out and get the baking done. Just let me do this, okay, *ma crème*? I want to help."

He put his hands on her shoulders and met her eyes, not seeing the usual light, life, or laughter in Claire's gorgeous eyes. She looked small and scared, almost shy, and he hated that. Hated that they were back in this place of danger and uncertainty, but this time without any protection for them.

But if he could keep Felicity away from Claire and Alan, it might protect them from the woman's claws. And that was something he was willing to sacrifice to do.

"It'll be all right," he told Claire, laying a hand on her cheek and kissing her brow softly. "I'm going back to the compartment to try to find more answers before I have to see her. We'll be in Dining Car 2 after that if you need me."

Claire gave a bare nod, and he didn't miss the ripple of a shiver that went through her. But she didn't touch him back, didn't say a word, and didn't relax her tense stance at all.

Hopefully, time with Alan could soothe her.

Then perhaps they could get back to the holiday ahead of them and pull something good out of this mess.

CHAPTER 11

"Any idea where Greg got to after he fled?" Claire asked Alan as they loaded up the scones onto her trolley.

"Nope, not a lick." Alan shook his head, something passing for concern mixing with his frustration. "But it wouldn't surprise me if he headed up front to demand the engineer figure out what's wrong with the train and get it moving again. His life's work is to make sure my schedule runs perfectly."

Claire was supposed to smile at that quip; she could hear the cue in it. But her face refused to behave, so all that happened was a noisy exhale through her nose. Not quite a hum, not loud enough for a honk, and not sniffling enough to be a cold. Just a sound, nothing more.

If Alan thought it was strange, he said nothing about it.

Thankfully.

"How am I going to serve this whole train by myself?" Claire mumbled, shaking her head. "It was hard enough last time with Jonny helping."

"Oh, how did the tarte tatin go?" Alan asked brightly, as though there wasn't a dead body on the train and a whole investigation ahead of them when the authorities learned about it. "Did they like it?"

Now Claire's face decided to work, and her smile came, even if it was small. "Yeah. Everyone was impressed, and the comments were good. Well, the ones about the food anyway."

Alan looked absolutely thrilled, and Claire wished she'd put a little more oomph into the description. Fluffed it for his ego. Gushed a little.

But she hadn't. Her words just lay there like frozen butter on a crumpet.

Weak and boring.

A knock sounded at the kitchen door, and Claire shook herself out of her funk, going to answer it while Alan ducked around the pantry door.

Greg stood there, acting as frazzled and nerdy as before. "Hi. Um . . . can I . . . come back in now? People want food, and they're yelling . . ."

Claire smiled and stepped back, letting him in. "Yeah, they've been doing that."

Only when the kitchen door was closed did she gesture to Alan, who stepped out of his meager hiding space. "Good timing, Greg."

Greg lowered his gaze like a puppy in trouble. "Sorry about earlier, Mr. Gables. Um . . . I've been trying to get some answers in the meantime. The engineer has no idea what kind of time frame we're looking at to get going again. He got pretty short with me when I kept asking."

Alan met Claire's eyes with a tight smile, which ought to have made her laugh. Usually, she would have done.

Not now. Not tonight.

"And the conductor told me off," Greg admitted as he scratched the back of his neck. "All I wanted to know was if we could get word to Mallaig, so they aren't wondering where we are. They're going to be waiting on us and believing we'll show up for the ceremony, and without any communication from us . . ." His breathing was growing more unsteady the more he talked, and his anxiety was rubbing off on Claire, making her sweat.

"It's fine," Alan told his assistant with a dismissive wave. "Well, not fine, but there's nothing we can do about it, so it might as well be fine. You can't make the train go if it's broken, and you certainly can't do anything about the ruddy storm outside. I imagine the officials will be checking with the train station, and they'll know our train hasn't arrived, which should alleviate concerns that we've ditched."

"I'm so sorry, sir." Greg's voice cracked, and he flinched at the sound.

Claire glanced at Alan, who seemed to be wondering if his assistant was unwell.

"I just said it might as well be fine," Alan said flatly. "We'll deal with it. Now, can you help Miss Walker?"

Greg nodded, swallowing hard. "However I can."

Alan pointed at the trolleys. "Please assist her with taking the scones out to the people and then go back to hounding whoever it takes to keep my career on track."

Claire bit her lip, then nodded. "That would be great, Greg. I don't want to do it alone, and for a lot of reasons, we don't want Alan out with the passengers."

Greg's head bobbed in another semi-nod. "Makes sense. And this way, maybe I can do some damage control with Alan's fans."

"That's the spirit!" Claire tried for enthusiasm, but it sounded like a day-care teacher praising shoddy artwork.

Oh well.

Alan shook his head at her quickly. "Come on, let's finish loading the trolleys. I'll stash some extra goodies for toppings here, just for those people you like."

"Why do you think I would like people?" Claire wondered aloud.

"You're you, lass, not me. Of course, you like people."

"I'm not a puppy," she grumbled, shooting him a dark look while he rummaged through the cupboards.

Alan clearly didn't hear her, since he gave no response.

But he probably would have gotten after her for the snark level in her tone alone had he heard it.

She couldn't help it. Jonny had been gone an hour now and was probably going to be occupied the rest of the night with his new friend Felicity. Worst of all, Claire was going to be the one serving this impromptu dinner to them and everyone else on the train. She would see their interaction and hear part of their conversation.

It was stupid, these feelings gnawing within her chest, and her mind told her repeatedly that she was being ridiculous for giving them enough weight to bother her, but there was no use. She didn't like what Jonny was doing, and she didn't like that he was willingly throwing himself at the feet of the woman who had been so blatant in her interest earlier. He'd said he was going to help, and maybe that was true, but he had to know what Felicity really wanted. He had to see that she would just be using him and her association with him for her own ends. She would chew him up and spit him out, and there was every chance it could make him go back to being the surly and brooding viscount all the time.

But this time, he might not give someone like Claire the time of day.

She could lose everything she had with him because of this. Because Felicity Farrow had legs for days, connections to use, and wiles to spin the sort of web that ensnared good-looking men with dopey grins on their faces. She represented the sort of stylish woman he could have at any time, and with how irritated he had been with Claire earlier—how closed off and cold—he might just be looking for a way out.

She could see him with exactly that sort of woman. Easily. The sort that would light up a red carpet and attend all sorts of premieres by his side, their faces and fashion being plastered all over the tabloids and social media spreads. A gorgeous couple that the world would bleed for and ship until their dying day.

And Claire would be one of those has-beens from a reality TV show who never made anything of herself or her career.

Had there ever been a more depressing prospect?

Or a more pathetic one?

She shook herself out of that thought. There was an actual dead body on this train, and she was sulking about her boyfriend and a snooty journalist. What in the torte was wrong with her?

Once the trolleys were loaded, Claire and Greg started to maneuver them out of the kitchen.

"Do you need anything else, Mr. Gables? Can I get you anything?" Greg asked, his tone eager.

Claire knew the young man was dying to be useful to his boss after such a disappointing venture so far. He was truly upset that the train was stalled and they were late to Mallaig, and he probably bore the sort of guilt that made no sense but was carried anyway.

Surely he didn't believe he ought to be capable of controlling train maintenance, did he?

"No. I have what I need," Alan said curtly.

Really, would it kill the man to be polite to his poor, young, guilt-bearing assistant?

Claire looked back at Alan once they were in the corridor. "Don't go anywhere, okay?"

Alan's smile was small and tight, much like his following nod, but he gave it anyway. It didn't touch his eyes, but at least it was a smile.

What was he thinking and feeling? Was he worried about Brian's death? Was he worried about Felicity snooping around? Was he just wanting to get off this train even if it meant his career might burn in the dumpster fire that was threatening to consume them all?

Sugar, this was all getting so complicated.

Her first steps with the trolley stuttered to a halt, her eyes widening.

Guess that meant that the cookbook wasn't happening, then.

So much for pipe dreams.

Or piping dreams, in her case.

She and Greg moved wordlessly through Dining Car 3, both of them avoiding looking toward the barricade in front of the bar.

Well, Claire almost avoided it. She felt compelled to look for evidence that a man had been killed there earlier in the day; but between Jonny's initial efforts and whatever the conductor and lead service agent had put together, no one would think a dead body had lain just beyond the makeshift wall that was now hiding an unsightly stain. The lights at the bar had all been switched off, so there was nothing to draw attention to the area at all.

Unless someone knew to look there.

Which Claire did.

Did anyone else know?

Well, Greg did now.

But surely he could hold it together while they passed out the tarte tatin.

He didn't seem particularly skittish or jumpy, just focused and determined. Like a university student who had been up all night and felt the caffeine burn off but couldn't go to bed yet because it was time for the exam.

Not that Claire had any experience with such a scenario.

Not at all.

Not ever.

"Okay, Greg," Claire said as they moved into the first passenger car. "Everyone gets one, and we can offer whatever toppings are here. We'll try to get this done quickly, so you can get back to hounding the engineer or whatever you like. Sound good?"

Greg dipped his chin but said nothing. He silently grabbed the scones in their paper wrappings and handed one to each passenger with a plastic smile that probably suited your average railway worker. He never met anyone's eyes, including Claire's.

She'd only known Greg a few hours, and already she knew this was not like him.

No one complained about the scones, and very few seemed to even care about the edible accoutrements they could top them with. But that could have been due to the pounding rain and rumbling thunder outside and the dark clouds that were even more ominous because of the minimal light of evening.

Creepy thunderstorm in the Highlands with no way to leave and a murderer and dead body on board—though none of the passengers knew about those last two things.

Agatha Christie, eat your heart out.

They moved into the next car with the same silent efficiency, their motion only slightly interrupted by the service attendants flitting among the standard compartments, bringing around pillows and blankets, sharing tablets with tomorrow's train schedule pulled up, or asking if anything else was needed. Everyone seemed to be speaking in harsh tones; though, so far, no one's voice was actually raised enough to be a shout.

Plenty of glares, though. And muttering. And every couple seemed to be arguing in whispers.

If they were arguing with each other, that meant they weren't yelling at Claire, so she'd allow that. Gladly.

To her surprise, no one asked about Dining Car 3 being closed. The death on the train must still be a secret, then.

Were people really not that curious about Dining Car 3 being closed when it hadn't been before? Or about the medical call directed there earlier? Claire had scampered there the moment a doctor had been requested, but clearly, she was in the minority with that impulse. People tended to mind their own business when they traveled, preferring to not get involved with something that could delay them, increase their stress, or ruin the ambiance they had intended. Claire understood that, certainly, but her curiosity was usually the thing that overrode her good sense and impulse control.

How else could she explain applying for *Britian's Battle of the Bakers* when she hated attention and pressure?

If she had exerted a tiny bit of self-restraint and ignored the call for a doctor, she and Jonny could be enjoying themselves in blissful ignorance like so many of the other passengers. She wouldn't have to worry that Alan would be arrested for murder or that someone was going to disturb the crime scene or that Felicity Farrow was going to steal her boyfriend . . .

Stupid curiosity.

Forget killing the cat, it was going to kill her sanity.

The next car held regular seats, and that meant more passengers, so her thoughts were taken up with handing out the potato scones to everyone on both sides of her. And looking pleasant while doing so. And trying to get Greg to pull himself together. And not thinking about Dining Car 2 up ahead, where her boyfriend was chatting with Journalist Barbie.

Details.

In the gangway of the next two cars, Claire turned the trolley slightly and folded her arms atop the handle on her side. "Greg."

His eyes flicked up in a show of attentiveness, but his gaze never made it past the handle itself.

"Talk to me."

Greg looked around nervously, like he was making sure no one could hear what he was about to say, which seemed silly because they would have heard the hiss of the doors behind them if someone was close enough to be snooping. Still, Greg was a skittish kid even when he wasn't bothered by something, so why shouldn't he have a paranoid reaction when he was?

Suddenly, a torrent of words left Greg's mouth: "I've met Mr. Donovan. He's a horrible person, and what he was planning to do to Mr. Gables is the worst sort of betrayal. But why haven't the train authorities said anything about what happened and where the body is now? If he *was* murdered, shouldn't we know? And now the train is stopped, and we could all be in danger . . . All of these people here for Alan . . ."

Claire's eyes widened as she watched panic literally take over the young man before her. "Greg. Breathe."

He inhaled a stuttering, wheezing gasp that immediately came back out like a sob.

"Try that again, slowly. Come on, breathe."

She motioned with her hands to try to help him with the action, keeping her eyes on him. It took four breaths, but eventually his eyes lost the light of terror and only looked very young.

"If it were me," Claire told him, "I wouldn't tell the public either. We wouldn't want the kids on the train to be scared, right? And we wouldn't want people to panic and make things dangerous."

Greg's throat visibly clenched, but he nodded.

"So it's probably just to keep everyone safe. Since Brian's dead, it's not as though anyone can help him now, right?"

"Right . . ." He blinked twice, still nodding. "Right. Okay. So we're going to continue keeping this a secret?"

He sounded like one of her young students, and, like a good teacher, Claire was going to reassure him.

"Yep, and we're going to stay safe," Claire said as serenely as she could. "So just breathe and try not to worry. Alan told you not to worry about the delay, right?"

Greg didn't blink, but his shoulders began to relax. "Right. But once we get to Mallaig . . . I don't know, what if he blows up at me? I had to turn my phone in, too, just like everyone else. I can't get through to them, and this was supposed to be his tribute, his honor parade, his grand moment. I don't want to let him down, Miss Walker."

"Greg," she said as firmly as a gentle teacher voice would allow. "You have nothing to worry about. Alan knows the situation. He knows about the phones. He knows about the storm and the damage and all of that, and he knows you can't control any of it. If he yells at you when this is over, tell me, and I'll yell at him for being an irrational boss and a rude human. He might not take arguing from you, but he'll have no choice with me. Okay?"

Greg's eyes were wide and round as he stared at her, a combination of awe and terror in his look.

Yeah, Claire got that. Earlier this year, she'd never have thought it possible that she'd be threatening Alan Gables, but here she was.

"Okay," Greg finally whispered in the least confident voice ever.

Claire tried not to smile. "Awesome. So all you have to do is make sure the interview is wrapped up and that Miss Farrow has everything she needs. Neither Alan nor you can make the train go, so let it go. Okay?"

Impossibly, one side of Greg's mouth twitched upward. "Okay. Thanks, Miss Walker."

"Any time," Claire quipped with a nod. "Now, let's get these scones out to the next car. We should be seeing Felicity Farrow, so you can ask her if she needs anything else for the interview. I'm planning to ignore her."

Greg smiled fully now as they worked to get the trolley into the next car. "Don't like her?"

"Don't know her," Claire admitted without shame, "but first impressions were lacking. I will give her props for being able to walk well in those shoes of hers, but more than that . . ." She shrugged as if it was the only nice thing she could say.

Greg's laughter was wheezy and high-pitched and never needed to be heard again, but at least it was the sound of amusement and not that of a sobbing child in a dark corner.

"Mr. Gables wasn't happy with her either," Greg told her, pulling his trolley into the dining car. "Miss Farrow tried to create a scandal around him a few years ago, I think for harassment of contestants of the show in its early seasons. The story never broke because she couldn't find any reliable sources, so you wouldn't know about it. It made her his enemy after that, but the magazine didn't have anyone else, and she is a name, so what can you do? She likes to stir things up, so she'll probably spin this delay to her advantage against him. I've been told to play nice and get her what she wants to avoid that, but, like you said, I can't make the train go."

Claire's ears perked up, and a cold tingle spread from her chest into her fingertips, somehow connecting to her lips and making them curve in a devious way.

What could they do? Oh, there was a lot they could do, none of it productive but all of it satisfying.

If only she had a phone and reliable Wi-Fi. She would rabbit hole so hard into cyberspace on this one, and her online sleuthing was way better than her real-life sleuthing. She could lose herself over the nuggets Greg had just dropped into her palm, and with Alan as her friend and future cookbook partner—unless he wound up in jail on a wrongful conviction, of course—she had the best kind of motivation. Why not burn this bridge while the other one was on fire too?

En flambe was totally the way to go. Maybe that should be the title of her first cookbook, just for some really snarky fun.

What a delicious thought.

Slow and steady, though. Felicity Farrow hadn't actually

committed a crime against Claire yet, unless one counted the undressing eyes she'd made toward Claire's boyfriend and the sneering smirk that seemed permanently stamped on Felicity's stupid face.

Those weren't actual crimes, though, just misdemeanors in the Classy Laws.

Which weren't actually enforceable or worthy of vengeance.

Not sober, anyway.

Hashtag pub life.

Hashtag IYKYK.

Hashtag sorry not sorry.

Claire shook her head like a dog coming in from the rain, scattering her ridiculous hashtags from the cobwebs of her brain. Scones first, then solving the case and getting off the train. Then plotting vengeance against Felicity Farrow.

One step at a time.

The passengers in this car were more interested in the condiments than the others had been, which made for a slower progression of the trolleys. Then there was the flurry of people at the bar, which made sense with Dining Car 3 out of commission. A few people laughed easily with the bartender, the lubrication of alcohol easing their frustrations and making life that much more entertaining, but others sat moodily at their tables, drinking to forget or to cope.

And then Claire's eyes tracked something else, and her chest immediately filled with fire and ice, the tension of that combination resulting in pain in her sides.

Felicity Farrow sat on the edge of her seat, her trim, lanky legs crossed and on full display for anyone to see. She trailed two fingers up and down Jonny's forearm with pointed familiarity as she leaned across the table in deep conversation with him.

There was no sign of distress or frustration in her posture, her hair, or her face. In fact, her hair was the slightest bit tousled and somehow more alluring for the nearly blown-out look it presented. She might have been on some hot date in London's swankiest club instead of stuck on a broken train. She was listening to Jonny, her eyes wide, her lips parted just enough to give a glimpse of perfect, pearly white teeth.

She was absolutely riveted by whatever Jonny was saying, and he wasn't pulling away. He was leaning in as well, elbows on the table, shoulders relaxed and easy.

Forgoing her present section of passengers, Claire swept two scones into her hands and marched past Greg to their table, setting the paper-wrapped scones before them. "Dinner, courtesy of Alan Gables. And me."

Okay, that wasn't strictly necessary, but it felt fantastic.

Felicity looked at her with a curious tilt of her head. "Cara, right?"

"So close," Claire replied through clenched teeth. "Claire."

"Right, sorry." Felicity giggled and waved her hand as though the truth didn't matter. "Did you say Alan helped with these?" Her eyes flicked to the scones before going back to Claire. "I haven't seen him since the interview. He's not turning his back on all these people, is he? Not when they've all come just for him and are now stuck here without him. This delay must be crushing to them, and he's staying away? Not very friendly, considering . . ."

"It's his recipe." Claire didn't look at Jonny.

Couldn't. Wouldn't. Didn't want to know.

Felicity, however, looked at Jonny with a broad smile.

"Well, I won't say no to some free Alan Gables food. How about you, Jonathan?"

Claire's eyes almost bugged out of her head. Jonathan? Nobody in the world called him that unless he was in trouble, being teased, or on official business. Politeness meant he was "my lord" to strangers, and his friends all knew to call him "Jonny."

But he hadn't even twitched, as far as she could tell.

Why could Felicity call him Jonathan when no one else could or would?

Jonathan was a much colder, distant name than the warm and approachable Jonny.

Don't read into it, don't read into it, don't read into it.

"I'd love a potato scone," Jonny said, straightening in his chair without the rush of someone being caught by their girlfriend in an awkward situation.

Just normal body movements.

Not panicking, not panicking, not panicking.

"Miss Farrow!" Greg's voice chimed from behind Claire. "So delighted to see you again. I was just talking to Mr. Gables about—"

"You've seen him recently?" Felicity broke in, a hungry expression on her face.

Claire looked at Greg with a raised brow.

He paled immediately. "Erm, not that recently. Earlier, I mean. J-just after your interview with him." He cleared his throat. "Did you speak with Miss Walker about Mr. Gables yet? I know you wanted to interview her."

"Not now, Greg," Claire grumbled, her face ready to burst into flame.

"Oh, yes, I would simply *love* to ask Claire all about Alan," Felicity all but cooed. "Jonathan, pull up a chair for her, won't you? This will only take a second, and then we can get back to the much more fascinating, incredibly pressing topic of *us*."

Oh, this Barbie . . .

But Jonny was nothing if not efficient, and a chair was quickly put behind Claire. He stood like the gentleman he was and helped her sit, which made Claire feel completely stupid in her jeans and pullover.

"I'll keep going with the scones, Miss Walker," Greg told her. "You can catch up when you're done."

"Yes, dear, she will. Go ahead." Felicity didn't even bother looking at him but simply straightened and turned her recorder that sat in the center of the table in Claire's direction. "So, Claire Walker, tell me everything you know about Alan Gables. Good, bad, and, most especially, ugly."

CHAPTER 12

Jonny berated himself for not hiding the cutlery in this dining car. He'd known Claire would be coming through eventually, but he hadn't expected Flaky Pastry Greg would be idiot enough to remind Felicity of the interview. Literally everything about Felicity grated on Claire, and Felicity was already in a snappy mood.

But there was no time to warn Claire of the dangers of peeving this woman.

Not that she was looking at him anyway.

She was shaking, and he could see the tension in every single one of her muscles, as well as the bouncing of her right leg against the floor. She was coiling like a viper, and he was very much afraid she was going to strike and cause a scandal.

Maybe even a bigger one than the murder on the train, if Felicity was offended enough. The press and social media held a scary amount of power, and Claire would be live bait.

She needed to be very, very careful.

"That's a bit of a general question, isn't it, Felicity?" Claire said with a slight curl of her lip. "Is there something more specific you would like from me?"

Jonny bit down on the inside of his cheek to keep from

making any sort of sound or actual facial expression. Claire's tone had been perfectly polite to any normal ear, but Jonny could hear quite clearly the absolute ice in every syllable.

Felicity, however, was a consummate professional. She only smiled more broadly. "You are absolutely right—my mistake. Tell me about working with Alan on your series of *Britain's Battle of the Bakers*. How was he off camera, for instance? Encouraging? Rude? Fair? Abrasive? Demeaning? Inappropriate?"

Jonny carefully eased himself back against his chair, which allowed him a better view of Claire without drawing blatant attention to her. If he wanted to keep distracting Felicity when this was over, he'd need to play his cards as strategically as possible, and if he could get a sense of what Claire would say, he could probably back her up.

Unless that would give Felicity insight into his relationship with Claire, which was entirely possible.

And not what he wanted his distraction to be about.

At all.

"Alan can't act, Felicity," Claire laughed, the sound light and somehow still covered in ice. "He is incapable of being anything but himself at any given time. I'm sure any of the bakers from any of the other series would agree with me. You know how in the show he gives a little bit of feedback when we're talking about our plan for the bake?"

Felicity nodded as though she was interested, but her eyes were completely vacant of that same energy. She was clearly not a rabid fan of the show.

And then, strangely, the toe of one of her impractical stilettos tapped against Jonny's shin and began slowly—pointedly—making its way up and down his pant leg.

Just what this awkward situation needed.

More awkward.

"Well, that's how Alan is off camera too." Claire crossed one leg over the other, still bouncing beneath the table. "He only gave a little feedback, just enough to make us consider shifting our direction. And then after the bakes were over, we heard his thoughts when the cameras were rolling, just how you see it. He really didn't talk more than that on set, unless he was giving instructions."

"Does Alan have favorites, Claire?" Felicity asked her, showing a little more teeth in her smile.

Claire smirked and drummed her nails on the table. "I am sure he does. Just like the fans do. But Alan doesn't let on that he has favorites. He is very professional that way."

"Standoffish?" Felicity pressed. "Rude? I mean, he doesn't even smile unless something is practically perfect. Wouldn't you call that cruel and demoralizing?"

"No, I wouldn't say so." Claire shook her head, her smile bordering on a sneer. "He liked to let us do things our way and learn from our mistakes. And he didn't want to show favoritism in a competition."

"He told you this?"

Claire opened her mouth, then closed it on a hum. "No, Felicity, he hasn't. I will admit I made those assumptions myself. But Alan was never harsh or personal in his criticism. No attacks. He was fair, and he knows what he's talking about."

Felicity's eyes narrowed, and her smile became closed-lipped. "Hmm. And what about since the show? Has Alan been any different toward you since the series ended?"

"Yes, he has." Claire slowly drummed her fingers one by one, her attention never straying from Felicity.

When it was clear she wasn't going to offer up anything else without provocation, Jonny bit down on his cheek harder, this time to keep from laughing.

He'd known for a while that Claire was a secret spitfire, but this was masterful.

"In what way?" Felicity inquired in the tightest voice Jonny had ever heard break through a smile.

Claire's index finger began to tap against the table like she was sending a message in Morse code. "He has become a mentor, in his way. He checks in and makes sure I am not too overwhelmed with the publicity that comes with *BBB*. And he is constantly making sure I am still baking because I enjoy it and not because of some expectation I need to live up to. Only last month, I asked for his advice on a recipe, and his feedback was encouraging, constructive, and thoughtful. He didn't have to take that much time to help me, and I certainly did not expect anything like that when I left the show. But I have spoken to a few others who have been on previous series—we've met at various events—and they have said the same thing."

"Which is?"

"That Alan Gables cares more about how we do after the show than how we do on the show," Claire told her simply, her finger stilling at last. "His concern is genuine and not limited to the filming schedule. He may not be the most effusive or demonstrative person, but I will take something genuine over something showy every single time. Wouldn't you?"

Felicity's eyes widened, no doubt from the shock of being asked a question herself. Had she been alone with Claire, she might have brushed it off, but Jonny saw her eyes flick to him, and, based on the conversations they'd had before Claire showed up, he knew she wanted to keep him on whatever leash she thought she had.

"Yes, I most certainly would," Felicity said in a falsely bright tone.

Claire nodded once, her middle finger now joining her index finger in a random tapping pattern on the table's surface.

Felicity stared at Claire without speaking for a moment, then her smile spread enough to show teeth once more. "What would you say are Alan's worst qualities, Claire?"

Starting with the worst? That was a bit of an obvious opening to her true intentions, wasn't it?

"He's harder on himself than anyone else," Claire said softly. "Which is probably why he doesn't smile often. He is never satisfied. But that isn't all bad, is it? Not if it leads to a fierce determination to be his very best at all times, which it does."

Felicity's eyes narrowed. "And his best qualities?"

"His creativity, integrity, and the ability to see through complete and utter nonsense with perfect clarity," Claire recited as though she had been prepped for these questions.

One of Felicity's eyebrows twitched, which made Jonny wonder if she hoped for a fraction of Claire's talent in brow mobility. Or if she even knew about it.

"Integrity," Felicity repeated in a dark tone. "Really?"

Claire's fingers danced more quickly on the table. "Isn't that the word for when someone is exactly the same to your face as they are behind your back? When the person you see on camera is exactly the same off it?"

Oh, goodness, she was on a roll.

Don't smile, don't smile, don't smile.

Jonny had never been prouder of another person in his entire life than he was of Claire at this moment. If Alan could only hear this . . .

"There have been rumors, you know," Felicity mused, though it was perfectly clear from the expression on her face that this was all planned, "that Alan's business is in trouble. That Alan himself has been less than honest. Not to mention the odd demand for secrecy onboard this train. What else could he be hiding amid all the rumors about him?"

If Jonny hadn't known Claire so well, he would have thought she had no reaction to the statement. Her face never moved, and her posture never changed. But he did know her well, and the bouncing of her leg slowed for a moment, and the tips of her ears turned pink. He couldn't see her eyes, but he knew they had taken on a more grayish hue to their green depths.

Which meant Felicity should probably duck and cover, but he wasn't going to announce a warning any time soon.

"There have always been rumors about lots of people and lots of things," Claire snapped, losing her smile entirely. "Fortunately for me, I don't care about rumors. I don't pay attention to them. I don't know anything about Alan's business because that's not what our friendship is built on. And I don't care about business, which probably means I will never be as successful as I'd like to be as a baker. But you know what, Felicity? That's fine by me. I'd rather keep my love of baking than lose my soul to the business of it all."

"We were talking about Alan," Felicity pointed out, unfazed by the monologue. "Not you."

"Were we?" Claire's tone made the question a statement—a challenge.

A shiver raked Jonny's spine, and he ground his teeth together to try to offset the tension building in his chest.

"What do I know about Alan's business?" Claire repeated. "Nothing. Because Alan's business is his business and not mine. Now, is there something else you would like my thoughts or opinions on? Because I'm starving, and these potato scones that Alan suggested we have would really help to shut up the inner Queen of Snark I'm holding back right now."

Felicity's smile became completely feral. "I meant no offense, of course."

Claire raised one of her ever-nimble brows. "Of course."

"What do you think you know about Alan Gables that I do not?"

Claire's fingers drummed on the table in an ominous roll of taps. "Did you know that, besides being the greatest baker the UK has produced, he sponsors scholarships at each of the major culinary schools in Britian so that deserving students can attend, no matter their financial situation? Did you know a portion of his cookbook profits go to a charity that funds school food programs? Did you know he insisted that Dame Sophie Layton-Hughes be his partner judge on the show because her career was taking a nosedive and he thought she deserved better?"

Based on the round eyes and gaping mouth, it was clear Felicity hadn't known any of this, and seeing her shock was pure satisfaction.

Claire laughed once. "If you didn't know any of those things, Felicity, I think you'd better pay more attention to your job and less attention to getting your diseased claws into the viscount here. Alan Gables is my friend, and if you come for him, you come for me. And you do not want to come for me."

Felicity sneered. "Careful, pet. I know more about Alan Gables and the skeletons in his closet than you could ever hope to. Why, earlier today I heard some very interesting things in Dining Car 3. A few choice words, you might say. Betrayal. Embezzlement. Scandal. Ruin." She smiled in the most chilling, superior manner Jonny had ever seen. "I could take those words alone and make all the headlines I want with a simple snap of my fingers. You wouldn't want to put your mentor's sins on display because of a little tantrum, would you?"

"Tantrum?" Claire repeated as her brows snapped down. "You haven't begun to see the sort of tantrum I am capable of. I have nothing to lose, Felicity, so your threats won't work. I don't care if you want to ruin me in the press because at least I can face myself in the morning without the devil appearing in my eyeballs, unlike you. So take your ridiculous heels and your atrocious perfume and shove them in your piehole, or I will do it for you. We're done here!" She shoved to her feet, sending her chair crashing to the floor.

Felicity sat back with a bemused smile, her fingers reaching for Jonny's hand again and tracing absent patterns on the back.

"And stay the croquembouche away from my boyfriend!" Claire bellowed over her shoulder as she moved to her trolley, maneuvering it out of the dining car and toward the next group of passengers.

Jonny watched her go, his heart on fire and ready to burst out of his chest. His girlfriend had never been so stunning, so impressive, so perfect, and it was killing him not to nudge someone nearby and say, "I'm with her."

Or pick her up and kiss the ever-loving breath out of her.

Or throw her an actual parade.

As it was, the more primal, hidden part of him snarled in possessive delight and growled *Mine* at the top of its lungs.

Surely it was normal for those feelings to bring about the current perspiration along his scalp, wasn't it?

"Is she okay?" Felicity asked in a particularly chirping tone. She giggled and shifted in her chair until she was fully facing Jonny once more, leaning against the table. "She seems a bit unstable."

Ah, the old gaslighting technique. How original.

"Claire was known for her candor during her series on the show," Jonny told her without any hint of apology in his tone.

"Is that what we're calling it? Huh." Felicity's lips pursed. "How very polite of us."

Jonny laced his fingers together in his lap. "She was a fan favorite because of it."

Felicity's brows quirked in blatant mockery. "Viewers have never been known for their intellect or taste."

Jonny thought the same might be said for those who read popular magazines, but there didn't seem to be a need to bring that up at this moment.

It would not serve.

"Did Alan like Blackfirth Park?" Felicity asked as she rested her forearm on the table, her fingers tracing patterns on the tablecloth near where his hand had been before.

Like she was inviting it back.

"He seemed to," Jonny replied as he pretended to think back on it. "The Historic Kitchens have always been a big draw to the estate, and Alan is well-versed in culinary history. I actually have hopes of him doing a documentary special on them. But you'll have to keep that between us. I wouldn't want the story breaking before the details are ironed out."

Though it could cost him his left kidney, Jonny grinned and winked at the woman across from him, just for emphasis.

Her smile grew like she was the Grinch himself, and she nodded in a slow, rhythmic manner. "Oh, my lips are sealed for you, Jonathan."

He doubted that.

Still, he sat forward, setting one hand near his glass on the table. "What do you think? Would he do it? And would the public like it? You are right in the thick of public opinion and creative content. I have to think about what's best for Blackfirth, which is always in need of public support and funding, and with us already having filmed the show on site, it seems like an easy win to me."

"Alan is very popular," Felicity told him, taking his hand and lacing their fingers intimately. "Very. A silver fox to many of the female viewers."

"But he's not that old," Jonny pointed out, smiling quizzically.

Felicity shrugged. "Doesn't matter. He's over fifty, ergo he's a silver fox. His cookbook sales are at an all-time high. He's fully in his era, so it's the perfect time to capitalize on that for your estate. Do it sooner rather than later because popularity can be fickle, and you never know what sort of scandals can topple a career. I would get those contracts inked this winter and film in the spring. I want you to get everything you can for your estate, Jonathan, as soon as possible. Every single penny." She leaned forward and covered their hands with her other one, curling her hold around him completely. "Believe me, I know what I am talking about. You want him on this, because your other option is Dame Sophie, and she will not get your documentary the same ratings. And none of the other

British bakers will have the same appeal as the judges on *BBB*. And if you have them talk about the legend, same as you have with me, you'll be absolutely golden."

"Huh." Jonny leaned back and crossed one leg over the other before prying his hand carefully out of her hold and folding his arms. "And to think, I figured you didn't like Alan from how you were talking to Claire about him."

To his surprise, Felicity scoffed loudly and took a long drink from her wine glass. "Alan Gables has all the sex appeal I seek in an exposé, and I am ambitious enough to pretend I like baking for that. People believe anything if you can write it well enough. But I'll tell you, in all confidence, Jonathan: I would much rather be spending my time with you. Every single minute of my time, and I would spend that time creatively too." She winked at him over her wine glass, her smile curving in an almost menacing way.

Rather the way Jonny's stomach was curving. In a nauseating way.

The sooner he could escape this interview and return to the blessed normalcy of his life, the better.

CHAPTER 13

The scones had been a huge hit for the passengers, and the compliments—few though they were—had been effusive. It was bizarre how baked mashed potatoes got more praise than an exquisite tarte tatin, but people would rather eat comfort food than fancy stuff when they were stressed.

Claire ought to look for macaroni and cheese after this. She might earn herself a knighthood for it.

Greg had been incredible in distributing the scones, his efficiency and dislike of small talk making him the perfect assistant. She'd sent him off as soon as they were done, and, after assuring him that she was fine, watched him head toward the engineer's office. He was going to get himself yelled at again, and he would probably turn into a child when that happened.

But she wasn't going to worry about it now. She had just made her way back through the entire train with the empty trolleys and had not seen Jonny or Felicity anywhere.

She didn't want to think about where they could have gone or why. She didn't want to know what had happened after she'd verbally slapped the woman in the face. She didn't want to know what Jonny thought of her outburst. She didn't want to consider how the outburst could have put both Alan's career and her own in the dumpster by the morning. She didn't want to think about any of it or reflect on her words or actions or look ahead to the future.

She wanted to sit on the floor of a dark room and eat junk food and cry.

And then take some medicine for the headache she'd get from crying.

And then eat more junk.

It was all just too much. The murder, the journalist, the food, the boyfriend, the stress . . . All of that on top of her own insecurities, overthinking, and inability to properly communicate her thoughts on any of the above was just too much. She didn't have trains of thought; she had stations of them. With at least seven trains in each.

Each with their own timetables, delays, and replacement bus services.

Her dad had always joked that she played hopscotch in her mind while everyone else walked, and there was some truth to it. How many times had she been three conversations ahead of those around her because of the connecting thoughts racing recklessly forward in her head? Explaining herself had become a way of life, and all it had done for her was make her realize she was just a strange bird.

A pigeon compared to the flamingo that was Felicity Farrow.

Claire gritted her teeth as she hauled the trolleys toward the kitchen door. Would any man have a hope of understanding how infuriating it was to be jealous of a spiteful hussy with no redeeming qualities? Jealous because she had endless legs, grace in sky-high heels, perfect lips, an actual Barbie figure, and hair that had probably never been affected by humidity.

It was one thing to be jealous of people you liked. It was something else to be jealous of the devil herself.

Self-loathing was the order of the night, and she needed to settle in with popcorn and a sugar coma for appropriate ambiance.

Pity party, table for one.

Entering the kitchen, Claire turned the trolleys and parked them to one side, then went to the sink and grabbed a damp rag. Alan was working at the counter just as he had been before, only now his sleeves were rolled back to his elbows and his hair was messier.

If he found her silence odd, he said nothing about it.

He was working on small marzipan sculptures, and she was in no mood to disturb that.

Claire wiped down the trolleys, the monotony of it soothing. She moved the condiments back into the cabinets, and only when the trolleys were pristine and she had removed her apron did she go see what, specifically, Alan was doing.

Everybody in the baking world knew he was famous for his marzipan, but Claire had never seen him work it in person before. She'd worked in it herself, of course, and during the filming of *BBB* earlier in the year, she'd made a marzipan Nativity that Alan had examined with the thoroughness of an exam proctor. As was his right as the Marzipan King.

He hadn't smiled at her for it, but he hadn't been critical either.

Small mercies.

Claire tilted her head as she watched the master work. He was shaping small versions of a steam engine, and the detail he was carving into each was absolutely incredible. Because of course it was! This was the man who had formed Edinburgh Castle out of marzipan, so why should these small trains be any less amazing?

Watching him work with the marzipan was like watching poetry in motion. He was as much a sculptor as anyone who worked in clay, and his smooth, fluid actions with the marzipan were almost hypnotic. His fingers, calloused and rough from his years in kitchens, managed the most minute and delicate details with ease and skill.

Had there been classical music and an opera singer in the room, Claire could not have been more certain that this man was a maestro who lived and breathed to create.

And he wanted to be her mentor and partner with her on a cookbook?

Why?

She'd never be as good as this. Never. She could work all her life practicing this one skill and never match him. Never attain this level. Never be this successful.

She wanted a career like Alan's, but she'd never manage such heights. Dreams were supposed to be what she was aiming for, though, right? Not necessarily what became of that aiming?

She'd be okay with following in his footsteps and using his life as a pattern if she could attain a little of the same success.

That would be enough.

Claire folded her arms and cleared her throat. "What are you doing with the marzipan trains?"

"Every passenger gets one," Alan murmured. "Part of the exclusive package. Plus it helps me think and process, and right now, there's a lot coming back. A lot to process."

"I bet."

She had a lot to process, too, but had no outlet like marzipan trains. She just had those tangled trains of thought, racing through her mind, down her spine, through her very blood, and congesting her heart until she couldn't breathe. Overthinking so hard it hurt everything within her.

Not productive. Not artistic. Not processing.

Not anything.

"Penny for them, lass."

Suddenly, it was hard to swallow. Claire moved to lock the kitchen door before walking over to the cabinets and sinking onto the floor, leaning her back against the cheap wood. She exhaled slowly, the sound shaking as though with sobs, and closed her eyes.

She heard Alan move to the floor as well and felt his shoe tap hers, not quite playfully but more in a show of support.

Companionship.

Awareness.

She was not alone.

"I saw them," Claire whispered to the kitchen, the saliva in her mouth burning against her gums with the words.

"Who?"

"Jonny and Felicity." She swallowed, and it hurt. Almost didn't work. Almost choked and gagged her while burning every inch of her throat.

"And?"

Claire drew her knees up and rested her wrists on them, opening her eyes and staring across the kitchen floor at Alan. "She's into him. Very."

Alan's mouth curved wryly. "She has eyes, woman. What d'you expect?"

The direct answer made Claire laugh despite not feeling any humor at all. "Yeah, I guess. He is pretty attractive, right?"

"So they say." Alan shrugged his slender shoulders and leaned his head back against the cabinets. "How did he look?"

"Fine. He could have been enjoying himself, for all I know." Claire looked up at the ceiling as she felt her eyes burn, her exhale growing shaky again. "She was . . . she was touching his arm, and he wasn't pulling away. He was letting her."

"You ken what he said he was going to do, right? Distract her so she doesn't put her nose where it shouldn't be."

Claire nodded almost frantically. "Yeah, I know. My brain knows he couldn't be disgusted or jerk away from her or be rude, but did he have to be *that* convincing?"

Alan snorted loudly, the sound echoing in the small space. "You can't honestly believe he likes her."

"It's not her specifically. It's not." Her throat tightened on the half-truth, and she waited until the tension abated before trying to say more. "Leggy, put together, graceful temptress that she is, I am sure he can see through it."

"Yeah, you sound pretty sure."

Claire ignored the jab, wishing Alan had a little less discernment and a little more compassion. But then he wouldn't be Alan, so there was that.

More's the pity.

Claire bit her lip, clicking her tongue and lowering her gaze back to her mentor. "I don't care about Felicity Farrow. It's the idea of her. Someone like her. Someone gorgeous and designer-wearing and classy. Someone who could attend any event in the world, high to low, and effortlessly own it. Someone you picture living in a big house and wearing exquisite jewelry and walking red carpets. Someone who makes your jaw drop because how can they be real? That's who matches Jonathan Ainsley, Viscount Colburn. Seeing them at dinner together like that . . . They just fit, Alan. Like puzzle pieces."

There was a long moment of silence, and each heartbeat that passed without response pumped more ice into her veins.

"People aren't puzzle pieces, Claire," he rumbled softly.

Tears slipped from her eyes, and she angrily swiped at them. "You basting know what I mean."

"And you'd basting better listen to me," Alan snapped, startling her enough to make her hiccup.

He glared at her, his brows almost covering his eyes, and the creases above his nose dark and angry. She'd never seen an expression so murderous on his face, and it was almost terrifying.

"People don't fit neatly into place like puzzle pieces," Alan told her, his tone still harsh. "We're not that simple or that inflexible. It doesn't work like that because people change, and we change all the ruddy time. We change every single day. If this is a puzzle, it's one where the pieces morph as time goes on—and so does the picture."

"Meaning what?" Claire asked, more tears falling as fatigue set in.

He exhaled a wordless laugh and laced his fingers behind his neck. "Meaning the man that you brought onto the train today is not the man I met the first day we went to Blackfirth. Meaning you are not the same girl who made the finale in series twelve of *BBB*. Meaning I am not the same idiot who told Rose McGregor that there was no room in my life for her." He groaned and gripped at his hair a moment before letting his hands drop back to his sides. "We are not who we once were. None of us. We look back and see our regrets, but we also see our growth. We see what makes us proud and what infuriates us. But we also know ourselves better."

"So he will outgrow me," Claire whispered. "That's what I'm most afraid of."

Alan shook his head, the corner of his mouth twitching. "You're projecting your fears onto your future, lass. Has he given you any indication that his feelings have changed?"

A sinking sensation hit her stomach. "He . . . he's never said he loves me. Not once. I haven't said it either, because I didn't think . . . I don't want . . ."

"You're placing your value on someone else's feelings of you?"

"It's not that," she protested quickly.

Too quickly.

Alan's smile was too knowing, and Claire looked away. "I don't want him to feel trapped. And seeing him tonight, I feel like I'm trapping him. He's so miserable doing this, and if I ever make something of my baking, he's going to hate all the publicity. This isn't the life for him, and I wish . . . He used to call me 'love' every now and then, but it's been so long . . . I don't think he feels that anymore."

"Would you like me to expound on the utter simplicity and density that is the male mind compared to the minefield of complexity and overthinking that is the female one?" Alan offered, his voice dripping with so much sarcasm it was miraculous there wasn't anything to clean up.

"That's not helping," Claire snapped. "I know I'm crazy. I know! And it's just another reason he belongs with someone else."

"Even if it breaks your heart?"

"My heart should know better." Claire thumped her head against the cabinet a few times. "Stupid, stupid heart should have known better."

Alan shifted into a cross-legged position. "You've been with him for months. Has he ever given you reason to doubt him before?"

Claire shook her head noisily, letting it hit the cabinets on either side of her for emphasis. "Never. But we live in Blackfirth, and he's not that social. Opportunities are slim. And he always comes back from London exactly when he says he will, so why would I think anything else? But even with all of that . . . Alan, I always expect the other shoe to drop. He likes this random baker who is different from everyone else, but when does the novelty wear off and reality kick back in?"

"Good heavens, Claire. You expect him to get bored?"

She nodded as firmly as humanly possible. "From day one, I knew it wasn't forever. Couldn't be. Not me, not for him. I just didn't expect to fall so hard for something without a warranty."

He cleared his throat almost awkwardly. "Claire, my lass, nothing in our lives or our love has a warranty. And if you really loved Viscount Hots-for-You, I think you'd see him more clearly than this."

"He's the best man there is," Claire admitted on a sob. "That doesn't mean he'd ever want me the way I want him. Not when there is so much out there better suited for him. And I can't tell you how stupid it is to be feeling this when there is a dead body a few cars down. But emotions . . ." She held up her hands in surrender, closing her eyes for a long moment.

Alan's exhale was long and slow. "You're not going to be convinced of anything tonight, are you?"

Claire swallowed fresh tears. "Nope."

"Okay. Want some trifle?"

She tilted her head as she looked at him, blinking wildly while also slapping her forehead. "We forgot to serve the trifle!"

He nodded his head, his face relaxing into something rather warm and comforting. "It was supposed to follow teatime service, but you had a lot going on at the time . . . Want some?"

Claire felt renewed burning in her eyes and a matching tingle in her lips. "Yeah. I'd love some."

Alan pushed to his feet and opened the fridge, pulling the bowls out and setting them on the counter before removing the cling film. He turned and brought a spoon to Claire, presenting it like a baton to a conductor or a wand to a fairy princess. Then he went back to the counter, but instead of spooning the trifle into a smaller serving, he brought one entire bowl to her and set it between her knees and her chest. Then, of all things, he took the other bowl and sat down once more against the cabinets, his own spoon in hand.

He dipped his spoon into his enormous bowl of trifle and took a massive bite. "Go on, lass," he encouraged around the mouthful, nudging his head toward the bowl she limply held. "We're eating our feelings tonight."

They were silent a long moment, and then Alan asked, "Want to hear more about my girl that got away?"

If Claire hadn't already been crying, she would have burst into tears right then. "You don't have to tell me anything about your past, Alan. Just being here with me while I cry is enough."

"Uh, trifle," he reminded her, hefting his bowl a little. "No one should eat feelings alone."

She managed a watery laugh. "Sympathetic trifle eating still doesn't mean—"

"Look, I'm not often in a nostalgic mood, let alone one where I'm willing to recount the part of my life with the one that got away, so I need you to help me out and take advantage of the fact that, at this moment, I really want to talk about her while I sit on the floor and eat this trifle." Alan raised a daring brow at her, taking another large bite of trifle and clearly waiting for a response from her.

Who was this ridiculous, thoughtful, curious Scotsman, and what had he done with Alan Gables?

Claire scooped a heaping spoonful of trifle pointedly. "Well, if it will help you, Alan, go right ahead." She took the bite of trifle and did her best not to moan at the delicious flavors of chocolate, cherries, and berries hitting her tongue in bursts of gloriousness.

And tried not to cry at the way he'd deflected the conversation away from her brokenness.

And tried not to smile at how sweet all of this was.

But mostly, the trifle.

It was a ridiculously good trifle.

"So," Alan began, as he continued eating his own trifle, "Rose had the greatest smile I've ever seen. Her whole face smiled, not just her mouth. She had this dimple, and I always wanted to just tap my thumb into it and see what happened. My mother adored her. My sisters adored her. *I* adored her. Absolutely adored her from head to toe."

The rawness in his tone tore at Claire's heart, and her

tears around another bite of trifle weren't for her this time. "Then how could you let her go?"

It was Alan's turn to thump his head against the cabinets. "Because she'd always been there, Claire. She was a fixture in my life, like my left arm. But because I couldn't see how much I needed her, I stupidly thought she was expendable. I actually used my left arm. Needed it. But I didn't think I needed Rose. She distracted me from success and glory. So she had to go. I guess part of me thought she'd always be there, and when I got where I wanted to go, we could pick up where we'd left off."

"You didn't think she'd go."

"I didn't think she'd move on," he corrected in a hoarse voice. "I didn't consider her life, her dreams, her goals . . . Her anything. It was always about me. I'm a selfish man, Claire. Selfish, soulless, heartless, stupid . . . and alone. There will never be anyone else. I tried a few times, but it was over before it ever went anywhere. Because I need Rose. Only Rose. And there's nothing else to be said."

"Alan," Claire whimpered, hating this side of him and adoring it all the same.

He closed his eyes and sighed. "Eat your trifle, lass. I'm going to try to think up happier stories so I don't find us whiskey in a minute. The last thing we need is alcohol on top of our trifle."

Claire looked at the bowl and smiled to herself. "I don't know, it might pair really well."

His soft snicker sounded a little reluctant. "We'll put it in the cookbook, then. 'Heartbreak trifle. Whiskey optional.'"

"But encouraged."

"Oh, definitely encouraged. Elevates the whole thing."

CHAPTER 14

The pounding in Jonny's head was absolutely brutal, and he'd been drinking only sparkling water all night. Not even a good flavor, just the basic one. He had needed something more distracting than still water to keep him sitting at the table and then to keep his wits about him while he had to meander through the train like a tour guide beside the bulldog dressed in pink.

The residual sensation of bubbles on his tongue had helped distract him from the looks he received while walking beside her. Not that anyone knew who Jonny was dating, or even knew Jonny himself, but Felicity Farrow attracted attention wherever she went. How she carried herself was a powerful draw, and she was well aware of how attractive she was. She knew her power and wielded it well.

Which meant anyone with her would also be seen, and Jonny had never felt so ogled in his entire life.

Even the husband-hungry American women he'd once despised for setting foot on his estate in thinly veiled attempts to find him hadn't given him this feeling.

But his time with Felicity was over now, and he'd barely

managed to escape the encounter with her without agreeing to breakfast together in the morning.

He'd do it if he had to, but he wanted to get back to the easy, natural, refreshingly normal life he had with Claire. There was no need for walls or guards or pretense with her. No acting or hiding. No expectations other than that he be himself.

Freedom. That's what it was. Claire represented the freedom to be who he was and not who anyone else thought he should be.

She had found parts of him that he had forgotten about, pieces he had hidden so well that they were foreign at first, corners of his heart and soul he didn't even know about. Yet she was oblivious to how extraordinary a creature she was. She had once joked about being a mediocre baker, and he let her, but there was nothing mediocre about her. Not her baking, not her looks, not her humor, nothing.

Not a single thing.

But he would admit, not everybody saw her that way. And he loved that. He loved that he was one of the few people aware of her brilliance and rarity and magnificence. He'd shout it out to the whole world if he didn't think there would be a stampede of others to get to her.

He was just possessive enough to keep that secret for himself.

Finders keepers, after all.

That wasn't too caveman, was it?

He moved through the dark train carefully, not wanting to disturb any of the other passengers who were trying to sleep amid the raging storm outside. The Highland winds battered the windows and walls while rain pelted the roof. It was as hypnotic as it was deafening, like waves against the shore. And with thunder rumbling in the distance, it was the perfect ambiance of night.

Some would sleep very well; others would be too distracted.

Jonny would be one of the content ones.

It was a dark and stormy night . . .

He chuckled to himself as he entered the VIP car and moved toward their compartment.

"What has you so chipper?" Claire's sleep-roughened voice asked as he entered.

The lights in the compartment were dim, but he could still see her curled up on the bench, one of the train's blankets tucked neatly around her. "I was just thinking."

"Dangerous," she murmured before he could finish.

He smirked in her general direction. "Cute. No, I was just thinking of the phrase 'It was a dark and stormy night,' considering everything."

She chuckled easily, and the sound warmed him as he sat on his bench and removed his shoes. "Yeah, I'll give you that one," she said. "But who's the writer of this mystery?"

Jonny sputtered once. "Not me, that's for sure. I'll stick with the numbers, thanks."

"Don't look at me," Claire insisted. "I can barely word my recipes."

"Guess it's someone else's job then. We'll take notes for them." Jonny leaned back against the bench, finding the small pillow propped by the window and the blanket folded near his feet, settling himself in.

A comfortable silence filled the compartment, punctuated nicely by the rain and wind against the windows, the rumbling, rolling thunder outside, and the occasional burst of lightning. But then something else joined the space between them, something that had Jonny shifting for a better position and teasing at his brain, something that would undoubtedly keep him awake until he could identify it.

A pointed flash of bright lightning illuminated their compartment for a blinding moment, drawing his gaze to the reflective surface of the window of the compartment door.

And the new word written upon it.

Backward from this perspective, as it had been written on the front.

"Erm, Claire?"

"Hmm?"

Jonny cleared his throat. "How long has 'danger' been written on the glass there?"

"Somewhere between scones and trifle," she said, sounding sleepy. "Wasn't there when I left the compartment to prepare dinner, but it was there when I got back. Security checked the compartments for threats, but there wasn't anything to find."

Jonny ground his teeth together hard. Another threat to Claire, and not a ruddy thing they could do about it. No cameras, no access to police, no protection whatsoever.

There was already one dead body on this train. Was someone trying to make her another?

"Stop freaking out, J," Claire mumbled. "It won't help."

"How are you so calm?" he snapped, jerking his head to look over at her.

He swore he could hear her shrug. "I'm not. Not at all. I just don't have any more tears to cry tonight."

Wait, what?

"You . . . what do you . . . ?"

"Shh," she urged in a low, gentle voice. "Not tonight, J. I'm exhausted. Please."

He couldn't argue with that, but the idea that he had somehow missed her crying was unsettling and went against everything he was trying to be for her. Against everything he believed in. Everything he felt for her.

But he also couldn't make her talk about it when she didn't want to. The stress of the day had only built as the hours had passed, between the dead body, the angry passengers, Felicity, the delay, not to mention the messages just for her. It was too much, surely. Who wouldn't have broken at least once? Jonny had needed a walk earlier, so why shouldn't Claire have needed a moment of emotional release?

He could talk to her about it tomorrow.

"Claire?" he finally said, his voice low.

"Yeah?"

Was it his imagination, or was her voice a little smaller than normal?

"Thank you for not wearing disgusting perfume that makes me want to choke and die."

An explosion of laughter came from the opposite side of the compartment, and the tension vanished in that moment. Jonny grinned at hearing it, and, for the moment, all was right with the world.

"You're very welcome," she giggled. "Are you dying for a shower right now?"

"Ugh." He made a face and shuddered. "Absolutely. Or just to be hosed down. Honestly, I can taste it when I swallow."

Claire made a gagging sound. "Gross. I'd pat your hand, but it's too far."

"Funny, I can feel it anyway. You're so compassionate."

"I know."

They fell silent again, but it was much better this time. Much more comfortable. Much more natural.

Much more them.

"Felicity knows something," Jonny announced without preamble.

"I should hope so," Claire muttered. "Imagine getting to where she is without knowing something."

Jonny snorted a surprised laugh. "I mean about Alan. She knows something, and she's definitely out for blood and not tributes."

He heard Claire moving and waited for her to settle back in. "Did she say anything after I left?"

"After you brilliantly shut her down, took a stand, and stormed out like a goddess of war, you mean?"

Claire's grunt of discontent only made Jonny smile more.

He turned his head to look at her as best as possible. "I mean it. I almost gave you a standing ovation."

"Thanks," she grumbled before sighing. "But what else did she say?"

"Well," he started, exhaling roughly, "she thought it was a great idea to have Alan host a documentary about the Historic Kitchens at Blackfirth. She knows he's popular and called him a silver fox. Actually, she's really into him, even though she could not care less about baking. Something about sex appeal."

"I am going to interrupt this lovely conversation and beg you to move on before I get sick," came a gravelly Scottish voice from the floor.

Jonny sat bolt upright and glared down at the darkness,

not seeing anything. "Baguettes and Bordeaux, what the hot cross buns are you doing there?"

Alan cackled—actually cackled—a gristly, choked series of sounds. "That just made my entire year, my lord. Ah, I needed that after today."

Jonny's heart rattled like a pinball in his chest, frantically pattering against every hard and soft surface possible while his lungs burned in an attempt to find any and all air to exchange.

His life had just been shortened by five years, he was positive of that.

Was his hair still the same color, or had it all gone white?

"I was expecting more of a shriek than that," Claire mused aloud to the darkness. "A yelp, at least."

Jonny glared at her, one hand going to his chest as though he could force his heart back into position and proper cadence by his palm alone. "A little warning would have gone a long way."

He would swear she shrugged against her bench. "I never found the right opening."

Oh, she was enjoying this, was she?

Great.

"Murderer on the train," Jonny emphasized with great care. "Remember? Have a little compassion on the ignorant."

"As I recall," came Alan's drawling brogue from the floor, "someone here suggested I do exactly as I am. Why are we to be blamed for his forgetfulness?"

After the day they'd all had, this was the sort of stuff they were up to? What had happened to the danger and the mystery lurking in every car of this train? What about being trapped in the middle of actual-nowhere Highlands?

These two were *pranking* him?

How long had he been gone on his distraction mission anyway?

"Oh my days," Jonny groaned, scrubbing both hands into his hair and pulling a little. "Okay." He inhaled slowly, held it for a count of four, then exhaled a long, cautious breath. After repeating that twice, he looked toward the floor again. "I hate you, Alan."

"I know."

"Aww, bonding!" Claire cooed with a laugh.

Jonny flicked his eyes between the two of them, his thoughts stammering with incoherence. "I feel like I've missed something here."

"Aye, that'll happen from time to time," Alan said without concern. "But do go on, my lord. Felicity knows something?"

Sensing he wasn't going to get a straight answer from the co-conspirators any time soon, Jonny sighed, rolled his eyes, and settled back against his bench. "Right. Felicity." He cleared his throat. "She said to film sooner rather than later. Like it would be too late if we waited too long to have Alan do this, and she wanted me to get every penny possible for the estate."

"Huh. Was this an actual idea you pitched, or did you just pull it out of your ear?" Alan asked him.

"My ear," Jonny replied with a smirk. "But it's not a bad idea if you're interested. I could have the paperwork drawn up next week, and we could have this all prepped by Christmas."

"I accept. Thanks, my lord."

"No problem. You want to stay at the estate?"

"Sounds lovely. Your cook there is fantastic, and I wonder—"

Claire snorted quietly and shifted her trainers against the bench with a harsh squeak. "Back to the task at hand, fellas."

"Sorry," they chimed in unison.

Jonny tucked one hand behind his head, frowning up at the ceiling. "What did she say to you, Claire? Something about rumors?"

"I was just trying to replay that," Claire said heavily. "My face is getting hot because of it, and all I can remember clearly is what I snapped back at her."

"That was such a good part," Jonny laughed.

Alan made a grumpy sound. "I miss all the best stuff."

Jonny turned on his side, grinning. "Felicity said there were rumors about your business being in trouble, and she was totally saying it to get a reaction, right? Except Claire says something about how rumors are everywhere about everything, and that your friendship wasn't built on business, so why does Claire need to care? And then—"

"Wait, wait," Claire interrupted, sitting up quickly. "She said Alan's business was in trouble, with rumors about it being less than honest. How could she know that?" She looked toward the floor. "Who all knows about the skimming?"

Alan was quiet for a long moment. "Just me, I think. Only learned today, remember? But Brian could have leaked whatever he wanted before he talked to me."

"Crepes alive," Claire grumbled. "This just gets worse and worse. Did Brian know Felicity was going to interview you?"

"Potentially. I mean, my calendar wasn't a secret in the company, and he is—or was—still on the board."

"Alan, you said that Brian was planning to drop his bombshell at Mallaig, right?" Jonny said slowly. "So if Alan is telling the truth—"

Claire snorted loudly. "*If*? Okay."

"Then maybe Brian had a backup plan in place," Jonny went on, choosing to ignore Claire's disgust at him. "Maybe he planted some information for Felicity to suspect problems early?"

He heard Alan shift on the floor. "You're saying he was going to give her some cockamamie story about me embezzling money?"

"Why not? Everybody would read a story about their favorite baking judge, even if it's about his downfall." Jonny found himself grinning again in the darkness. "Especially if he's pretty much universally declared to be a silver fox."

A slender fist rose from the floor toward him, and he tapped it with his own.

"That right there is not going to help clear Alan's name," Claire pointed out, her finger wagging in their direction.

"Sorry," they said again.

Claire's eyes zeroed in on Jonny. "We've gotta get more info on Brian. What he had in store, if he planted the story for Felicity, if more actually happened to the money . . ."

Jonny shrugged. "I put the briefcase back in Dining Car 3 behind the bar. We can go through it again in the morning, maybe, but that's just what he had at hand. If the conductor would let us look at his suitcase, maybe we'd find more, but I doubt we'll get that lucky. Too bad we can't get to Brian's phone."

Alan barked a laugh from the floor. "They'd have taken that first thing with everyone else's."

"Except . . ." Claire said slowly, her tone growing thoughtful.

Jonny squinted, but the dim light made it impossible to decipher her expression. "What?"

He could practically hear her smile. "Was Brian a rule follower?"

Alan snorted loudly. "No."

"And is it a company phone?"

Jonny's jaw muscles pulled as his mouth fell open. "Oh good gravy!"

"I think I love you, Claire Walker," Alan announced.

"I'm kind of the best, aren't I?" she preened, quite possibly flipping her hair. "And I doubt Conductor Lisa actually confiscated anything, since no one mentioned the briefcase missing earlier, and the refrigeration car is just beyond the kitchen, seconds away from here, so . . ."

She was up and out of the compartment before Jonny could finish blinking, the door clicking shut as her footsteps retreated down the corridor.

"Surely she didn't," Alan began hoarsely, the thought going unfinished.

Jonny laughed weakly. "No way. She'd never . . ."

But why else would she just leave the compartment like that, especially when the thought was fresh and her ire apparently still up from her Felicity Farrow confrontation?

"She could be in so much trouble," Alan whispered to the night.

"But if we don't know what she's doing . . ." Jonny offered in the same tone.

Alan snapped his fingers. "Plausible deniability."

"We're going to let her take the fall?" He winced even as he said it, feeling like not only the worst boyfriend that ever existed but also a sorry excuse for a man.

Jonny laced his fingers over his stomach. "I'm willing to give you the benefit of the doubt on the money, Alan. If you say Brian doctored the documents I've seen, I'll believe you. For now."

"I'll accept that," Alan said after a moment. "I've given you no reason to trust me, but hopefully I've also not given you reason to doubt me. And if Claire does miraculously manage to find Brian's phone, I can give you that proof. Technically, it *is* a company phone, so . . ."

"Plausible deniability," they said together.

Again, up came Alan's fist, and again, Jonny bumped it with his own.

The compartment door opened, and Claire entered, blinking at them in the dark. "Yeah, still not okay with whatever it is making you two do that."

Jonny barked a laugh. "I thought you wanted us to be friends."

"I do. But it's creepy to jump to that already." She shook her head and closed the compartment door, then moved to her bench and sat down again.

Jonny wished he could turn on the lights so he could look at Alan in shared confusion, but he would settle for staring in Claire's direction and hoping the pressure would get to her.

Then, of all things, her face lit up. Actually lit up.

Because there was a phone in front of her face.

"Any idea what Brian's passcode is, Alan?" she asked as though checking a weather forecast.

"Holy crap," Jonny breathed, unsure if it was in horror, amazement, or pride.

Or all three.

"Let's see," Alan mused with laughter rife in his tone.

"The company setting is 001234, so try that. If not, go for his birthday—24-08-73."

Claire typed away and grinned rather devilishly at the screen. "I'm in. Birthday for the win!"

Jonny sat up and swung his legs down, the tip of his foot hitting something pointy on the floor. "You are not," he managed, keeping his eyes on Claire's glowing skin.

"That was my funny bone, you pretentious viscount," Alan growled.

Jonny kicked his foot out intentionally, and it collided with something else, which earned him a stinging swat. "Friendly viscount, thank you." He returned his attention to Claire. "You totally did not just get into the phone of poor, dead Brian."

"Poor, dead Brian," Claire and Alan repeated solemnly.

All that was missing were drinks to toast him at this strange wake of sorts.

"I totally did so," Claire assured him in a singsong voice, waving the phone at him, though he couldn't make out anything on the screen. She pulled it back and settled into her bench like it was the plushest couch known to man. "Alan? Think he set up two-point security?"

"No possible way," Alan told her, giving each word its due pronunciation. "His phone never left his person, so he probably never saw the need."

Jonny tilted his head in curiosity. "Never? What about—?"

"I don't think any clarification is needed," Claire announced loudly, her eyes widening as she worked at the phone. "Sugar, it's like being back in the classroom with you two."

"Okay," Jonny said slowly, "but what age?"

"The man has a point," Alan agreed.

Claire cut them off with a fist pump. "Email!"

“Work or personal?” Alan asked, sitting up for the first time.

“Both, as it happens.” Claire showed him the screen. “Any requests for my first hunting venture?”

“Financial records,” Jonny said at once. “Let’s see if we can get Alan off the hook for at least one thing tonight.”

“Aww, thanks, friendly viscount.”

“I will kick you again,” Jonny warned.

Claire shook her head and handed the phone to Alan. “I don’t even know what I’m looking for. You dig.”

Alan heaved a dramatic sigh. “So much for plausible deniability.”

CHAPTER 15

As it happened, Alan knew exactly where to look for the financial records—the correct ones—and was able to bring those up for Jonny to see in full detail.

The ones in the briefcase had indeed been modified to make Alan look guilty, but the originals, as proven by time stamp, revealed that the deceit was all Brian's.

Thank you, time stamps.

After scouring the financials, they'd dug into Brian's personal email accounts for anything he had sent about Alan.

Turns out, he vented about Alan a lot.

Like . . . a lot.

There was an email thread specifically about taking Alan down, but there was no identity attached to the other party in the thread. Just the screen name Contact.

Not much to go on.

But the emails did mention the train, a story, and a meeting.

There were exactly zero messages between Brian Donovan and Felicity Farrow, much to their disappointment. Whoever Contact was must have brought Felicity on.

Unless Contact *was* Felicity, but Claire, for one, doubted the woman could have hidden that well.

For the sake of being thorough, they'd checked for any texts containing the words *Mode Magazine*, journalist, interview, or train like they'd found in the emails.

Zilch.

The search had occupied them all until it was so late that they'd reached a level of hilarity resembling intoxication, which hadn't helped the investigation whatsoever.

But it had given Claire a set of sore abdominal muscles that screamed at her when she woke at what felt like the crack of dawn.

They hurt almost as much as her neck and back did from the uncomfortable bench she'd slept on, but at least she'd slept some.

Small mercies.

Claire sat up and craned her neck from side to side, groaning at the series of satisfying pops the motion elicited. She had never been an exercise aficionado, but she could use a good, long walk around the Blackfirth grounds to not feel like she'd slept in a tiny box all night. Her body hated her at the moment, and that wasn't going to make for a good day.

She could already feel where her headache would be in a few hours.

She rubbed the spot absently and looked out the compartment window. The train wasn't moving, and the clouds in the sky were sailing by quickly, giving occasional glimpses of blue sky. The rolling, sometimes jagged hills were gorgeous and majestic, as though displaying the most primal part of Earth itself just because.

Walking out there would have been glorious.

Possibly painful and death-defying, but there were ways around that. She'd have to come back when there wasn't a murderer afoot.

She made a face as she considered that murderer and the dead body in the refrigeration car.

How did that settle overnight?

A shudder raced through her, head to toe, and she shifted her attention to the two men in her compartment.

Jonny lay across his bench, still asleep, mouth parted and a slightly congested breathing escaping his lips in guttural bursts. It was unfair, really, how he could still be that attractive while making such sounds. His face was completely relaxed, making him look younger and more innocent, and his disheveled hair only added to the effect. He would always be a handsome man, no matter what age or life did to him, so maybe it was only right that he practically snored when he slept.

It would have been too cruel otherwise.

Claire glanced down to find Alan almost spread-eagle on the floor, his head lolled to one side. He was more of a purring sleeper, though he still looked as grumpy as he did when he was awake. Classic Alan, always himself even when asleep.

He would never know what their conversation over trifle had meant to her. No one had ever opened up like that just to make her feel better or to sympathize with her, and if anyone had suggested that Alan Gables would discuss broken hearts and romantic expectations with her, she would have laughed until tears drowned her. The fact that he'd done it with an excessive quantity of comfort food in hand had made it even more unreal.

And even more special.

It hadn't convinced her that Jonny would somehow see her

the way she wanted to be seen or that he'd never trade her in for a better, fancier model of girlfriend, but at least she wasn't crying about it anymore.

She didn't believe for one second that Felicity Farrow was his cup of tea, but that didn't mean she felt any differently about the woman.

At all.

Claire grunted moodily to herself and pulled out Brian's phone, thumbing in the code and opening his email again. There had to be something in here that she could work with. Something that would give them insight into who might have killed Brian.

She searched for Alan's name, which returned way more emails than she wanted to look at, but that was the risk when including company emails.

She narrowed her eyes at the screen, hunting for any sort of filter.

Ah, perfect. She could exclude certain email addresses from the results.

She found Alan's business email and plugged that into the excluded addresses, then watched as the bulk of the messages fell away.

That should never have been a cathartic experience, but here she was, breathing more easily over someone else's email accounts.

Bizarre.

Thumbing through a few emails, she found an interesting thread among them. Brian was absolutely brutal when it came to his former friend, and he had made plenty of plans around this trip into the Highlands. He was careful in his discussion of it, but once Claire recognized the context, it was pretty clear.

Had he known it was Felicity Farrow doing the interview? How else could she have had a hint about the trouble with the business except to have been tipped off?

Claire shook her head as she thumbed through more emails. Everything she saw would only make Alan look more guilty, and if she didn't know better, she would have thought that Brian planned his own death.

Oh, sugar . . .

What if he had?

If he was gone, no one would suspect the financials were a setup. And even if someone eventually did, Alan's reputation would have been permanently damaged by the time it happened, and he would never recover his footing. For a man who hated him as much as Brian had, it would have been the perfect vengeance.

But he couldn't have planned to be knocked into the corner of a bar with exactly the right amount of force to die.

If he had been shot or stabbed, that would be one thing. But the head wound?

No way. Not possible.

Or was it?

"Nobody should frown like that this early in the morning," Alan said in a low, growling tone. "What is it?"

Claire met his eyes, hesitated, then gave in and told him everything she'd found and her fears about a bigger conspiracy that didn't make any sense. Jonny woke up during the discussion but didn't add anything to it. He only looked at Claire and smiled in understanding or encouragement.

He was good at knowing when to speak and when not to. It was one of the things she loved most about him honestly. He wasn't always trying to fix everything and take charge, or acting without thinking, or getting overly involved in things that didn't need his touch. No, Jonny was perfectly happy to let Claire vent everything and then ask what she wanted him to do when it was all out of her system. Most of the time, all she'd wanted was to vent anyway, and being held by him afterwards solved almost everything.

It wouldn't help her here, but the reminder that he was supporting her was enough.

When Claire finished, she sat in the silence with them, her thumbs tapping absently along the outside of the phone. "So what do we do now?" she eventually asked.

Alan ran a hand over his hair, smoothing it more than ruffling it. "Probably time to start looking at the people on the train, right? Suspect time?"

Claire nodded, setting the phone down beside her on the bench. "Do we need to get a list from Lisa?"

Jonny surprised her by holding a finger in the air like a child in the classroom. "Greg should have one, right? If Alan is supposed to be schmoozing with people, there would be a list of who is here and all that."

Alan pointed at Jonny. "That. Yes."

"Suppose they get the train fixed," Claire suggested. "We'd be at Arisaig in, what, two hours?"

"Tops," Alan agreed with a nod. "It's a small place, so their police presence might be minimal at best, but I doubt they'd want to take us all the way to Mallaig before getting Brian off. Then again, we could pass Arisaig altogether, given the circumstances. Mallaig is only about fifteen minutes further."

Jonny scratched at his morning scruff, exhaling roughly. "Any idea what the actual issue is keeping us here? I know they said they couldn't get a crew out last night and communication was an issue, but now . . ."

Alan lifted a shoulder. "Could be anything with these historic trains. The fact that they couldn't fix it last night means they might need to send out a standard train to get us to Mallaig while towing this old girl along."

"Basically, we probably don't have much time." Claire pursed her lips, nodding to herself. "Okay. I'll have to put together something for breakfast for the train. Might as well get started on that now. Sooner started, sooner finished. Alan, any ideas?"

His brows snapped down in thought. "Easiest would be some sort of French toast. There's leftover rhubarb and blueberries, so we could make a compote for it. And there should still be plenty of potatoes if we want to add a hash side. Not a ton of protein to choose from, since we didn't prepare for that, but at least it'd be hearty."

Claire stared at him for a long moment, blinking slowly. "I fully expected you to say porridge, not gonna lie."

Alan grinned at her, looking decades younger. "Why be basic when you can be bougie?"

There was no helping the snort that escaped her, and she wagged a scolding finger in his face as she fought waves of laughter. "Never—ever—say that again, Alan Gables. Oh my scones, that was so wrong."

"Hey!" Alan protested. "Unexpected body in the bagging area or not, this train is still supposed to carry my name on the food. I'm not putting porridge anywhere near those mouths. They can get that somewhere else. Bread, eggs, cream, nutmeg. That's all I need. Think you can handle that, short stack?"

Claire's eyes widened so quickly it was painful, and she gaped at her mentor in amused shock. "What did you just call me?"

"I'd run if I were you, Alan," Jonny muttered with a friendly swat to his arm. "Now."

Before Alan could move, however, there was a knock at the compartment door, which slid open to show Lisa, the conductor, looking pale.

"Oh good, Mr. Gables is here too," she said with a slight nod.

When she didn't say anything else, Claire prodded warily. "Lisa?"

She closed her eyes for a long moment, then looked directly at Alan. "There's been another death. And this one can't be called an accident."

Alan stumbled back and sank onto the compartment bench next to Jonny. "Another . . . "

"You were all seen with the victim yesterday. Can you come to Dining Car 3 to confirm the identity?" Lisa asked before Alan could say another word.

They all mumbled acceptance and rose, following her down the corridor into the next car.

"How did we not hear anything?" Claire whispered to the two men. "We're not that far, and . . . Why was anyone in Dining Car 3 in the first place?"

Alan took her arm and squeezed gently. "Easy, lass. Let's see what we're dealing with first."

She nodded shakily, uneasiness and dread threatening to consume her entire body.

Creepy threats in her train compartment and an accidental death were one thing. But another dead body?

That was not okay.

Who was gone now? Lisa said it hadn't been an accident, but maybe it was an illness.

Please let it be a heart attack. Please let it be a heart attack.

The doctor from the day before was in the dining car, as well as a security guard, but no one else. The body on the ground was covered with a sheet, which was somehow more chilling than it had been walking in to find poor, dead Brian the day before. Claire's knees went numb as they approached, and her fingertips began to tingle.

As though he could feel her anxiety, Jonny gripped her upper arms and steadied her as he helped her move forward, then kept his hold on her when they stopped.

"Ready?" the doctor asked with a calm look at all three.

Faces from throughout the excursions in the train the day before flashed through Claire's mind, each one looking more dead than the next. It could be any of them, given all that had transpired. It could be none of them and simply be the face of a worker she hadn't met. It could be—

The sheet was pulled back, and the cheekbones that could have sliced bagels lay dusted in day-old bronzer and blush. Perfect lips parted on a last breath. Tousled blonde hair was matted against the floor.

Eyes wide open and frozen on the space above her, Felicity Farrow bore wide, purple bruises on her throat in the shape of hands.

Claire stared at the body for the space of twelve heartbeats and three breaths. "That . . . is not who I expected to see."

Jonny cleared his throat behind her. "That is Felicity Farrow. Journalist for *Mode Magazine*." His grip on Claire's arms tightened perceptibly, and she wondered what else he wanted to say.

"Confirmed," Alan muttered, running a hand through his hair.

The doctor sighed and covered her face again. "Rigor mortis hasn't fully set in. Without anything to fully establish a timeline, my best guess is six to eight hours ago. And this one was no accident, conductor."

"Yeah, ta, Doc." Her voice was hoarse, and she shook her head. "I'll take you to fill out the forms. Maybe we can get a decent signal to the Arisaig authorities over radio now that the storm is over." The two of them stepped out, and the security guard followed, only to take up position just outside the door, blocking the window into the room.

"I have so many emotions right now," Claire whispered aloud. "So many . . . conflicting emotions . . ."

Alan glanced at her, the corner of his mouth ticking. "Don't . . ."

"May she rest in peace," Claire said immediately, lowering her head. "But I think we all know the elevator of life took her down and not up."

Jonny snorted behind her, his mouth immediately going to the back of Claire's head.

"We are *not* laughing about someone being dead, you sick people," Alan hissed.

Claire shook her head, not feeling in any way close to laughter and yet shaking as though she was holding it back. "Shock, Alan. Shock and inappropriate coping mechanisms. This isn't funny at all. I wanted to stab her with one of her heels, but I never wanted her dead."

Jonny exhaled slowly, then stepped back from Claire.

"Okay, so this is getting worse, obviously. Who kills Brian by accident and then definitely kills Felicity on purpose?"

"Not it," Alan announced.

Claire flapped her hand at him, smacking him squarely in the chest. "We know that, dough brain. You were in our compartment all night. None of us would sleep through someone getting up and getting out."

"Do you still have Brian's phone, *ma crème*?" Jonny asked as he stepped to Claire's right.

She nodded, pulling it out from her back pocket. "Why?"

"I think we need to try to get a message to Watson, even if this isn't his jurisdiction." His thumbs flew quicky over the screen as he took in a measured breath. "Accidental death is one thing, but murder . . . Yeah, I'm gonna try, even if the signal doesn't let us."

"Go for a short message," Alan suggested as he stepped around Felicity's figure and pulled back the sheet to look at her neck. "Should go through more easily with low signal."

The door behind them opened and Greg hurried in, his face filled with concern. "What's going on? Why are we in—?" His eyes fell to Felicity's form, and he staggered back two steps. "M-miss Farrow? What . . . how . . . ?"

"Take a breath, Flaky Pastry," Jonny told him without looking up. "Sit down if your knees are shaky."

"Sound advice," Alan praised, pointing at Jonny.

The two of them air fist-bumped.

"Stop that!" Claire shrieked, the shaking almost-laughter of shock still rippling through her. "Okay, focus. Who would want Felicity dead?"

"How much time do we have to create the list?" Greg asked as he took a seat on the floor, pointedly looking away from the body. "And really, without getting detailed, anyone on the train could be on the list, especially if they'd been sitting around her if she was in a mood."

Claire rolled her eyes and looked at him. "I mean actually dead, Greg. Not someone who wanted to punch her lights out."

Greg held up his hands in surrender before shoving them in his hair and hunching over. "Dead bodies on a train. Why not? Delayed in the Highlands. Sure! Can't contact Mallaig. No bother!"

Claire blinked at the mumbling young man before looking at Alan. "Is he okay?"

Alan didn't even look up. "Not really, no."

Zero sympathy from that quarter, then.

She looked over at Jonny. "What are you saying to Watson?"

Jonny smiled a little. "'Murder on our train. Manual strangulation. Please advise.'"

Now it was Alan who snorted.

"Please advise?" Claire repeated.

Jonny was completely unperturbed by his own stupidity. "What? We need his advice, so I asked for it."

Claire shook her head and squatted down near Felicity, sighing as she looked at her unmoving corpse.

"I really didn't want her dead," she mumbled, twinges of guilt and shame firing throughout her body. "Nobody deserves that. Especially to die facing their attacker while their air is being cut off." She shuddered as a chill washed over her skin. "Terrifying."

"How do you know she was facing them?" Greg called from where he was.

"Hand positioning on the bruises," she replied easily.

"Finger marks are going toward the back of the neck. The killer watched the life drain from her."

"Great," Greg mumbled, going even paler. "Sick and twisted bloke on the train. And we fed him. Just great." He hunched forward, gripping at his hair. "What are the odds of this becoming a haunted train after this?"

Jonny rolled his eyes and put his hands on his hips. "Okay, so first question: Why is the body in here? A guard should have been stationed here 24/7."

"We have to talk to security." Claire stood up before groaning and tipping her head back. "Except we also have to do breakfast for the train. It's not like Lisa and company are going to tell the passengers that a second dead body has been discovered in Dining Car 3 especially since they don't know about the first body yet."

Alan and Jonny looked at each other. "Unexpected body in the bagging area," they said together.

Greg gasped. "That is horrific!"

"Thank you, Greg," Claire announced with a nod of approval. "Someone has their humanity intact."

Alan stood and walked over to Greg, surprising them all by holding a hand down to him. "Come on, Greg. I need the list of guests and passengers for the next part of this. Claire, head to the kitchen, and I'll meet you there. Viscount, I could really use some coffee."

"Me too!" Claire chirped, raising her hand.

"All the coffee in the world isn't going to help me," Greg grunted as Alan hauled him to his feet. "But I'd love some."

Jonny hummed a short laugh. "As long as I don't have to talk to anyone, I will happily fetch coffee."

Alan nodded as he and Greg returned to the compartment car, leaving Claire and Jonny alone with the corpse.

"Well," Claire suddenly began, "I don't know what we call her. We already have poor, dead Brian. What does that make Felicity?"

"Dearly departed Felicity?" Jonny offered with a half smile. "Cold, stiff Felicity? Unalive Felicity?"

Claire smirked. "I think 'dearly departed.' She'd prefer the formality."

They shared a smile, and for a moment, Claire forgot all about the fears that had been so prevalent the day before. They were a playful, teasing couple, and had been from the day they'd met, so the reminder of who they were was timely and much needed. And bittersweet.

Because the fears weren't gone. They were just tucked into a corner of her mind that she was choosing to ignore at the moment.

She loved that man across from her. She loved him a lot.

But since when had loving someone ever meant they would love you in return?

He was a good guy. They would always be friends and on good terms, she was sure of it. But she would always wish it was more, even if she never told anyone but Alan.

She wouldn't have told Alan, of all people, if he hadn't been the version of himself that had appeared in the kitchen last night. She wouldn't have thought he'd care about that part of her life. But his stories about Rose and his regrets about losing her had struck something in Claire, and she wanted to do something about it.

"Alan told me about that girl from his past last night," Claire admitted softly, surprised that her voice broke.

Jonny heard the catch, and his brows immediately creased in concern. "Yeah?"

She nodded, swallowing quickly. "He misses her. A lot. I wouldn't have pegged him as a romantic, but J . . . Crepes alive, he still loves her."

"Can you love someone you haven't seen or talked to in twenty years or whatever?" he asked hesitantly. "Don't get me wrong—I hope so. But a lot can change in that time."

Claire bit her tongue to keep from snapping at him for being a jerk, mostly because she knew he was right. If Alan and Rose ever managed to be reunited, she wanted it to be a glorious, romantic event, but Jonny was logical and sensible, and baggage was a real thing. If Alan had crushed Rose as much as he and Brian thought he had, she might never want to see him again. She might be hardened beyond belief, hiding her broken heart. Or she might be gloriously and wildly happy with a devoted husband and six children who worshipped the ground she walked on, and Alan Gables was just that guy on the baking show.

Not the Alan from her childhood. Not the Alan she had loved. Not the Alan who had broken her heart.

Meddling in other peoples' romances, especially without all the information, was a surefire way to lose friends, honestly. And look like an idiot, to boot.

Just like Felicity meddling in Claire's romance had made her Claire's enemy.

Dearly departed Felicity Farrow, that is.

May she rest in peace.

"I'd better get to the kitchen," Claire murmured, rubbing her arm uneasily. "And, if you really don't mind, maybe get me two coffees? I'm struggling."

"You got it." He winked at her and nudged her forward, his fingers trailing down her arm to link with her fingers while they walked.

Croissants, it was like his fingers were twining around her heart when he did that.

Walls. She needed walls if she was going to save herself from the coming heartache. But it was impossible to build walls, let alone maintain them, when he was around.

For now, she'd just enjoy the feeling of his hand in hers.

While it lasted.

CHAPTER 16

"Viscount, I mean this in the nicest way possible. Get out of my kitchen."

Jonny glared at Alan's glowering face, wondering if it would be too rude to take the man down in this space and show him what a man of his stature and ability could do to a middle-aged twig.

Not that it was an unreasonable request. Jonny wasn't exactly helping out here. Bringing them their requested coffee? Yes. Making conversation, yes. Asking intelligent questions about their process, yes.

Assisting them in making breakfast for the train?

Nope. Not even a little bit.

He knew where his strengths were, and they were not in making French toast on a mass scale or creating a fruit compote to top it.

But he was good company.

Or so he thought.

"J," Claire said in a sweet tone that instantly soothed his ruffled feathers. "Go help Greg. Alan sent him to chat with the security guards about who worked the VIP section last night."

She turned slightly to face him, looking beautiful but exhausted. She'd redone her hair into a loose plait, and he loved seeing her so casual. He didn't like the dark shadows under her eyes, but he was pretty sure most everyone on the train would have them after last night. And her smile was so soft, so tender, so perfect.

He was so far gone with her. She could have asked him to find her a goat in the hills outside and milk it for them, and he'd have done his best to make it happen.

He hesitated, looking longingly at the list of passengers, which now sat beside Claire's workstation in the kitchen. Truth be told, he was more interested in looking at the suspect list than talking to security, but there would be time for all of that later.

Alan came over to the counter beside Jonny, taking up the travel cup sitting there for him. "Nice blend," he commented after a long sip. "Better than I thought we'd get on a train."

Jonny shrugged. "That's basically what I said too. The bartenders are running around like mobile drink dispensers and making everyone think this is a regular Starbucks, but whatever soothes the rattled masses, right?"

"I'll drink to that," Alan echoed, raising his cup in a hint of a toast. "Many thanks. Now, seriously, get out."

Jonny held up his hands, though one carried his own cup of coffee. "Going. I'll take Greg his cup too. Later, *ma crème*."

Claire waved at him with a light wink and went back to her work.

Out in the corridor, Jonny allowed himself to take in a long, slow breath.

So far, this entire trip had been a lot more than he'd bargained for. Death would do that, of course, but there was also something about the ominous messages to Claire that had him spooked. It was possible that they were only warnings for her, that nothing would truly come of them, but it didn't feel that way. Things seemed far more threatening now that Felicity had been murdered, and he had spent most of the night before trying to figure out why anyone would need to threaten Claire.

She wasn't the sort to have enemies, especially ones from her personal life. She was too nice, too fun, too quirky of a human being to form any sort of negative relationships in life.

Benji from her series of *BBB* didn't count, even if he did try to kill her. That was different.

Why would someone feel the need to threaten Claire? On a train of die-hard Alan Gables fans, why would Claire be a problem? She had been one of his favorites on the show; anybody could see that. Claire ought to be fairly popular with the Alan-loving crowds. Granted, some of them were a little on the intense side, so if they didn't like that Claire had been chosen to bake with Alan on this trip, that could be an issue, but who else could Alan have chosen?

People made no sense. Maybe that was why Jonny had never been particularly fond of them in general.

Among other things.

Sighing to himself, Jonny moved through Dining Car 3, noting that Felicity's body had been removed. Not that the public would know anything about it, but everybody deserved dignity in death, and being laid out on the floor of a train car didn't seem the most appropriate thing in the world.

But that was another level of frustration to this whole

thing: That train car floor now held evidence of two murders. If there had been any sort of cut on Felicity or if the blood on the floor hadn't dried completely, the original crime scene would be contaminated. It probably was, regardless. And what about any fibers or the like? Weren't all those crime shows always going on about fibers? Fibers from Felicity's clothes were probably mingling with fibers from Brian's clothes right now.

Wouldn't a second dead body in the vicinity change whatever evidence might have been found from the first death?

Watson would know more about this than Jonny, of course, but there wasn't time or ability to discuss any of it with him. Jonny would be lucky if the email to him went through at all, let alone if Watson could answer it. Or help in any way.

Minimal details meant minimal help, and minimal communication meant they were still on their own.

Unless Watson had a genius plan for creating a better way of communicating in the middle of the Highlands.

Once out of Dining Car 3, Jonny paused at the sight of the guard currently on duty. "Hey, mate. Have you spoken with a young guy with VIP access this morning?"

The guard looked at his VIP badge first, then at his face. "This morning? No, but I just came on a few minutes ago. Why?"

Jonny offered a tight but polite smile. "Have you been informed of what happened last night in Dining Car 3?"

A telling wince crossed the guard's face. "Yeah. We were all informed in our morning staff meeting. I think the conductor was looking for our shift calendar to talk to whoever was stationed here at the time, but with the delay and all, the schedule has been a bit of a free-for-all. I mean, clearly someone has been here around the clock, but nobody wants to admit they were the one on duty when such a tragedy occurred."

Jonny tried for a casual stance, leaning against the wall of the car. "Any trouble with people trying to get into the VIP section?"

The guard snorted loudly, which was answer enough. "Of course. Especially after the train stopped. Cabin fever mixed with the already crazed nature of the Alan fans. There's only six of us security guards, and we hand off and report. So we've got Red, who I'm pretty sure is in love with Alan and not in a cute way. Like stalker-obsessive delusional. She's a special bird, tell you what."

Jonny chuckled easily, picturing the woman who had confronted him the day before. "I think I met that one."

"Well, aren't you lucky?" The guard laughed once. "Then we have Jacque. We think he's the French version of Alan—hence the nickname—but not a professional version. Like the Vegas version of Elvis, right? Might not even be French, but he's trying hard."

"Huh. Haven't met that one." Jonny shook his head, not at all disappointed in his ignorance there. What would a French Alan be like? The Scottish one was complicated enough.

"He's not very pushy," the guard explained. "He just stands out."

"Fair enough."

"Then we've got Fanboy," the other man went on. "And Fanboy wants to *be* Alan, but he's so obsessed with Alan that he flutters between imitation and adoration constantly. I swear he's wearing an outfit plucked from Alan's wardrobe on an episode last series, but I can't prove that without going back and watching."

Jonny tilted his head in thought, faces of irritated passengers flickering through his mind like a slideshow. "That guy get in your face a lot?"

"Oh yeah," came the instant reply. "Aggressive as anything and demanding that we give him his fair share of time with Alan. Thinks we're keeping him back here locked up and forcibly away from his fans. Said he was going to put together a rescue mission or some such. Absolute nutter. He even said he doubted the food was Alan's because he's never read anything about a tartan tart something or other."

"Tartan tarte tatin," Jonny recited without thinking.

"Yeah, that." The guard paused to dramatically roll his eyes. "And since Alan wasn't around to explain himself or his recipes, Fanboy believes it's a conspiracy cooked up by Miss Walker and he's been tricked into being here—"

Jonny straightened immediately, pushing off the wall. "He *what*?"

The guard nodded slowly, his eyes holding zero amusement. "Oh yeah. Late into last night, he was getting super agitated about her. We had to threaten him with restraints. He was pretty sloshed last time I saw him. Not sure if he went to the bar in Dining Car 1 or 2, but somebody plied him with good stuff, that's for sure."

Well, well, well. Hello, prime suspect . . .

Pursing his lips, Jonny forced his anger and adrenaline back and down, safe within the confines of his control. There wasn't a single person on this train he could fully trust except for Alan and Claire, and he had only recently been willing to trust Alan. Who's to say that one or two security guards weren't involved in the deaths and threats? Or hadn't been bribed to look the other way, for whatever reason?

"Anyone else besides those three annoying the guards?" Jonny made himself ask, though he really wanted to go find Fanboy and tie him to a chair while asking specific questions with something threatening in his hands.

"That uppity journalist lady, for sure." The guard growled darkly. "She asks so many questions, none of which we could answer, and she's always cozying up to whoever is on duty like she's some sort of seductress. I mean, that might work for some, but she's so blatant. I felt like I needed to shower with bleach. After the conductor announced that we'd be spending the night on the train, that journalist lady marched right back here and plastered herself to my side, practically scaling me like a monkey on a tree. I swear she started sniffing my neck as she asked question after question about what was going on." He shuddered at the memory, and Jonny choked back a laugh.

Clearly this morning's tragedy had been reported to the security staff, but not the identity of the victim.

Dearly departed Felicity.

"Hansen was guarding with me at the time. Poor kid wasn't sure if he was scared or wanted to be sniffed at next." The guard reluctantly chuckled, lowering his head for a moment. "She'd eat him alive and spit his bones back out in a nice, tidy pile if she sunk her teeth into him."

"Mm-hmm," Jonny agreed on a hum.

"How I'm going to explain the perfume reeking off me to my wife, though . . ." He made a gagging face before smiling ruefully. "Still, I only had to deal with her twice yesterday. That was enough, believe me. I'm sure she tried the other guards multiple times too."

Jonny was pretty sure about that as well, knowing all too well how Felicity liked to get her way.

"Any idea who was dealing with her last night? She was pretty upset after the dinner delivery if I recall."

From personal experience. Witnessing it himself. Trying to escape her after Claire had taken a seat at their table and practically slayed her.

He'd managed to steer Felicity away from any further interaction with Claire by tucking her into a corner of the bar in Dining Car 2 with a couple of men willing to listen to her story of dismantling a model's image of class and good behavior through amateur sleuthing and bribing a handful of contacts. She had zero shame about her actions and had delighted in telling them that she had also enjoyed a six-month relationship with the model's boyfriend after the fallout.

None of the men around the table could have passed for a model, but they were certainly keen enough to give her six months or more of attention, if she'd accept.

It was painful, being around such a person for hours. The more time he'd spent with Felicity, the more he'd found that there was not a single redeeming quality about her. Not that he could find, at any rate. She didn't deserve to be strangled to death, of course, but had she been the only victim on this train, the list of suspects would have been massive.

As it was, the authorities might still consider Alan the prime suspect in both Brian and Felicity's deaths. But he couldn't believe Alan would risk torpedoing his career in such a way.

The man had both humanity and sense, which could not be ignored.

Soft tutting sounds brought Jonny back to the present, focusing on the guard once more, who seemed to be thinking rather hard about his coworkers and their improvised shift schedule.

"Either Danny or Rob would be my best guess, but they might have made some kind of deal to switch. I know Hansen switched with David for mid-train duties at dinner because David had a headache." He flicked his gaze to Jonny with a rueful smile. "I know that's not much help."

Jonny shrugged. "No, but it's good to know the shifts are as messed up as everything else on this trip. We'll just have to talk to everybody."

A grimace crossed the older man's face. "Sorry about that. But better to be thorough than to miss something, right?"

"So says my friend the detective sergeant," Jonny joked, even if it was the truth. He clapped the guard on the shoulder and strode further into the train.

Greg should be around here doing the same thing; maybe he already knew which security guard had been stationed at the VIP section last night. Flaky Pastry was a decent guy, even if he was a kid in more ways than one. He might not know what questions to ask, but he worked hard for Alan and clearly cared enough about his reputation to stress himself into illness. He'd help them get to the bottom of whatever mess this was just to make sure Alan still wanted him on the employment books.

It was still early in the morning, so many passengers were not awake enough to notice who he was as he wandered around with his glaring VIP credentials. No one was going to provoke him into crankiness—he hoped—and no one was going to yell at him about Alan Gables, especially if they were hoping for a decent breakfast in the next little while.

Small mercies.

So right now, for this moment, Jonny Ainsley, Viscount Colburn, could be just an ordinary passenger walking easily through a mostly silent and unmoving train.

It was very nearly bliss compared to every other time he had walked the train.

Midway through the cars, he found the second security guard on duty. He was stationed here more for crowd control and maintaining order than for checking badges, but his hulking presence and the Mace on his belt were a reminder to everyone on the train that they did need to have some restraint.

Or decorum, at least.

"Morning," Jonny greeted, dipping his chin at the guard.

"Good morning, sir," came the polite, easy reply. "Something I can help you with?"

With an opening like that, how could Jonny possibly refuse?

He grinned at the man. "Actually, yes. Have you talked to a young guy this morning? Scrawny, lanky, dark hair, possibly twitching?"

The rumbling laugh from the guard was unexpected. "Blimey, he was twitching, wasn't he?"

"I haven't decided whether he's stressed, anxious, generally a wreck, or secretly claustrophobic on this train," Jonny mused aloud.

"All of the above, likely." The guard jerked his thumb behind him. "He went that way to find the other security guards. You trying to figure out what happened last night in Dining Car 3?"

"If we can, yeah." Jonny folded his arms across his chest. "What did he tell you?"

The guard gave a half shrug. "Asked me where I was last night, what my shift was, that sort of thing. He asked who's been annoying us about the VIP section, so I told him what I knew about that, but really, I didn't have much to add. So he said he was going to talk to the others and to let him know if I heard anything."

Sounded like what Jonny would do. Maybe Greg wasn't useless after all.

Good to know.

"I'll just follow his breadcrumbs, then," Jonny quipped as he held out his hand for the other man to shake.

"See if you can calm him somehow," came the chuckling suggestion. "He's going to have a heart attack before thirty-five if he can't ease up."

Jonny exhaled slowly, embracing the drama. "Mate, if only I knew how. He's his own kind of special."

Thunderous laughter erupted from the guard, making him less threatening than before in nearly every way. Yes, he had Mace and who-knew-what-else in his arsenal, but he looked and sounded like a jolly giant who regularly dressed as Father Christmas during the holidays. Was that something that could be forgotten under the right circumstances?

Hopefully, they wouldn't need to know.

"Name's Tate if you need anything else," the guard told Jonny, still laughing.

"Thanks, Tate. I'm Jonny." They shook hands again, and Jonny headed farther into the train with a smile he didn't have to fake.

Then he heard the voices of irritable passengers in the next car, and his smile faded with a heavy sigh.

It would have been a great train were it not for all the people.

Alas.

CHAPTER 17

"Done and done."

Claire propped her hands on her hips and looked at the incredible stacks of French toast she'd managed. It was all on a buffet tray, but it still looked like she'd used a ruler to make everything Jenga-straight and sturdy. Not a single piece had been burned or overdrenched, and not even Alan Gables would be able to find fault with the uniformity of something as freehand as French toast.

It was the little things in life that made the world go round.

"Do you want a parade?"

Okay, maybe Alan would have found fault, but Alan was a faultfinding genius who could see lint on the king's shoulder, so he didn't count.

She glared at him darkly. "There is nothing wrong with taking pride in your work."

He rolled his eyes like a teenage girl. "You made French toast, not mille-feuille."

"You love my mille-feuille," she reminded him as she jabbed a finger in his direction.

He waved his rhubarb-and-blueberry-compote-coated spoon toward her. “Not here, though, is it? Just French toast. Stop congratulating yourself and get the plates.”

Grumbling, Claire did as he instructed and stacked the second tier of the trolley with plates.

“Are you going to venture out of the kitchen to serve with me today?” Claire asked as she checked the number of forks.

“Probably shouldn’t, but all these people are on the train for me. But with someone killing people associated with me—if your conspiracy theory is correct—who knows what could set them off again? Somehow, I’m at the center of this, so do I show myself to the public and act like all is well? Or do I stay here and cross my fingers that my lack of engagement will hold off whoever is after me?”

Claire pursed her lips in thought. As frustrating as it was, she didn’t have an answer for him. This train ride was supposed to be part of a larger tribute to him, complete with a fabulous spread in a magazine—a spread meant to show the world that Alan had a personable side—but a crime had been committed instead. His best friend had been betraying him for years, and his career could very well take a sharp left into the proverbial wall when they all got back to reality.

How could anyone offer much comfort or advice under those circumstances?

Maybe there wasn’t anything to say.

Maybe it was time to do something instead.

“Having a thought,” Claire said slowly, letting her eyes go unfocused as she stared straight ahead.

“Congratulations. Again, do you want a parade?”

She snapped her fingers and pointed in his direction. “Shut up, Alan, and let the thought come.”

"Is there a labor and delivery process going on here? Having a thought like having a baby? *Push*, Claire!"

She was torn between snarling and snickering but settled on lowering her head and doing some combination of both.

"Did it work?"

Claire shook her head and blinked, looking up at him with a grin. "I hate you so much."

Alan put a hand to his heart. "Thank you."

"Anyway," she said with some force, trying to warn him off and failing, "what if we *don't* hide you anymore? Like you said, none of the security guards or train personnel have the authority to arrest you, and they don't even seem to think a crime was committed, at least when it comes to Brian's death. Jonny and I are investigating, mostly in a preventive way, but no one else is."

Alan stirred the cooling compote with a thoughtful expression. "I'm listening . . ."

Claire bit her lip. "You said something earlier about needing people to see you as a whole at this point in your career. Something like that, right?"

"I did."

"Are you thinking about retiring?" she asked, crossing her fingers that he wouldn't hide behind vague answers and dismissive actions this time. That he would be direct with her. Full disclosure.

That he would trust her completely with the truth.

"No," he said simply, his voice lower than normal. "I just regret that I have spent so much time being the strict judge and nothing more. That my solemn demeanor in that role was taken to be my whole personality and being."

Nodding, Claire smiled as her fingers uncrossed. "Then

let's give these people the whole you. Let's get this train ride back to what it was supposed to be for you. Come on out there with me and serve French toast with fresh compote to the stranded passengers on this train. Talk to the people. Be the Alan nobody gets to see."

His smile was slight and soft. "But what if not everyone likes Alan Gables?"

Claire shrugged. "Alan Gables doesn't care. But he's better than people think. He's the guy who sits on the floor with a pathetic, crying girl and eats trifle out of the bowl with her. Not gonna see that on a series of *Battle of the Bakers*."

"No, they cut the bit when I did that with Helena in series ten. I asked them not to, but alas . . ." He winked, his smile growing. "If you think this will work, lass, I'll do it."

"Let's do it, then. And I won't have to manage all the French toast alone, so hooray for me!" She fist pumped and grabbed a container for the compote, holding it while Alan poured.

"See if there's some icing sugar in the pantry," Alan suggested with a nudge of his head. "It won't hurt anyone to have that dusted on top."

"You big softie," she scoffed. She found exactly what he was looking for, bringing it back over. "Alrighty. Aprons on?"

Alan gave her a bewildered look. "We're taking berry compote and icing sugar out into the public on an unstable, overloaded tray on a train that could start moving at any moment. Yes, aprons on."

Claire held up her hands in surrender and backed away toward the aprons. "Okay, fine. Sheesh, someone's protective of his laundry."

"Clearly you haven't lost enough beloved clothing items

due to baking mishaps." He smirked and held out his hand for an apron.

What a bizarre world this was turning into. Alan Gables was snarky on any given day, but she had never expected this. Laughing and teasing with her like they were old friends and giving her advice of the heart and listening to her when she advised him.

Did complicated times make for strange compartment fellows or what?

"Think Greg will want to help us?" Claire asked as she tied her apron around her. "Eager beaver that he is?"

"Doesn't matter," Alan told her, as though reading her mind. "What would he help us with anyway?"

"Plate distribution?" Claire suggested with a grin.

"And where does that go on a résumé?"

They'd only gone a little way down the corridor when one of the young service attendants appeared, her hair pulled back in a neat ponytail, her smile entirely too bright for the morning they were having.

"Hi!" she greeted eagerly. "Your friends talking to security suggested I come down here and see what you needed. We figured breakfast was about done."

Claire and Alan looked at each other, smiling the same knowing smile.

"Plate distribution."

And so they went, the three of them, into the next car, working like a well-oiled machine, shoveling out pieces of French toast topped with compote and icing sugar to the starving masses.

Well, the hungry, grumbling, and stranded masses, anyway.

But nobody was grumbling when the French toast was plated before them. Nope, that was when lips were licked and eyes brightened and dark romances happened between a person and their breakfast.

It's a thing.

And that breakfast was also making people happy; a few people swapped jokes, their tone bright.

Merry breakfast to all, and to all a good pair of stretchy trousers.

"Eh, I give the plating a six out of ten," one of the older passengers croaked with a wink at their new pal Lacey, plate distributor extraordinaire. Had he been reading Claire's mind?

Alan was brilliant with his retorts. He grinned like the man was his uncle and waved a finger at him. "I will have you know that this is a very French plating of your French toast, and you'd be seeing plates just like it in Paris."

"Sensitive subject, criticism?" came the reply, which had everybody in the vicinity roaring with laughter.

Including Alan.

Alan, who hated people in general.

He looked decades younger. Laughing and smiling, his sleeves rolled back, his top button undone, dressed in an apron, and spooning out extra compote to those who asked nicely. Was this the version of himself that had left Glasgow for culinary school? The one that Rose McGregor had fallen in love with? The one with big dreams and a desire to make something of himself? Or was this some secret version of Alan Gables that had been lurking beneath the surface all these years and just needed a chance to break free?

It was certainly not the Alan Gables anyone had ever seen

on television. Nor was it the one who had ever been interviewed.

If she didn't know Alan was a terrible actor, Claire would have thought he was acting now.

But it was no act. It was easy and natural, free of strain and pretense, like he'd been doing this for years.

And it wasn't for the television or the public or the papers.

It was for the weary passengers who had waited not-so-patiently for just this moment.

A teenaged girl in a London sweatshirt shyly asked Alan if they could take a picture together, and, to Claire's bewilderment, he agreed and handed Claire the girl's old-fashioned camera to do the honors.

Her fingers shook as she got the pair into focus and saw the light in both sets of eyes through the screen. Alan never smiled in pictures, what with his smile being something bakers on the show worked tirelessly to earn. He'd built his entire persona on being gruff and grumpy, unsmiling but for rare moments of the sun breaking through.

Not on this train, and not anymore, apparently.

That picture started an entirely different sort of interaction as they moved into the next car. More people asked for autographs with Alan, and a few people even asked for a signature from Claire.

The dining car was next, and Claire beamed as Jonny approached.

Alan and Lacey moved around the dining car to take plates of breakfast to those sitting within, while Claire stayed close to Jonny's side.

"What have I missed?" Jonny asked in a low voice.

"The return of Alan Gables," Claire said dramatically as

Alan threw his head back and laughed with a table of elderly women.

Jonny gave her a quick look. “No more hiding?”

“Nope. We’re back to the train tribute, as it should be.”

He grunted softly. “That should settle the cranky masses.”

Claire forced herself not to wince at his tone, and his words. This was an amazing opportunity for Alan, and an honor for him, but it was Jonny’s worst nightmare, apparently. He’d never want to do this sort of public interaction intentionally.

Not that Claire wanted to be serving a train of people her own recipes one day, but . . .

Would it have made a difference if Jonny had known how involved he would be before they had gotten on the train? Or agreed to the trip? If he’d been prepared to interact with strangers like this, would his mood be better?

Or would he always hate this?

Alan finished at the table and came back to the trolley, taking the handles. “Come on, crew. More cars to go.”

Claire took the other side and pushed the trolley toward the door as Lacey moved ahead of Alan to help manage the crossing.

Jonny rubbed at his jaw and glanced out of the window. “I think a team of engineers has arrived to fix whatever broke, so we’re in a tight investigation window.”

“We’ll just have to see what we can get and turn over whatever it is to the authorities.” Claire exhaled a sharp puff of air to get the tendrils of long bangs out of her face. “I never thought those words would come out of my mouth.”

“Agreed, but we can discuss our new side business another time. Think Watson will be an investor?”

Claire rolled her eyes as they all entered the next car of

passengers. "In what? Our own private investigation business? What are we calling it? 'Brains and the Baker'?"

Jonny flicked the end of her plait playfully. "Maybe. You're good at this, and I'm not half bad."

She gave him a despairing look. "J! We're nosy amateurs who know a detective. That's all."

"Gotta start somewhere," was his only response.

Ridiculous man. But he did make her smile sometimes.

Kind of like breakfast.

CHAPTER 18

"Uh-oh, incoming," Jonny murmured to Claire as they reached another car of passengers to feed.

Claire turned just as two kids barreled toward them with bright smiles. "Well, hi there!" she greeted cheerily, surprising Jonny. "Isla and Peter, right?"

They nodded eagerly, and Jonny restrained a groan.

Of course, Claire had already met some kids and made them fall in love with her.

If he weren't trying to finish up this breakfast dispersal of hers, he would have been amused. As it was, he wanted to get away from the people—one of whom could be a murderer—and get her safely tucked back into the kitchen.

He'd told Greg to talk to the last security guard on their list, since the poor guy had seemed desperate to do something to help his boss. But now Jonny wished he'd been more selfish and claimed the interview for himself and made Greg do the people engaging.

"And where is your mother?" Claire asked the kids, propping her hands on her hips and giving them the sort of warning look that only a parent or teacher could pull off.

"She's got a headache," Peter said at once. "She told us we could come meet Alan while she got some air."

Jonny raised his brow, though only Claire would see it, but she wasn't looking at him. Where in the world would their mother get some air on this train? The windows should all open, if actual air was what she needed, but it sounded like the woman was hoping to literally go outside somehow.

As if in answer to his unasked question, a woman brushed by him, head lowered, tucking her auburn hair behind her ear as she moved to the gangway—was there air somewhere beyond it?—behind them.

He watched her go, curious why she wasn't staying to meet Alan with her kids when everything about this train was all about Alan and meeting him. Supporting him. The tickets were ridiculously expensive, apart from the handful of lottery ones that had been released for the general public. Had this family been among those fortunate few who hadn't doled out mounds of money for this trip? Was this just one of those sacrifices that parents made for their kids?

That seemed ridiculous. This wasn't one of those cartoon shows on ice that had to be endured because the children loved it so much, while the parents were bored out of their minds. This was Alan Gables and *BBB*, national treasures both, and adults and kids alike were captivated by them.

But that woman was trying to make herself as small as possible as she made her silent exit.

Interesting.

"Well, I supposed we can take a moment for Alan, then," Claire was saying as Jonny tuned back into the conversation around him. "Jonny, Lacey, and I will plate up your breakfasts and take them to your seats, okay?"

The kids nodded with so much energy Jonny wondered if they'd had coffee.

Claire half turned and led them toward the man of the hour. "Alan? Got a minute?"

Alan flicked his eyes up the aisle then smiled, nodding easily. He finished his conversation with his current fans, then turned and faced the approaching kids. "Well, who do we have here, Claire?"

"This is Peter, and this is Isla. They're brother and sister, and you are their favorite judge," Claire said proudly, almost as if they were her own kids.

Alan scoffed loudly. "Of course, I am. I am the best, after all. Now, shall we have a quiz and see how much of a favorite I really am?"

Jonny shook his head in amusement as Claire returned to him, and together they and Lacey began plating up breakfasts for the kids.

The amusement and bliss were interrupted, however, by Red, who was marching down the aisle toward them, her steps muffled by the thick carpet.

"Do you need to get by?" Lacey asked in her bright, helpful voice.

"I need to speak with Alan," Red told her, each word cold and clipped.

Lacey was completely unperturbed, as a good service attendant always was. "Sure! He's chatting at the moment, but we should be to your seat with breakfast in a minute."

Jonny wanted to give Lacey a high five for that diplomatic response but settled for a satisfied smirk.

Red saw it and glowered.

Meeting her angry gaze, he clicked the tongs in his hand

and reached around Claire to lift two pieces of French toast from the tray and onto the plate Lacey had handed him.

Claire spooned compote carefully on top, followed by a sprinkling of icing sugar, and Jonny then handed the plate to the woman at their right.

"He decided to finally care about us?" Red sneered, though her breathing became a little more unsteady as she asked.

Claire exhaled loudly and dramatically. "Why not? It's been an upsetting trip, with all the delays, but that's not Alan's fault. He knows the passengers have suffered, so he's making it up to them now. Everyone wants to see him. Some understanding would go a long way." She looked Red up and down with a pointed glance. "Don't you want to prepare yourself for your moment instead of marching in and giving a poor impression of yourself to Alan?"

Jonny bit back a smirk as something twitched in Red's face, lighting her cheeks on fire with the sort of blush that only the highly embarrassed can manage. She wheeled around and marched back up the aisle without a word.

Bizarre woman. So angry and yet so passionate about Alan. Could she have done something to Brian and Felicity for Alan's sake?

Claire nudged Jonny hard, and he blinked, looking at her curiously.

"Plate," she hissed, gesturing for him to lower it so she could put the food on it.

"Right, yeah." He nodded and shook his head at the same time, letting himself mull over the idea while they served up a few more plates.

Soon enough, the kids were darting back to their seats and

Alan was back with them. "What was with the snarky redhead?"

Jonny grinned at him wickedly. "She's your future wife and wants to talk about the wedding."

Alan's face went so white Jonny had to bark a laugh at him.

"Stop that," Claire whispered, taking his wrist and tugging him as they moved the trolley. "We'll save you, Alan. Give her five minutes and an autograph and we'll say Greg needs you, okay? Behave, J!"

It took them a while to manage the full train, but eventually, they made it, and Lacey offered to take care of the cleanup.

None of them were going to argue with that.

The three of them returned to the kitchen and sank onto the floor with their own plates of French toast and ate in silence for a while. The act of socializing had been as exhausting as the serving of food.

Funny how none of them liked talking all that much, and yet the morning had been oddly invigorating.

"That was fantastic," Claire announced, surprising them all.

Jonny looked at Alan, who also seemed uncertain about that statement, and then they both looked at Claire.

"I feel like that should be sarcasm, and yet . . ." Alan narrowed his eyes at her, as though waiting for her to burst out laughing.

But she didn't.

She shook her head as she took another bite of her food. "No, I mean it. Having you out and about with breakfast not only helped to lift the spirits of everyone on the train, but you also gave them this new side of you to consider. Everybody knows you're the fan-favorite judge, but this? Your agent is so going to thank us for this when they get back from Ibiza. I expect a fruit basket at the minimum."

"One of those chocolate-covered fruit arrangements," Jonny chimed in. "I mean, this is a big deal."

Claire pointed at him but kept looking at Alan. "What he said."

Alan looked between them like they had lost their marbles. "Why would I have any say in what my agent decides to send you?"

"That's cute," Claire said with a series of very pretend laughs. "Pretending like everyone associated with him doesn't do exactly what he demands."

"Adorable," Jonny agreed.

Alan glared at Jonny, but he kept his mouth shut.

Jonny stood, collecting their plates and setting them in the sink to rinse. He glanced at the remaining baked goods on the countertop, and his entire frame stiffened and froze in one breath.

Every single gingerbread man had its head cut off.

No. He looked more closely and saw that the lines were jagged and uneven, not consistent on any of them.

The heads had been snapped off. By hand.

His eyes flicked to the corner of the counter where the gingerbread heads had been perfectly stacked.

"Uh . . ." He swallowed roughly. "Pretty sure I know the answer to this, but did these gingerbread men have their heads attached when you left the kitchen?"

There was silence for a moment, then some frantic scrambling before Alan and Claire were on either side of him, gaping at the decapitated biscuits.

"Oh my crusty croquembouche," Claire whispered as her hand flew to her mouth.

Alan waited a beat before adding, "What she said. And, if you'll take a look at the knife block, you'll notice one is missing."

Jonny did look, and by appearances, it seemed that the butcher knife was the one missing.

Of course it was.

He returned his attention to the defiled gingerbread men, and saw that one of the headless gingerbread men had letters carved into its body. Like whoever did this needed to make the point any clearer.

C-L-A-I-R-E.

A butter knife stuck out of its chest.

A wave of ice cascaded over Jonny's body at an almost glacial pace. He felt every centimeter of motion through his frame from the ends of his hair to his fingernails to the inside of his ankles. Agonizing, painful, debilitating ice that burned with a fierceness that robbed him of the breath in his lungs.

This wasn't just a prank anymore. Not just a warning or a threat.

This was a preview.

"Rude," Claire whimpered in a would-be light voice that convinced no one. "Now w-we can't serve gingerbread biscuits."

Neither Jonny nor Alan replied. They couldn't.

They all stared at the biscuit massacre for a long moment, then Alan moved over to the other side of the sink where his marzipan trains sat in a perfect line.

"Who, in the name of Glasgow's green grocers, touched

my marzipan?" Alan growled in the most dangerous tone Jonny had ever heard.

It was more terrifying and intimidating than Alan berating a contestant on *BBB*.

"They touched one of your trains?" Claire shrieked, darting over.

Well, as long as they kept all of this in the proper perspective . . .

Alan shook his head and jabbed a finger at something else, and Jonny quickly joined the pair.

A scrap of marzipan sat near the trains, and a fingerprint and a half could clearly be seen pressed into the dough, as if someone had leaned on the counter to study the trains more closely and had gripped the surface of the counter for balance. It wouldn't be too surprising; the models *were* intricate and amazing, as befitting the work of the Marzipan King.

But to have a fingerprint changed everything.

"Don't touch it," Jonny said slowly, keeping each word calm and concise, fearful of startling the obsessed and possibly feral bakers. "Claire, Brian's phone, please."

She handed it over without moving anything else, and Jonny quickly opened the camera app. He stepped as close to the marzipan as he dared and took as many clear pictures as he could.

"Sending these to Watson," he grumbled as he opened the email server. "Not saying the fingerprint belongs to the murderer, but threats on a train that is also harboring a murderer is a bit too coincidental for my taste, and I've had enough."

"Fair," Claire allowed, pointing a finger at him without meeting his eyes. "Totally fair."

"If the pictures even send," Alan reminded them. "Poor service, remember?"

Jonny waved that off. Whether it worked or not wasn't really the point. It was the action itself and the knowledge that he had done what he could under the circumstances, even if those circumstances totally sucked, that counted.

"What are you going to tell Watson?" Claire asked softly, leaning in.

"How about 'Fingerprint of possible suspect attached. Please investigate'?" Jonny knew their eventual return to Blackfirth would demand a full-disclosure lunch with their favorite detective sergeant.

Claire rolled her eyes. "You're an idiot, but sure, why not?" Shaking her head, she returned to her previous position on the floor and leaned her head back against the cabinets with a long exhale.

Jonny followed suit, sitting beside her, and, after a long moment of staring at his marzipan, Alan took up his position on the opposite side of the space.

Questions swirled around Jonny's mind. Questions he wasn't sure if he should ask aloud but couldn't keep from wondering anyway.

How much longer would they be here? What was the murderer—whoever they were—up to now? Was it possible that whoever it was had escaped into the Highlands around them? Who else was in danger?

How was he going to protect Claire if more death lay ahead?

She had to be a target; the threats were clearly pointing in that direction. Which meant it wasn't just Brian and Felicity who had committed some crime for which the murderer was seeking vengeance; Claire had also unknowingly offended this guy. But she had no prior connection to either Brian or Felicity. Nothing made any sense.

He had to figure out who was behind all of this before anyone else was hurt, including Claire.

Especially Claire.

"You know," Alan said with a frown, "if he wasn't dead, I'd be hard-pressed not to throw a punch in Brian's face for having Felicity try to expose me like that. When it was just him involved in this, it was one thing. But now other people who he pulled into his web have suffered because of it. I just . . . but you know. Poor, dead Brian."

"Poor, dead Brian," Claire and Jonny said together, solemnly.

They were so weird.

"So, moving on to the list of people on the train?" Jonny suggested, trying to keep his voice even despite the panic starting to eat away at him.

Claire sighed and reached up onto the counter for the list of names, taking a pencil from the drawer just above her head. "I suppose any females are off."

"Why's that?" Alan asked from his side of the room.

"Did you see the size of the handprints around Felicity's neck?" She scoffed loudly. "Those be man's hands, make no mistake. Unless there's a female professional basketball player on board."

"Doubt that," Alan commented absently. "Not quite my fan base."

Jonny met Claire's eyes, rolling his own, before they began putting small *X*'s beside the women's names.

That would take away over half the list, thankfully.

"I'd like to thank Greg for making sure pictures were required when the passengers applied for the trip. And for including ages on his list," Claire said with a rueful smile. "While we're crossing out the women, should we get rid of others? No kiddos. No men over the age of, what, seventy?"

"Probably," Jonny agreed, nodding.

"Any time you want my input, just say so," Alan quipped as he downed the rest of his coffee.

"Shut up, Alan," they said together.

Claire eyed the list of passenger names and pictures spread over several pages, shaking her head. "We can't exactly go question everyone, so we'll have to eliminate them some other way. I think we're looking at some sort of avenging angel. We've all had interactions with people on this train, so while marking off who we know it's not, flag your suspects. Alan, start on these pages, and J and I will do these ones. And if anyone looks familiar to you for whatever reason, shout it out. We'll swap in a minute."

"Right." Alan reached out for the papers. "How else are we supposed to kill time until the train moves again?" He grimaced. "Sorry, poor choice of words."

With perfect timing, the Tannoy clicked on over their heads.

"Ladies and gentlemen, pardon the interruption. We are pleased to announce that the mechanical issue that has kept us stranded is being fixed at this time. We anticipate departing within the hour. Thank you for your patience, and we will update you again as soon as we can."

The faintest sound of applause could be heard from the cars ahead of them, but no one was applauding in the kitchen.

A sense of doom and unease settled among them, and all three looked at each other.

"Right," Claire said slowly. "So we've got three hours or so until we're at Mallaig, and everything happens. Unless they have us stop in"—she looked at Alan—"what's the other place?"

"Arisaig," he murmured. "But with the delay we've had, they'll probably bypass it instead of pretending people want to stop and look around. Depends on if anyone is getting off at the station."

Claire nodded, biting her lip. "Right. Okay, why don't I go ask Lisa if we're actually going to stop there? I can pose the question like we're trying to figure out if we need to do another round of food or something."

"First of all, you're not going anywhere alone," Jonny said. "Not after the death of a gingerbread man named Claire. Please, come sit closer." He patted the floor next to him. "We can finish looking at these faces before we get a timeline."

Jerking a nod, Claire scooted over beside him, her small sigh making him wonder if she was as relieved by his request as he was by her response.

They marked off every guest on the first page for one reason or another, then turned to the second.

Claire paused and laid a finger beside a picture he recognized. "He's certainly got the anger."

"Fanboy? Yeah," Jonny said slowly, twisting his lips in thought. "But how would he have managed dealing with Felicity last night? Unless they bribed a guard or something. I don't know."

"He's passionate enough about Alan to act irrationally on his behalf," Claire pointed out. "And treat others poorly."

"That's for sure. I just . . . I don't know. We'll leave him as a possibility." He could only shrug, not sure why his gut was sticking up for someone he'd suspected before.

"Fair enough."

They turned to the next page, and Jonny started making marks when Claire gripped his arm.

She cleared her throat. "Alan, you said Rose had a dimple you adored, right?"

Jonny looked from Claire to Alan, who didn't twitch, look up, or pay any sort of attention to what they were doing.

That was how innocent Claire's question sounded.

"She did," Alan answered. "And she had a crescent-shaped birthmark on her jaw. It was my favorite place to kiss her. Very ticklish on that spot."

"Huh," Jonny grunted, trying to sound interested.

Claire immediately began squeezing his arm, her nails cutting into the skin.

"What?" he yelped, canting away from her.

She looked at Alan quickly, then back at Jonny, slamming a finger to her lips.

"What?" he mouthed in response, still tense with apprehension.

Claire pointed to a picture of a woman on their current list. A woman named Rose. "She. Is. On. This. Train." Her voice was barely above a breath as she whacked him on each word.

Jonny stared at her, unblinking for so long his eyes stung. Then he looked down at the picture, then back at Claire.

Oh. Holy tartan . . .

"Crepes alive," he whispered.

Claire nodded almost frantically, her hands flying to her mouth.

“What is going on over there?” Alan asked with a laugh.

“Erm . . .” Claire’s eyes shifted into full panic, and anxiety filled their emerald depths as she looked at Jonny for help.

He had very little help to give.

“Whiskey,” Jonny bleated before he’d actually thought through anything. “I forgot to ask what whiskey Brian was served yesterday.”

Claire’s expression turned incredulous.

“Why?” Alan laughed again. “Think we’re overproofing here and Brian really was that drunk?”

“Need to rule it out,” Jonny answered, trying to look apologetic. “And Claire is a pub girl, as you know, so she’s excited. Wants to know for her own interests.”

Based on looks alone, his girlfriend was going to kill him when they got off this train.

But she hadn’t offered a better story, so who was really to blame here?

“I’m gonna go find Lisa,” Claire muttered, standing up and shoving Jonny a little.

He batted at her hand in a weak defense.

Alan stood with a groan. “I’ll be your bodyguard and see if we can track down Greg. He probably has more information on the passengers besides what’s on this list, if I know him.”

Jonny watched as the two of them left him alone in the kitchen and smirked to himself. “I’ll just stay here then. Sounds good.”

CHAPTER 19

Lisa confirmed that they would be stopping at the Arisaig station, where the bodies would be removed from the train and the official investigation would commence.

This meant that once the train got moving again, they'd have two hours to get the answers they needed.

Lovely. Nothing like a good, short, very tentative time frame.

Claire did her best not to grumble under breath as she made her way back toward the kitchen, Alan on her heels, a smile plastered onto her face as though she worked for the railways and couldn't show any emotion other than contentment to the passengers.

"I require a moment of your time, Mr. Gables," intoned the most pompous voice Claire had ever heard.

Groaning, she pulled to a stop, knowing all too well that Jonny would have a field day if she didn't stick with Alan.

"Certainly, sir," Alan said in a tight but congenial voice. "Might I escort Miss Walker back to her compartment before we talk?"

The man, who had clearly dyed his hair to get a smattering

of gray in it to match Alan's coloring, only glanced at Claire before returning his eyes to Alan. "No, I don't care about her. And the way that boyfriend of hers was sniffing around the journalist, no one else does either."

Claire inhaled sharply, biting down on the inside of her lip to keep from shouting. Or crying.

Crying might have been more likely.

"Watch yourself," Alan snarled, his brogue growing more pronounced.

The passenger raised a brow. Or tried to, anyway. It made him look slightly constipated, but then she noted his carefully maintained scruff, the button-down shirt neatly rolled at three-quarter sleeves with the top two buttons undone, the perfect off-center part sweeping to the left . . .

Oh, baguettes. This was the one Jonny had called Fanboy. The passenger who wanted to *be* Alan so much that he had literally made himself look as much like him as possible.

Never mind that the man was at least three inches shorter, thirty pounds heavier, and had a darker complexion than the Scotsman.

Details.

"I have seen entirely too much of Miss Walker on this train," Fanboy told Alan with the sort of superiority that no one should bear. "I require at least thirty minutes of your time, Mr. Gables, for my trouble. You owe me."

Alan stiffened, his hands becoming fists at his sides. "I owe you? How do you figure?"

Fanboy's brows lowered. "I paid an extreme amount of money to be here *for you*. It was the least I could do to support your efforts, yet all I have received in exchange is some medical issue that closed the back of the train, a breakdown preventing us from arriving at Mallaig on time, and mediocre meals to tide us over. As though that would suffice. We have seen you exactly once, sir, and that is unacceptable. Miss Walker does not deserve to breathe the same air as you, and yet we have seen *her* to excess. Send her back to clean up the kitchen and salvage this excursion."

"Uh-huh," Alan said slowly in a tone that made Claire wary. "And your name is . . . ?"

Fanboy puffed out his chest. "Darren Child."

Alan reached back toward Claire, his hand finding her forearm and holding tight. "Claire Walker is the most promising amateur baker to come out of *Britain's Battle of the Bakers* in ten years. I consider her to be a friend as well as a colleague, and anyone who wants to support me would do well to support her. And now that I know of you, Darren Child, and your attitude toward those I mentor and associate with, I can safely ban you from anything having to do with me or her and save myself the effort of further conversation, as well as from the risk of diminishing my IQ, my standards, or, quite frankly, my will to live. Excuse us."

Claire gaped as Alan turned to pass her, tugging her hand to follow.

"No, wait, please!" cried Fanboy, his stern demeanor gone in a blink. He stumbled toward them, his eyes filling with tears. "Alan, you're my hero and my inspiration, please . . . Please don't leave me . . . Alan!"

But Alan only swept out of the car, clutching Claire's hand and marching them back toward the kitchen. He never uttered a single word.

Once they reached the security guard, Alan finally let go of her hand and smiled. "Think you can manage walking down to Viscount Hots-for-You alone now that we're in the secure part of the train?"

Claire smiled at him, but it didn't feel real. It was simply a matter of muscles shifting in her face, with no real indication of her feelings.

Alan had defended her against a rabid fan. Shut down the insults about her and taken a stand without hesitation or question. He'd certainly left an indelible impression on Fanboy.

When Felicity had insulted Claire, Jonny had just . . . been there. No reaction. No defense. No words at all, really.

No anything.

Alan didn't like people, but he defended her. Alan was trying to make himself more likable, but he had said something. Alan didn't have the relationship with Claire that Jonny had, but he still had shut Fanboy down.

Was Jonny done with her now? Was he trying to figure out how to tell her? Had he already checked out of the relationship?

He still cared about her, obviously, but Jonny was a surprisingly caring guy. He would never want to see her hurt, emotionally or physically, and would find a way to break up with her in a kind way. He would probably pull the 'It's not you; it's me' card, even though there was nothing actually wrong with him, and therefore there could not be a situation where he was the issue in a relationship.

Which meant she was the issue.

It didn't matter if it was the image of Felicity Farrow, or the risk of Claire becoming a public figure, or Jonny realizing he could do so much better than her. Jonny thinking about any or all of those things was enough to make something very clear to Claire.

She had to know. Now.

Claire shook her head as she walked away from Alan and into the VIP section. It was time to confront Jonny about all the insecurities she had and all the gunk that this trip had dredged up. She needed to know *now* if Jonny was even remotely feeling like she was good enough for him. If he was satisfied with what they had. If he was considering leaving this relationship of theirs.

What he wanted. What she wanted. What they were. Where they were going.

If they were going anywhere.

Sugar, she felt pathetic. Was this what other women dealt with in their relationships? Or was she just a particularly messy woman who really ought to sit down with a therapist and work through a few things?

Loads of things. All the things.

One thing was for certain. If Alan was serious about working with Claire and launching her career, Jonny would need to be forewarned. He hated the press, and having his girlfriend at the center of attention wasn't going to go well for someone who hated publicity. He should probably get out of the relationship before any of that could happen, just for his own safety and sanity. Claire wouldn't want the resentment to build and build until it exploded and ruined their chance of an amicable breakup.

She still wanted to be his friend, if her heart could survive it.

Big if, that.

"Settle, Claire," she urged herself. "Let's not jump to conclusions."

That would be the more rational side of her talking. The other side had already written her monologue and was preparing the waterworks.

Slow and deep breathing was the only way she managed to keep herself steady while she headed for the kitchen. It was impossible to stop her thoughts from whirling like a child with a sugar high on a carousel, but her feet kept moving and her jaw remained clenched. No wobbling, no trembling, no burning eyes, no lightheadedness.

She could do this.

She had to.

The further back into the train she went, the quieter everything became, and the more her thoughts intruded her consciousness. She would rather be back in the pavilion on *BBB* than have this sort of conversation, would rather give a speech she was unprepared for to a room full of teachers, would rather face the actual murderer on this train . . .

If there was a coward's way out, she'd consider it.

She'd hate herself for considering it, but she would.

Her heart thundered against her chest as the kitchen drew nearer, and her palms began to sweat. Her ears filled with a faint rushing sound that only her breathing drowned out while her toes seemed to have gone numb deep within her trainers.

She didn't want to know. She needed to, but she didn't want to.

Memories of her relationship with Jonny flashed through her mind like a frantic montage at what was surely the end. Laughing in the kitchen at Blackfirth. Eating crème brûlée in the Historic Kitchens. Snuggling together while watching past series of *BBB*. Long walks hand in hand. That wild first kiss after her near-death encounter with Benji.

Every sweet and simple kiss since.

Okay, *now* her eyes were burning. But she would get through this.

One more slow breath, and Claire pushed the kitchen door open.

Jonny hadn't moved from his spot on the floor, and for that she was grateful. If she was standing and he was sitting, she would be in a position of confidence and authority, which might make this whole thing more manageable.

"Hey, what'd the conductor say?" Jonny asked with a brief glance in her direction before his eyes dropped back to the list of passengers.

Claire's throat immediately clogged with a lump, and she swallowed several times in desperation. "Erm," she eventually choked out, "we're stopping in Arisaig."

He nodded without looking. "Well, that's fair. Too bad we won't see much of it, but they probably want to wrap this up quickly. Where's Alan?"

She tried to respond, she really did. Tried to nod too.

But nothing happened.

Her throat tightened around the lump that wouldn't dislodge, and before she had an actual heart attack or panic attack, the words came flying out of her mouth. "Are you going to break up with me?"

Jonny's head jerked up so sharply he whacked it on the cabinet behind him. But instead of rubbing the place where he'd hit, he looked at her with wide eyes. "What?"

Panic set in. Cue the rambling.

"I mean, I know that eventually you'll break up with me," Claire added hastily. "It's a given, considering you and considering me, and I'm more wanting a timeline of things than anything else because it's just getting harder and harder to not be sucked in, and I'd rather have some sort of self-respect when this is over so I'm not starting from the bottom of the barrel next time. If that makes sense."

Sense was clearly not seeping through because Jonny just stared at her, his mouth hanging open.

Awkward silence sat between them, not moving, yet impossible to fully ignore.

Like roadkill.

"What?" Jonny said again, the word a harsh whisper.

Claire's teeth dug into her bottom lip. "Just tell me, okay? I realize Felicity Farrow wasn't exactly your cup of tea, but someone like her will be, and I don't want to be the emotional piñata for whoever is next for you. So let's just call this what it is and pick the expiration date so I can avoid being hurt too badly."

Jonny got to his feet, his eyes never leaving hers. "Can we back up a minute?" he asked, his voice rough and unsteady. "I'm lost."

"How?" Claire asked in return, wishing she had some strength to throw into her voice.

"How what?"

"How are you lost?" she ground out.

His brow snapped down, his blue eyes becoming stormy, almost gray. "Oh, I don't know, because my girlfriend marched in here and started rambling about a breakup and my next girlfriend and Felicity Farrow, of all things, and I have no idea how any of those topics are even coming out of her mouth!

Call me crazy, Claire, but I thought we were having a great relationship until sixty seconds ago."

Oh. Well, when viewed in that light . . . Perhaps a different question might have been a better opening.

Claire fingered the end of her plait nervously and nodded once. "Me too. But I know it won't last, and maybe this could have waited a few more months, but dearly departed Felicity got to me, and—"

"Surely you don't believe I had any interest in that hyena."

She cracked a smile at his clear disgust. "No, I know you better than that."

He folded his arms, still frowning. "But apparently you don't know me well enough for the rest of it."

Stung, Claire gritted her teeth for a moment. "Jonny, I live in the real world. And in the real world, a guy like you doesn't end up with a girl like me. You get with the Felicity-esque types. Fashionable and leggy and expensive and posh. Not the girl who leaves pairs of glasses everywhere and prefers T-shirts and still gets zits from stress and shops in thrift stores. But you're such a good guy, and this has been like a dream, but it's just going to make it harder to walk away when you're done. So I'm just . . . looking for clarity."

"I'd like clarity too." Jonny closed the distance between them, placing his hands on her upper arms and gripping tightly. "And I'm going first. What, in the name of Dame Sophie Layton-Hughes herself, gives you the impression that I am going anywhere? Ever?"

Claire's eyes widened. "You . . . you're not—?"

"I'll tell you what I'm not," he overrode, his eyes flashing. "I'm not the guy who is constantly looking for something better or exploring other options. I'm not interested in stereotypes and expectations. I'm not playing any sort of game, and I am certainly not biding my time. Whatever insecurities Felicity Farrow knocked into you, I am asking you to knock them back out again because you are what and who I want. Have I ever given you reason to think otherwise?"

"N-no," Claire whimpered as tears welled up and clogged her throat.

Jonny stooped just a little, his hands moving to cup her face, his eyes fixed on hers. "Then why, sweetheart? Why are you asking me these things, and why are you expecting to be thrown away like I'm using you?"

"It never made sense," she cried, gripping his shirt in her hands. "You being interested in me. I couldn't see it, and still can't, so it just eats away at me. I don't want to believe you'll find the perfect model girlfriend and leave me to bake alone for the rest of my life, but I can't h-help it. And you hate being here, doing these things with all these people. Facing them and dealing with them for Alan, but I might have to do things like this if I succeed the way I hope to. You'd be so m-miserable doing that with m-me."

His thumbs quickly swiped away her tears, his expression shifting to one of tender concern that warmed her suddenly freezing body. "I could never be miserable with you. Ever. I do hate being out with the passengers, but that's because it's for Alan, and Alan hasn't won my enthusiasm and pride and devotion. You have. I would talk for twenty-four hours straight to the most annoying people ever—Fanboy and Red included—if it was about you or for you."

Claire hiccuped, covering her mouth.

Jonny tapped her chin with his thumb. "And as for us

making sense . . . It doesn't make sense to me that someone as amazingly talented and extraordinary as you would be interested in me, but you know what? I love that. I love that it doesn't make sense because it means I'm lucky. And it means I get to feel like a regular guy instead of whoever Viscount Colburn is supposed to be. Because I *am* just a regular guy, Claire. A regular guy who has the most spectacular, funny, warm, brilliant, beautiful, and sometimes straight-up bizarre girl by his side. What more could I even want?"

Tears were streaming like waterfalls down her cheeks, and controlled breathing wasn't going to calm anything down. "I want you too. I love you, Jonny, and I didn't want to say it first because I was certain you didn't and couldn't. You don't even call me 'love' anymore, so why would you—?" She couldn't finish and shut her eyes on more tears.

His thumbs continued to sweep across her skin, softly and sweetly. Then his hands slid farther back and tightened against her face. "I can see that we've been communicating in very different languages here, so let me see if I can spell this out for you in the plainest terms possible."

Claire swallowed and waited.

"Look at me."

She bit her lip, her eyes squeezing more tightly closed.

"Claire, *ma crème*, I'm not going to say anything until your beautiful eyes are on mine." His thumbs brushed her cheeks again, applying a bit more pressure.

She couldn't resist.

She opened her eyes, a few tears falling as she did so, and met his tender gaze.

His mouth curved in a crooked smile. "I love you. I am in love with you and falling more in love with you every single day. I have no intention of going anywhere or finding anyone else. Ever. I love you enough at this moment to know you're it for me, and I don't care about anything else. All those things you mentioned? I don't care. I love you. And that means you're mine. But it also means—and I want you to listen very carefully here, okay?"

Claire tried to nod, her hands flying to his wrists and holding tight.

"It means," Jonny breathed in a low voice, leaning closer until their foreheads touched, "that I am yours. Just yours. Only yours. Which means if anyone is doing any breaking up here, it's going to have to be you, and I'm going to ask you not to do that because there would be no getting over you."

His lips brushed hers once, twice, then sealed over them for a brilliant, blinding, soul-stirring kiss that had Claire tightening her grip on his wrists to keep herself from melting into the tile floor.

This wasn't just a kiss. This was a claiming, a confession, an exclamation point to everything he had said.

This was the engagement ring of non-engaged people who haven't even discussed matrimony.

This was a showstopper of a kiss, and the pièce de résistance of the conversation.

Maybe of the relationship as a whole.

Claire's entire body began to buzz and tingle in furious delight, her thumbs moving all on their own to stroke the skin of Jonny's wrists in encouragement. Or gratitude. Or some sort of spasm because *holy smoldering crepes alive*, this was the kiss of the century and what else was a girl to do?

At least she wasn't fainting.

Yet.

Jonny broke off and touched his forehead to hers again, his breath dancing across her suddenly sensitive skin in hot bursts.

"Any questions?" he rumbled after they'd both managed to settle some.

Claire's thumbs continued to stroke his skin while she hummed dreamily. "Nope."

"Okay. Good." He kissed her quickly and straightened, his hands brushing down to rest on her shoulders. "I'll try to be clearer with my language with you, love. I'm sorry you've been doubting."

She shook her head and swiped at her cheeks. "No, I'm sorry. That wasn't fair to you, and clearly I need to work on some things."

He smiled and touched her jaw. "Only in seeing yourself the way I do. Everything else is perfect."

Claire rolled her eyes and swatted at his hand. "Perfect? Please."

"Perfect for me, which is all that matters." His wink was as playful as it was sensual, and Claire shivered at it.

"I, erm . . ." She cleared her throat and rubbed at her upper arm. "I may still be stinging from when Felicity said to leave the real men to the real women, and suggested I was forgettable. That one got me pretty good, no lie."

"Claire, my love." Jonny took her hand and brought it to his lips before pressing it to his heart. He was still smiling, but his eyes had taken on a serious light. "You are the most real person I have ever met, male or female, and I would love to be left to your care. So *that* I agree with. And as for being forgettable . . ." He smirked slightly. "Maybe she had a bad memory. No one, having had the pleasure of meeting you even once, could ever forget you."

Claire tutted at his words, as the other option was to burst into tears again and fall at his feet over the sweetness. Her cheeks flamed, not getting the memo that they weren't going to have an emotional reaction, but her knees locked on command, so at least that would keep the falling at bay. Now, if only she could do something about her heart trying to jump into Jonny's arms . . .

Be still, heart.

Huh. Maybe that was what the saying actually meant.

Good to know.

Alan strode into the kitchen at that precise moment, only slightly pausing at the pose Claire and Jonny had going on at the moment. "What's the word?"

Jonny looked at Claire, then back at Alan. "Gritty risotto."

Claire snorted a laugh and clapped a hand over her mouth.

Alan looked mildly concerned. "I don't even want to know." He pursed his lips and exhaled through his nose. "Well, I can't find Greg anywhere. He's not in any of the places where we've met before. With a murderer on this train and now a time limit, we probably ought to look everywhere for him."

"Jonny cut the list down," Claire told him. "Care to take a look, Alan? See if anyone looks familiar?" She held back the page with Rose on it, which might prove to be a terrible idea, but she needed Alan to focus.

Alan took the pages and looked at the circled photos and names, frowning. After examining all of them, he shook his head. "Nobody is making any sense to me, and nothing is sticking out as significant. We could just be dealing with someone delusional. But you've got seat assignments, see? Let's go chat with the passengers, see if anyone was hanging around poor, dead Brian *and* dearly departed Felicity." He rubbed a hand over his hair, exhaling slowly. "And I'll go back to the conductor. We're going to need all the help we can get."

"And Claire goes nowhere alone," Jonny insisted, taking her hand and squeezing hard. "I don't trust that she wouldn't be victim number three if given a chance."

"Agreed," Alan clipped.

The ground beneath their feet shifted suddenly, jolting them with such force that they all stumbled, and then . . .

The gentle rumbling of the train met their ears as a faint buzzing spoke of motion.

They all looked at each other, eyes round.

"Two hours, you said?" Claire asked Alan.

"Or thereabouts." He ran a hand over his face. "Two hours to find Greg, find the murderer, and get answers for the authorities in Arisaig."

The weight of all that was left to do thumped onto Claire's shoulders like the heaviest, most poorly packed knapsack in the world.

"Then we'd better get started."

CHAPTER 20

Talking to strangers on purpose was not Jonny's forte. Nor was it in his bag of tricks. Nor his comfort zone, his area of expertise, his field of interest, or his wheelhouse, whatever that was. And this was different from asking the repeated question of if they wanted biscuits because that did not invite conversation. That was a simple question, answer, move-on situation.

Now he was practically begging for conversation.

If he were to break out in hives, he would not be at all surprised.

It might be preferred actually.

How did one bring about hives?

Jonny had talked to at least five passengers who had been labeled "possible" by Alan, but none of them had any clue where the VIP section even was on this train. They hadn't been to the dining cars, and the most recent person Jonny had talked to didn't even drink, as validated by his wife. Neither seemed to mind the questions and hadn't asked too many of their own, though that could have been due to Jonny's sour expression.

Perks to being Viscount Grumps.

Claire and Alan were checking on the other possibilities, which meant Jonny could look for Greg now, if he wanted to.

Poor kid. A big trip like this had been meant to be a celebration of Alan, and it had gone disastrously wrong. It wouldn't be in the least bit surprising if Greg was cowering somewhere on the train mid-panic attack now that they were on their way to Mallaig. The organizers of the event in Mallaig were probably, and understandably, already upset with Alan and his team for not showing up on time, and Greg would be the one to address all of that.

Greg didn't look like he could address a class of five-year-olds without sweating.

Greg, who was basically flaky pastry.

Greg, who was a puppy at Alan's heels.

Greg, who was one of the only people who could get into the VIP section without issue and—

Jonny's eyes widened, and he slapped himself in the forehead. Greg, who could pass for a hipster and might hate that someone on the train was creating trouble for Alan. Greg, who would recognize Brian Donovan straight off.

It was a massive conclusion to jump to, and it sounded absolutely impossible, but it stuck to the forefront of his mind like Velcro.

Jonny tucked himself into the gangway nearby and looked for the nearest security guard. He had spoken with four of them earlier, and Greg—before he'd gone missing—had assured him that he'd spoken with the other two, so Jonny hadn't seen the need to seek them out specifically.

But at this moment, he needed to know for sure what these two had seen.

He raced to the middle of the train, relieved when the security guard posted there was unfamiliar.

"Can I ask you a question?" Jonny blurted out when he reached him, not bothering with any sort of greeting.

The guard shrugged. "Course, mate."

Jonny exhaled a short breath. "When my friend talked to you this morning about watching Dining Car 3 last night, did he seem okay?"

Confusion lit the other man's features. "When who did what now?"

"Talk, skinny, dark-haired guy. Looks like he's seventeen," Jonny told him as he made a "let's hurry this up" motion with his hand. "We were asking all of the security guys about last night."

"I didn't talk to anybody this morning," the guard assured him, eyes wide. "Which is dumb, since I was the one on Dining Car 3 last night."

Jonny feared his kneecaps would dissolve completely and send him crashing to the floor. He leaned against the nearest wall, praying it would keep him up. "You . . . What?"

He nodded slowly. "The only guy I've seen like you described is the assistant to the baker, and he's been running all over this train. He had Felicity Farrow with him last night, and he said they were going to be doing more interviews in the back of the train. She had been trying to get back there on her own all trip, but since she was with him and he had credentials, I figured it was okay. I was off shift before they ever came back out. I wasn't sure if they were lying about an interview and just going back there to hook up or what. She was pretty eager and holding his hand like they were eloping, you know? But she doesn't seem—"

"Hold it," Jonny interrupted, trying to catch his suddenly unsteady breath. "He brought Felicity into the VIP section last night?"

"Yeah. After the dinner stuff and when most everybody else was sleeping." He nodded earnestly.

Throat dry, Jonny tried—and failed—to swallow. "And you really didn't talk to anyone about this today but me?"

The guard shook his head. "I'm supposed to meet with Lisa, our conductor, when I finish this shift and before we get to Arisaig, but that's it."

Jonny shoved a hand into his hair, nodding jerkily. "Okay. Okay. Th-thanks, mate. What's your name?"

"Rob. Need more from me? Happy to help."

"Not yet. We'll see." Jonny somehow managed to shake his hand, and then turned away, his mind close to breaking with the mix of thoughts filling it.

Not only had Greg had lied about interviewing the two remaining security guards, but he hadn't even talked to the one actually on duty. Greg had been with Felicity in Dining Car 3 before she'd died. Greg wanted everything to be perfect for Alan all the time.

All. The. Time.

With a jolt in his stomach, Jonny bolted back toward the passengers, pausing at the service attendant break room, which had been empty before. He dodged passengers like he was in a Matrix film, scrambling his way as fast as possible up the aisles and through the few cars between him and his destination. Was running strictly necessary? Probably not, but with Arisaig getting closer every minute, the risk of something going wrong was too high.

So running like he'd lost a child was happening.

Claire and Alan were side by side, chatting with passengers and blissfully unaware that the world was currently spinning backward.

Claire's eyes flicked to him as he approached, her brow creasing in confusion.

"Why are you panting?" she asked with a smile.

"Running," he said simply. "And I have a really crazy thought that sounds less crazy the more I repeat it in my head."

She bit her lip as she looked up at him. "Do you need me to follow you and validate your crazy?"

He let his hands graze her sides as he moved by her, making her breath hitch, which made him grin. "You can follow me anytime and anywhere. But I'm not sure if I need validation or elimination of the crazy."

She smiled at him. "Let's go discuss, then. Wow, for once it's not my crazy. I don't know what to do with this."

"Nice." He brushed his lips across her brow and hurried up the aisle with a quick nod to Alan that he had Claire. He tried in vain to swallow the burning sensation of adrenaline hitting the sides of his throat. Linking his fingers with hers and tugging, the pair of them moved with fast steps to the nearest gangway.

"Greg," Jonny whispered when they were alone.

"Where?" Her confused gaze darted around the area. "You found him?"

Jonny grabbed her chin and forced her eyes to meet his. "Greg didn't talk to all of the security guards this morning. He lied to me. I just talked to the guard who was on duty at the VIP section last night, and he said Greg hadn't been around at all this morning."

Claire's eyes widened as her mouth formed the word "What?" without any sound at all.

Releasing her chin, Jonny nodded and turned her around to start walking into the dining car behind her. "Greg went into Dining Car 3 last night with Felicity, and they did not come back out. Or, at least the guard I just spoke with didn't see them come out. He went off duty shortly after they entered. I don't know what to do with this. I just . . . Greg is one of the few people who can get in and out of the VIP section without issue. Greg would know Brian. Greg would be furious if he'd somehow learned about Brian's plans. But Greg is Greg, so . . ."

"We need to tell Alan," Claire whispered. "Nobody else on the train has seemed anywhere near this suspicious. The last two people Alan and I talked to don't even care that they're here. They just came for their wife and their mother, respectively, and they're furious about the delays. They're so cranky, they make you and Alan look like the happy emoji."

Jonny's pulse was pounding harder now. He wanted to run. He wanted to go full Tom Cruise and sprint through every single one of these cars without jostling a single person because somehow the way would be perfectly clear and smooth while he flew to save the world.

Because the public never panics in a Tom Cruise film. Even when he runs like that.

But no, this was real life, and avoiding panic had been the entire theme of this trip ever since Brian had been found dead. It wouldn't help anyone to ruin that in the last stretch before Arisaig.

Walking and smiling it would be.

"Here's something I don't understand," Claire murmured as they stood outside the passenger car, motioning for Alan through the window. "Brian outweighed Greg by a decent amount, so how did Flaky Pastry manage to have Brian hit his head so hard against the counter that he died?"

Jonny exhaled slowly with a faint whistle. "I'm not sure,

but they were on a moving train, right? Brian might have been tipsy, but he wasn't plastered. But if Greg caught him by surprise or got him off balance—"

"We've gotta find him," Claire ground out. "He might bolt the minute we get to Arisaig."

Jonny made a face. "But why would Greg be making threats against you? What have you ever done to Greg?"

Claire shook her head. "Here, check your email on Brian's phone. See if Watson got back to you."

Jonny took the phone from her and quickly logged in to his email account. The tension in his chest lessened when he saw the message sitting in his inbox. "He wrote back."

Claire scooted closer, plastering herself against his side to read along.

> *Why is it always you two? Don't touch dead bodies. Reaching out to Arisaig authorities, since that should be your next stop. Fingerprints match Gregory Andrews—no criminal record. Prints on file for background check before employment with Dishable Inc. Stay safe. Bring back whiskey for me and we're even.*

"Crepes alive," Claire whispered. "I was hoping you were wrong."

Jonny closed the email and shook his head. "So was I." He put his arm around her shoulder and pulled her even closer, fear and uncertainty gripping him as he realized that the man responsible for two deaths was gunning for Claire too. And they had been close to him for almost the entire trip.

He could not—*would* not—lose Claire. Not to Greg and his threats, not to another woman, not to anyone.

How could she have ever thought he would want someone else? It had been a sucker punch to his soul when she'd talked about him breaking up with her as though it was somehow inevitable. Nothing was inevitable except for his falling in love with her. That had been in someone's cards for him from the day they'd met, and no one would ever convince him otherwise.

Blimey, he'd have proposed to her right now if he thought it would do any good.

That was where he was. But Claire had some serious insecurities that he needed to take the time to ease her out of. Time and his attention would reassure her that he wasn't going anywhere and that she was perfect for him. She couldn't be more perfect for him, actually. She made him human, as his sister, Gabi, loved to point out, and she hadn't thought anyone capable of that.

Just Claire.

Always Claire.

Forever Claire.

And now he was a sap.

Oh well.

The nearest door slid open, and they found themselves face-to-face with Alan and the conductor.

Alan grumbled. "That was not fun. That guy was a French pastry chef who wants to collaborate, and his seatmates swear he's been in his seat the whole time, apart from visiting the lav. They were playing Jenga, of all things, during the time everything went down in the bar."

"Jenga on a train," Jonny muttered, shaking his head. "That's insane."

"And yet, I want to try it now," Claire mused with a nervous giggle.

Alan snorted and folded his arms. "You have anything?"

Catching how Claire's eyes flicked to him, Jonny cleared his throat. "I am very much afraid that we've got a problem. Greg. He's behind all of this."

Alan's eyes went wide and then he swore and turned away, his hands going to his hair. "Why? How? I know you wouldn't say this if you weren't serious, but—"

"He would do anything to protect you," Jonny went on. "He lied to me about talking to all the security guards. The one actually on duty last night said he saw Greg going into Dining Car 3 with Felicity. Greg had credentials to get by, which is the only way Felicity could have gotten through. He knew she wanted to expose you, and he heard us taking earlier—"

"And he hasn't yet sent Claire the contract for the cookbook, which I asked him to do months ago," Alan mumbled.

"He *what*?" Claire shrieked.

Alan looked at her. "I had an email prepared to send to you ages ago, along with the contract. Every time I asked him about it, he said he would get right on it, but then he would bring up something else more pressing. I didn't think anything about it, but I wonder . . . He never said, but . . ."

"You think he wanted the focus to be only on you?" Jonny asked.

Wincing, Alan gripped the back of his neck. "Maybe. I know I haven't been the best boss, and he takes it. He doesn't sweat a thing. He just fixes what I ask and continues to be as dedicated and devoted as ever . . . Fire and brimstone, did I do this? Did I create him?" He grimaced and went to the train door, staring out at the Highlands.

Jonny doubted he was actually seeing anything at all.

It was not a great weekend to be Alan Gables, certainly, but this was a crushing blow, and Jonny could say nothing to make it better. First Alan's partner and former best friend tried to ruin him, then that partner wound up dead before justice could be served, then the woman who was supposed to sing his praises but was actually working to destroy him ended up dead, and now it appeared that his devoted assistant likely caused those deaths.

It was too much.

There was no telling what Greg's motivation was or if what had happened was an accident or intentional. Or, quite honestly, if Greg even had anything to do with it.

Only Greg could give them those answers.

"I haven't seen Greg since he told me he'd questioned the last two guards," Jonny offered. "But he has VIP access, so checking the back of the train is probably our best bet."

"Unless he's been up front again," Claire pointed out hopefully. "He was so upset about the delay to Mallaig, wasn't he? Asking all those questions yesterday?"

"What questions?" Lisa asked with a frown. "I've had a few conversations with Greg this trip, but I didn't see him up front with me or the engineer after we left Glenfinnan."

Jonny jerked in surprise. "Bistro said what?"

Lisa looked puzzled.

"They swear in baking terms," Alan explained on a weary exhale. "Don't worry about it."

Ice began to slide down Jonny's spine. "Alan," he said slowly, "are you sure you can't remember where you were when you got hit yesterday? Like what part of the train you were in?"

Alan tilted his head in thought. "I had come out of Dining

Car 3 and was starting up the gangway toward . . ." His eyes widened. "I was in our compartment car."

Jonny pressed his tongue to his teeth, exhaling a slow breath. "VIP section. No one in unless they're a worker or have a pass. And Dining Car 3 was locked down by then, so not even Felicity could have gotten back there."

They all met the gazes of each other as reality sunk in.

Greg. Of all people, of all possibilities, Greg.

"We need to find him," Claire announced softly. "Ask him questions, if nothing else." She turned to Lisa, setting her jaw. "Besides the private compartments, the kitchen car, and the refrigeration car, what else is beyond the VIP security checkpoint?"

Lisa removed her hat and scratched her scalp. "Well, Dining Car 3, obviously, and then we have a storage car and the luggage car, which is for the larger bags that don't fit in the overhead. Other than that, nothing. And the luggage car needs a key for security reasons."

Alan made a choked, scoffing sound. "Greg could find a way in without one, trust me. He's opened locked doors plenty of times, and I never asked questions. Why didn't I ask more questions?"

"Shut up, Alan," Claire said without raising her voice even a notch. "Okay, let's get back there, preferably with some security guards. We don't have a ton of time, and Greg knows way more than he should."

No one argued with Claire, and the four of them continued the trek toward the back of the train, hopefully to find Greg and end this once and for all.

CHAPTER 21

Claire didn't miss the way Alan tensed when they entered the dimly lit storage car. She doubted anybody could miss the way Alan's shoulders shot practically to his ears and his spine stiffened while he inhaled sharply.

It was one of the most dramatic reactions she'd ever seen from him.

And she couldn't let it go without trying to help.

She reached out to grip his arm. "Breathe. I know you woke up in here and that was probably terrifying, but please breathe. And don't worry, I'll shank anyone who comes at you."

As she'd hoped, that made Alan laugh, even if it was only a reluctant rumbling that could easily have been the Scottish reaction to indigestion.

"Thanks, lass. That's scary, but thanks anyway." He patted her hand on his arm.

Claire raised a brow he would barely see. "Everybody thinks nice can't also be scary, but here I am."

Again came the rumbling half laugh, and then a sigh. "You know, it was probably Greg who hit me. That'll come out of his paycheck."

"What's the going deduction for knocking your boss unconscious, I wonder?" Claire mused aloud.

"Pretty sure it's 30 percent of the gross of the paycheck amount," Jonny quipped from behind them. "Plus more for emotional damage fees."

Alan reached a fist out behind him. "Word."

Jonny bumped it with an acknowledging grunt.

Claire threw up her hands. "You two seriously need to stop. This bromance is so awkward and strange, and I've had it."

"You can't stop fate, lass," Alan told her. "And you wanted this for us."

"Clearly, I wasn't thinking." She forced herself not to smile because it would ruin her protests, but secretly—or not so secretly—she was thrilled and entertained by the friendship that had developed between Alan and Jonny. They were both important to her, and having them get along for their own sakes and not hers was a dream come true.

But there was no need for them to know that.

Irritation looked good on her, she was certain.

If anything did.

Lisa and the two large security guards she had called to join them had their torches out and on, sweeping the beam of light from side to side as they moved deeper into the darkened car. Why she hadn't opted to flip on the overhead lights, Claire wasn't sure, but she wasn't going to argue. They were almost to the end of this; she could taste it on her tongue.

It tasted like metal and bitter coffee and anxiety.

If Greg was in here, he might have heard them coming over the creaking, grating sounds of the train beneath them, but there were no sounds of rushing around or any movement at all. If he was in here, he was hiding.

So many questions poked at her mind like impetuous children on a road trip. Repeatedly and incessantly prodding because there was nothing better to do and no answers to sate them with. She and Jonny had done all they could up to this point, and they had enough information for logical conclusions, but answers—real answers—could only come from Greg now.

And if he didn't give them now, before they reached Arisaig, it might be too late.

Greg had been difficult to get a read on when she'd first met him, but after five minutes of observation and conversation, she and Jonny had dubbed him Flaky Pastry. An efficient, task-oriented assistant who either had a hero complex with Alan or a high pain tolerance because Alan's brusqueness didn't seem to put him off at all. He must have been good at his job for Alan to work with him, let alone tolerate him. That he was in this situation now was difficult to comprehend.

He didn't seem the murdering type. Not unless he was a psychopath who hid those impulses well.

Yeesh, what if he was straight out of a true crime podcast?

A wary shudder coursed through Claire, and she forced it back as much as she could. Innocent until proven guilty, right?

Or innocent until proven creepy, anyway.

She couldn't forget the threats against her, and the demented decapitation of her gingerbread men. And the fact that one of the largest butcher knives was still missing.

The stabbed gingerbread man with her name on it was a pretty freaky harbinger of doom.

There were no sounds except what they were making themselves and the noise of the train against the tracks, but there was something strange about this space. Crates upon crates sat against the walls, spare trolleys were locked together, and wrapped stacks of boxed supplies were seemingly everywhere. She could even see the outline of a fridge, but Claire doubted it was connected to anything. Dark containers lined the other wall, and tools of all sorts hung from hooks nearby with small walkways weaving between all of it.

A hodgepodge of things, and someone could hide in here for days without being found.

"Check if anyone is in there," Lisa murmured with a gesture toward those dark, towering containers. "It's all the mechanical stuff, but you would be able to sit in there for a while if you're small enough."

Claire nodded and held Jonny's arm as one of the security guards walked over.

"If he jumps out, I'm going to scream like I'm in an Alfred Hitchcock film," Claire whispered. "Just so you know."

Jonny wrapped his arms tightly around her. "Noted. I got you."

She patted him as she tried to swallow the newfound burning at the back of her throat. "What, you won't jump?"

"Oh, I'm sure I will," he assured her. "I'm actually holding you like a teddy bear because I'm scared."

"You two are children," Alan rumbled.

He was probably shaking his head too.

"Inappropriate humor," Claire whispered. "Bad coping skills. You should know this by now."

Alan only grunted in response.

The guard was back in a few moments, shaking his head. "Nothing in there."

"What do they have for weapons anyway?" Claire asked Lisa as the security guard led the way, the second one bringing up the rear.

"Mace," Lisa said. "And some zip ties for restraints."

"I suddenly regret asking," Claire whispered.

Their protector swept ahead of them with determined, unafraid steps, his torchlight waving over every inch of exposed space. He shrugged when they reached the end of the car.

"Looks like the luggage car is where he'll be," Lisa said. "Figures. Last car of the train." She focused on Alan. "You sure he'd be able to pick the lock and get in there?"

Alan nodded. "I don't know how he'd do it, but he could, yes."

Lisa returned his nod and turned on her heel, opening the door to move them into the gangway between cars. She hesitated only a moment before opening the door to the luggage car.

No key necessary.

The space wasn't particularly full, Claire noted as they entered. Just a few large suitcases neatly laying in rows and the occasional duffel bag. But the journey from Fort William to Mallaig on this particular train was usually more for locals on day trips, so that wasn't too much of a surprise.

What was a surprise, however, was seeing Greg sitting at the end of the line of suitcases, leaning against two that were stacked atop one another, his eyes on them as they entered.

No fleeing.

No panic.

No hiding.

His young face was lined with strain, though; Claire could see it clearly. His shoulders stooped and sagged, everything about his posture and his bearing spoke to complete and utter defeat.

For a moment, her chest seized up at the thought that he might actually be dead, but the next moment she heard him sigh loudly, so her fear quickly dissipated.

"You found me," Greg announced flatly. He waved at them before slumping again. "Figured you would."

"We have some questions," Alan told him as they all continued toward him. Slowly. Carefully. Warily. "It'll be okay. We can figure this out."

Greg looked at Alan for a long moment, then smiled.

But not like the nice, sweet, anxiety-riddled Greg that Claire knew.

This was a very different Greg smiling now.

And crepes alive, it was the creepiest grin she had ever seen in her entire life.

"Figure it out?" he repeated with a maniacal laugh. "I figured it out a long time ago! I solved all the problems before you even knew about them! Do you even know how much work is involved in taking care of your problems, Alan? Sorry—Mr. Gables. Professional at all times."

"I wouldn't say that, exactly," Jonny muttered.

Claire gripped his hand, trying to silence him.

Please don't tap the glass; it may startle the psychopath . . .

Greg giggled a little, the childlike quality of it creeping her the heck out. "Mmm, I see we've continued with the 'keeping precious Claire with a buddy at all times' thing. And

I was so hoping that I could go three for three on this trip. I know you got my messages, Claire, and yet here you are. Don't you listen, teacher?" He pulled out the missing kitchen knife and began tapping the blade against his thigh.

Because that wasn't at all creepy.

"No need for knives, Greg," Alan assured his assistant in a soothing tone. "Can we just talk?"

Greg's insanity settled almost entirely as he looked at Alan. "I'll answer anything you want, Mr. Gables. Alan. My mentor. My boss. My . . . everything." He wrinkled his nose and snickered. "That sounds like I'm in love with you. I'm not. Promise. I'm just the only one who cares more about your legacy and career than anything else in this world. Or anyone."

He shot a dark look at Claire, and he was so different from the anxious young man she'd soothed the night before that her stomach curdled.

"Can you put the knife down, Greg?" Jonny asked as they continued to approach, their steps slow and cautious.

"Can? Yep. Will? Nope." He popped his *p* on both answers, twirling the tip of the blade against his thigh. "How do you like that, Viscount?"

Claire grabbed Jonny's arm with her free hand, clinging to him in two places. She didn't believe Greg could actually get to her, not with everyone else in the room, but she needed to ground herself to something real and good and safe or she was going to start panicking hardcore.

Jonny was the only real thing she had right now.

Alan moved to sit on the floor of the car, surprising her. "Okay, Greg. Will you tell me what happened with Brian first?"

Claire followed his example and sat on the floor, Jonny coming to sit behind her and pulling her into his chest.

Lisa and the guards remained standing nearby; though one seemed to be surveying the distance between Greg and everyone else, eyeing a way to intervene.

Greg sneered without looking at Alan, his eyes on the blade. "How about we discuss Claire first?"

"Fine," Alan murmured again. "Go ahead, Greg."

Greg's eyes flicked to his boss, staring at him for a long moment. "I had no problem with Claire before you started talking cookbooks with her. You don't partner with anyone, which makes *me* your partner. Me! Not her. I don't get any credit for it, and I don't need credit. But I'm the one who preps the recipes. I'm the one who handles all the approvals. I'm the one contacting photographers and ensuring your contracts are perfect. Each cookbook since I've been hired on is my lifeblood in your name. And you were going to take that away from me for someone who doesn't even know how to handle marzipan correctly."

Claire inhaled sharply, then clamped a hand over her mouth. She didn't need to set Greg off when he already hated her, but if this was where his hatred of her had come from, why wasn't that anger directed at Alan?

"But if she said no," Greg went on, his words picking up pace, "then you wouldn't have anyone else. I didn't send the contract because if it never got to her, this wouldn't happen. Then you insisted on telling her about it on this trip. You don't like any other baker as much as you like her, so all I needed was to scare her away from the cookbook. That was my big plan. Scare her away from you. From us. From our perfect partnership."

Cakes and a custard, that was it? That was the big crime she'd committed against him?

How had that led to murder?

"Okay," Alan acknowledged, his voice somehow still steady and low. "I get that. Now what about Brian?"

"I was at the bar in Dining Car 3 when Mr. Donovan came in," Greg began in a surprisingly calm voice. "Didn't notice him at first; I was just having a break with a gin and tonic. It wasn't until Mr. Donovan ordered his second whiskey that I looked at him. I knew who he was right away."

He looked away, shaking his head, some of his earlier madness disappearing and bringing the man he'd been before to the surface. "And then you came in, Mr. Gables, and the two of you started to talk. I ducked away from the bar so you wouldn't see me, but I heard everything he said to you. All his threats about taking you down and making the business go belly-up with your prints all over everything . . . I couldn't let that happen. I stayed where I was when you left, and then went back to the bar when I was sure you weren't coming back.

"Mr. Donovan ordered his third whiskey," Greg told them. "The bartender went to the back, and then Donovan looked at me. He said he knew who I was, and that I'd overheard their conversation, and that nothing could stop him from doing what he was going to do, no matter who I talked to. I told him there wasn't a need to do this, and that he should leave Mr. Gables alone, especially on this train."

Greg shuddered, shaking his head. "He didn't like that. I . . . I lost it. I shoved him in the chest, as hard as I could. It was stupid because he outweighed me by so much, but since he wasn't expecting it, he fell backward, and his head hit the corner of the bar counter. He went down and didn't move. I tried to find his briefcase, but he must have dropped it behind the bar or something. I could hear the bartender coming back, so I bolted."

Greg raised his head a little, his gaze landing somewhere in the vicinity of Alan's shoes. "And then I freaked. Didn't want you to know what I'd done, Mr. Gables, so I hit you. I don't even remember what I hit you with. I just grabbed something and hoped I could knock you out."

Alan rubbed at the bruise on his head almost absently but didn't comment on it.

"Once I'd dragged Mr. Gables to the storage car, I wanted to stop the train." Greg closed his eyes and leaned his head back against the suitcases, his mad smile returning to his lips. "I don't even know what I broke, I just started tossing things into the wheel mechanisms. The first two attempts just made a lot of noise, but the third time, something broke off, and the train stopped. With the storm rolling in, I figured it would take a while to fix, and maybe I could come up with a plan."

He laughed eerily. "And then I realized . . . there wasn't a problem at all. I was a genius. I'd solved the problem with the business, and with Mr. Donovan dead, no one would bring the mess back to Mr. Gables. So I poked at Claire again, needing to secure my future and keep her away."

Jonny rumbled a growl that Claire felt against her back, and she placed a hand on his knee, squeezing gently.

"I played my timid part again, let you all try to solve this like the brave little detectives you are." Greg's expression took on a dreamy aura. "And then . . . Felicity Farrow. I hated her so much. She was going to bring Alan down. She was going to get with Donovan and spread the lies he'd tell, and she would get more popular for it. Make a fortune. Continue her toxic Barbie lifestyle. I was eavesdropping on the conversation she had with Claire in the dining car last night, so I knew she'd discovered that something corrupt was going on within Dishable. So I thought, why not fix that problem too? I'd taken care of Donovan, even if it was an accident, and I could take care of her too."

A chill erupted in the pit of Claire's stomach and raced down to her toes as she listened to Greg. As she watched him. He had gone from defending his boss and causing an accident to willingly choosing to end a life.

How did anyone devolve so quickly?

Greg slapped his knife against his thigh again, making Claire jump. "It was ridiculously easy to get her back there. All I had to do was play the scared little boy and give her a hint of some news to share." He shook his head. "Pathetic. But anyway . . ." He waved a hand like a gnat was in his face, and the gnat might have been named Felicity Farrow.

"She wasn't expecting my hands to find her throat, and she definitely wasn't expecting me to drag her down to the floor and watch the life leave her eyes." He exhaled loudly, his shoulders seeming to lose any and all tension. "It was magical. One minute the cat was clawing, and the next she was out. Beautiful. Right there on the floor with Donovan's blood still smeared into the carpet."

Claire gripped Jonny's arms, fighting the urge to jump up and run from the room. From the train. From all of it.

This was ugly. Cold. Unnerving.

And it could have been her.

"And Claire?" Alan asked when Greg didn't go on.

The snarl that immediately flashed across Greg's blissed-out face was disturbing, contorting his features like some grotesque Stephen King character. "Claire," he spat. "I was going to get her too. But strangling wasn't good enough for her. No, I wanted a slow bleeding out for her. I wanted to watch the life leave her body."

He looked at her, his snarl curving almost into a smile. "Did you like the scene I set out for you, Claire? Your quaint little gingerbread men were nothing compared to Alan's masterpiece in marzipan. I carved one of them just for you. Just so you'd know what was coming. But your boyfriend got all protective, and I couldn't get to you."

Greg sniffed and tapped his finger against the sharp point of the blade. "It's fine, though. I am the Avenging Angel of Alan Gables, and if I can't be anything else, at least I can be remembered as that. The most devoted. The most determined. The one who risked . . . everything."

Greg trailed off, absently twisting the blade of the knife against his finger.

The train lurched around a curve, throwing them all off balance for a moment, and one of the guards lunged at Greg, tackling him to the floor. He must have moved while they were listening to Greg monologue his crimes, doing so quietly enough and slowly enough not to draw attention, and it worked. The knife skittered across the floor, safely out of Greg's hands.

Alan leaped to his feet and moved to the weapon, pulling out a handkerchief before picking it up.

Greg didn't even flail under the guard's weight, but he did laugh as his cheek was pressed against the floor. "Hope you enjoyed the show, Claire. Watch out for trains. And knives. And creepy boys that sneak around in the night."

Claire stared at him in horror, unaware that a tear was rolling down her cheek until Jonny brushed it away.

"Don't," Jonny whispered in her ear. "Don't give him another thought or another tear." He kissed her cheek and stood, pulling her up with him. His arms tightened around her, and the increase in pressure brought the weight of comfort and security.

Alan looked over at Lisa, his mouth set tightly while the guards zip-tied Greg's wrists. "I trust he is safe, Conductor?"

Lisa gave him a firm nod. "He is. We'll keep him in our office with two security guards until we reach Arisaig. The authorities are meeting us at the station. We should be there in less than an hour." She gestured to Greg. "Get him up."

The guards dragged him to his feet, one holding Greg's shoulders and forcing him forward, the other taking the handkerchief-wrapped knife from Alan.

Greg allowed himself to be pushed forward without resistance, calling over his shoulder, "I'd kill for your approval again, Alan. And I did! Twice!" His loud laughter sounded unhinged.

One of the guards rumbled something and forced him to move more quickly, Lisa and his associate following at pace.

Alan exhaled roughly as they watched them go. "I wasn't expecting that, I admit it."

"Not sure any of us were," Jonny agreed, his hand tracing up and down Claire's back in gentle, soothing motions.

Claire bit her lip as they started out of the luggage car, keeping far enough back to avoid being overheard. "I don't understand any of that. How did Greg . . . Why did he . . . ?"

"Don't," Alan said at once. "Greg worked for me for years, and I never saw that side of him. I never saw how he thought about me or how obsessed he was. I certainly never saw him as a partner in my work. Maybe if I had paid more attention, been less of a grump, as you say, or an entitled jerk, I might have seen the work he'd done and appreciated it. Maybe that would have been enough to keep him from his delusions, but maybe not. Maybe it would have gotten him there sooner instead. Either way, if I didn't see it, how could you?"

"You're not to blame for Greg's actions," Claire scolded, though her voice held little severity to it. Only sincerity. "He made his own choices."

Alan nodded as he swallowed. "I ken that, lass. But now I'll have guilt for what my career and my actions have done to more people than just Rose. I don't know how I can make peace with that."

Claire felt Jonny's fingers poking her in the back and glanced up at him, a question in her eyes as she gave him a slight smile.

He winked and nodded in encouragement.

"Well," Claire said, heaving a sigh, "you aren't the spark of delusion, Alan, try as you might, so ignore that bit. Brian and Felicity were jealous of your success, so wash your hands of them. And as for Rose . . . I happen to know she's divorced, has two kids, and is on this train right now. Car 2."

Alan stopped so suddenly that Claire ran into his back. He turned to look at her, dark eyes wide. "Say that again?"

Claire grinned as Jonny laughed a deep belly laugh behind her. "Rose is on this train, Alan. She's not married. She's in car 2, and her kids are with her. You met them earlier." She peeked up at Jonny with a speculative look. "Lisa said less than an hour to Arisaig, right?"

"Pretty sure that was it, yes," Jonny affirmed, his smile crinkling his eyes.

"That's plenty of time to have a decent chat." Claire looked back to Alan, raising one of her very mobile brows in a dare.

Alan Gables stared at her, stared at Jonny, stared at Claire again, then turned around and ran, full tilt, through the storage car and beyond without another word.

"Huh," Jonny grunted as they started walking again. "Was it something we said?"

EPILOGUE

Arisaig was the most adorable train station Claire had ever seen.

From the windows, at least.

It was small, only two platforms, but everything was designed to be as historically accurate as possible, as though perfectly preserved in time. From what she could see, there were no ATMs and no ticket machines. Just the ticket teller at his desk, old-fashioned turnstiles, and classic signs and advertisements dotting the walls. The station itself resembled a cottage: fully whitewashed and simple, barely a blip on the gorgeous scenery around them.

She'd have to come back to Arisaig to have a look around sometime. But right now, she just wanted to get to Mallaig and get off this train.

They'd been at the station for twenty minutes so far, and she was ready for a nap. She and Jonny had watched Greg be escorted along the platform by armed guards, still wearing his loopy grin and no guilt for what he had done.

The conductor held out a bag to the police, slashed bits of paper spilling from its unzipped opening.

"Your contract," Jonny murmured as some of the officers

collected the pieces. "I heard them talking as they pulled Greg's things from the compartment. Alan must have given him a printed version for safekeeping, intending to give it to you on this trip, and Greg tore it to shreds instead."

"And kept it," Claire muttered with a shiver. "Like a trophy."

Jonny said nothing as he held her close.

Then they saw the wrapped bodies of Brian Donovan and Felicity Farrow being carried off the train, onlookers lowering their heads in respect as the bodies passed them on the platform.

Only when they completely disappeared from sight could Claire breathe a sigh of relief.

Jonny heard it and kissed the top of her head. "That was some trip, huh?"

She leaned against him, groaning. "That was the most stressful trip I have ever had in my life, and I was once stranded in Amsterdam without any luggage for twenty-four hours at Christmas."

"There are worse places to be stranded than Amsterdam at Christmas," he mused, tugging her closer and resting his chin on her head.

"No luggage," she emphasized. "That means no toothbrush, no deodorant, no change of clothes. Do you know what it feels like to walk into a hotel that is hosting a Christmas gala wearing jeans and a hoodie with only your wallet and phone for company? I looked like a hobo, J."

"But a very cute hobo, I'm sure."

She poked his ribs hard but made no effort to escape the circle of his arms.

He laughed, the sound a little wheezing, much to her

delight. "The most adorable, feisty little hobo, my love. Would you like to visit Amsterdam at Christmas with your luggage this time?"

"Maybe," she grumped, hiding a smile against him. "I don't know. Find out if there's a gala first."

"I can do that." His fingers began to toy with the end of her plait, instantly making her sleepy. "Would you go to said gala with me?"

She shrugged. "Maybe. If I can find a non-hobo outfit."

He tugged at her plait playfully. "Stubborn little scone. Gabi can find you something stunning in five seconds, and she'd love the assignment."

"The point is moot if there is no Christmas gala in Amsterdam to attend," Claire protested as she gave up her pretense and laughed.

"I am fairly certain that there will be a Christmas gala somewhere in Amsterdam," Jonny retorted dryly.

A knock at their compartment prevented Claire from flinging snark back in her boyfriend's face. At the same time, the train jerked forward, beginning its trek out of the station and on to Mallaig.

Alan's head appeared as the door opened, a hesitant smile on his face. "Any room at the inn, lovebirds?"

Claire reared back into Jonny's arms. "Don't use a biblical reference ever again, and if you call us lovebirds one more time, I'm having you committed somewhere with padded walls."

"Sounds like a lovely vacation, if you ask me," he mused, his mouth curving up.

"As long as we understand each other." Claire waved him in.

The hesitation was back. "It's . . . not just me."

Claire flicked her gaze to the compartment door window before biting her lip. An auburn-haired woman stood there, her face obscured by the frosted nature of the glass.

"Come on in," Claire insisted, gesturing to the other bench.

Alan glanced back with a nod and pushed the door open, moving to sit on the bench while Rose Ferguson, formerly McGregor, followed with a shy smile and a wave to Claire.

"Hi, Rose." Claire was barely able to restrain herself from clapping her hands. "It's so good to see you again."

Rose chuckled and tucked a curl behind her ear. "It's good to see you, too, Claire. I'm sure you remember my kiddos. They talked about you constantly after meeting you last night and started recounting their favorite moments of you from the show."

"Aww, that's sweet. It was fun." Claire smirked as Alan snorted. "What? It was!"

"I don't seem to remember it that way for much of the shoot," Alan mused, stroking his jaw.

Rolling her eyes, Claire put up a hand as though she could block Alan from her sight and from the conversation. "It *was* fun, except for this one judge who didn't like anything. Mood killer, that one."

Rose grinned, and Claire instantly got a vision of the young woman she must have been. The one with enough spunk, sunshine, and charm to make two friends fall for her without any effort at all. Claire saw the light that Alan could have used in his life, the laughter he had been missing, the support he must have craved, the friendship he had mourned.

All of it was there in the corners and dimples of this woman's smile, and in her bright, dancing eyes.

"So," Jonny drawled, dragging the word out knowingly, "how's it going?"

Claire whacked his knee with her knuckles, making him jump. "Behave!"

He mumbled incoherently as he rubbed at his knee.

Alan, however, cracked a wide smile and looked at Rose. "We've talked. I've apologized for being a reckless, selfish fool, and for staying silent and away all these years. I chatted with the kids again. They don't really know who I was to Rose yet, or at least not the whole picture, but we may get there. And now we're all going to spend some time together on the Isle of Skye once we finish the unveiling at Mallaig. See where this goes, and if . . . some things can truly be forgiven. And mended."

Claire all-out squealed and clapped this time. "Oh sugar, I love this. Love, love, super love this. All of this. Sorry, a good reunion and second chance thing is my jam and my clotted cream, and I am going to stop rambling and gushing now because someone is going to blush and it's probably me. I am so sorry." She slammed her palms to her cheeks as though the burning had already started.

"Way to keep your cool, love," Jonny deadpanned. "Really, no one would ever know how you really felt."

Rose laughed, the sound easy and warm, and clearly well-used. "It's fine. I'll admit to being a little giddy myself." She flicked her eyes to Alan shyly. "More than a little giddy, actually. It's been a long time, but some things . . . never really go away."

"For which I am eternally grateful," Alan murmured, his voice deeper and rougher than usual. There was no mistaking his feelings for the woman beside him; love was etched into every portion of his face. It lived and breathed in his eyes when they were on her. It was in the very air around him, somehow rosy and sweet without being in any way noticeable to the senses.

It just . . . was.

Claire's heart swooned and sighed in her chest, and she wanted something chocolatey to eat while she watched this unfold.

"A second chance is a miracle," Alan went on, as if Claire needed anything else to start keening like a fangirl. "One I don't intend to take for granted."

Rose met his eyes fully then, her smile showing absolutely no hesitation or reluctance as she reached out to take his hand. "Neither do I."

"Ohhh!" Claire clapped a hand to her mouth before she could turn any more pathetic than she already was, but this was just too good, and she was going to start crying in a second if they didn't stop being so cute.

"Crepes alive, Alan." Jonny whistled, shaking his head. "Do you need us to leave the compartment, or . . . ?"

That broke the romantic tension, filling the space with awkward laughter. Blushes crept into the cheeks of the couple across from them.

"You are the absolute worst, Jonny Ainsley," Claire whispered loudly, pushing against his arms, which refused to let her go. She shoved her elbow in his side for good measure.

"Yeah, but you love me," he murmured against her ear, which made goose bumps race across her skin.

She craned her neck, helpless to resist the sensations he raised. "Apparently," she managed in an unsteady voice.

He chuckled, kissed her ear, then cleared his throat and

leaned back against the seat more fully, dragging her back with him. "Not that we aren't delighted to hear these new developments, but you didn't exactly have to come and tell us, you know. Not our business, really."

Alan looked at Rose again, who nodded, before he leaned on the table and folded his arms atop it. "I realize this trip has had more plot twists than any of Claire's favorite novels and effectively ruined whatever you had planned for yourselves when we got to Mallaig."

"No lies detected," Claire quipped with a grin, lacing her fingers with Jonny's. "Go on."

"So I thought, and Rose agreed, that we should make it up to you." Alan tapped his fingers on the tabletop like he was prodding the proving of a dough. "How would you both like to come to the Isle of Skye with us? I'll arrange for your lodgings, and you can tour one of the jewels of Scotland and enjoy yourselves."

Claire felt Jonny go still behind her and seemed to freeze herself as she gaped at her mentor. "You want us to come with you?"

Alan scratched at his scruff. "Skye is gorgeous, and you can really get away from everything there. You'll love it, I promise."

Jonny shifted. "Not to be rude or anything, Alan, but, erm . . . You're not going to be with us the whole time, are you? That would definitely take away from a holiday together."

Alan's head fell back as he laughed heartily. "Kind of like I ruined a scenic train ride through the Highlands with business talk and baking assistance?"

"Like that, yeah."

He grinned at Jonny. "No, my lord, I will not be your tour guide or your chaperone or anything else. Maybe we'll meet up for lunch one of the days we're there, but I genuinely want the two of you to have a holiday together on Skye. Paid for, in fact. I don't know if you were going to get over there originally, or . . ."

"Yeah, but just a day trip," Claire told him, a bit overwhelmed by the offer. "We were going to stay in Mallaig for a few days."

"Always a solid option," Rose broke in eagerly. "Mallaig is stunning. You should see it for sure. But a retreat on Skye is unlike anything. You deserve a few days there to just be and not rush around like tourists. Please, let us do this."

Alan nudged Rose's elbow on the table. "Her aunt runs the bed-and-breakfast we want to send you to. We can refund you whatever might be lost with your arrangements in Mallaig but do come stay on Skye. It will be worth your trouble."

Claire looked up at Jonny and found his eyes on hers, wordlessly seeking.

He smiled down at her, that warm, delicious curve of his lips softening his gaze into something so adoring, so tender, so kneecap melting and resolve obliterating that it could only be love.

Love, which lit up her soul and set every conceivable part of her on fire.

Love *en flambe*, anyone?

"Sure," Claire whispered, hoping her eyes and her smile returned that love in equal measure for him. "It doesn't matter where we stay or what we do, so long as we are together."

Jonny dipped his chin, leaning close and nuzzling against her cheek before brushing his lips there in a path of tingles.

"Exactly," he rasped against her skin before raising his head and leaving her in a smoking, buzzing mess in his arms.

"Do we need to leave the compartment, or . . . ?" Alan asked in a suggestive tone.

Claire buried her face in Jonny's chest as she snickered, feeling his own laughter against her, rumbling through her ears.

"Ah, lass," Alan said, "that trifle won't be needed anymore, eh?"

Turning her head so she could see Alan while remaining nestled against the man she loved, Claire smiled. "I think trifle is multifunctional. Let me know when the next trifle is, and I'll be there." She scrunched up her nose. "Maybe not on a train next time."

"And not with dead bodies."

"Poor, dead Brian," they all said together. "And dearly departed Felicity."

Rose looked at them all in abject horror. "You three are absolutely terrible!"

"We know," they chorused before dissolving into laughter.

"Oh, and Claire," Alan managed around his continuing laughter. "Before I forget. We're still doing the cookbook together. We'll talk after this holiday is over, but I'm serious about it. And Jonny, if you're serious about the documentary at Blackfirth, I would be glad to host it."

"Did . . . did you just call him Jonny?" Claire squeaked, her tears of laughter turning to tears of something else.

Alan blinked at her. "Yes. Was I not supposed to?"

She shook her head quickly, holding up a hand. "No, no, it's fine. You just never have before, and that means . . . It's like you two are friends, and I just . . ." Her lower lip began trembling.

Alan's expression morphed into one of disbelief, and he looked at Jonny. "What in the name of marzipan is wrong with her?"

"If I ever find that out, mate, I'll let you know," Jonny told him in an unbothered tone. "I just kind of go with it."

"You called him 'mate'!" Claire wailed, hiccuping into her boyfriend's chest.

Alan coughed once. "Good crumpets. Time to go, she's lost it. We'll see you in Mallaig, kids."

"Bye now," Jonny called as he rubbed his hands over Claire soothingly, a suspicious quivering of his chest feeling a lot like his laughter.

But surely, he wouldn't laugh about his girlfriend crying, would he?

And why was she crying anyway? It was silly, even in her own brain.

Stress. It had to be stress from the entire case. And lack of sleep, because compartment sleeping was a terrible idea. Once she got some decent sleep at the bed-and-breakfast on the Isle of Skye, her sanity and emotional stability would almost certainly return.

It had been, without a doubt, the most complicated and confusing trip Claire had ever been on. Two deaths on a steam train in the middle of the Highlands while baking with her former baking show judge, getting stranded in a storm in those same Highlands, and finding out her boyfriend was wildly in love with her. Oh, and helping that baking show judge reconnect with his former flame, of course. It was enough to make anybody's head spin like an old-fashioned top.

But with that spinning had come a repositioning of a few things in Claire's life in a way that was going to open doors she had never expected. A future with Jonny. Career opportunities with Alan. A chance to see a part of the UK that she'd never planned on.

A budding sense of confidence and value she should have had long ago.

Sure, it had come with another close brush with death and crime, but that had to be a complete fluke and something that wouldn't be repeated again.

Right?

RECIPES

MARZIPAN

1 cup ground almonds
⅔ cup powdered sugar
⅔ cup superfine sugar
4 teaspoons pasteurized egg white
1 drop almond extract

1. Place ground almonds, powdered sugar, and caster sugar in a small bowl.
2. Add egg white and almond extract.
3. Mix well with hands until it comes together in a smooth paste.
4. Lightly dust countertop with powdered sugar.
5. Roll marzipan paste into desired shape.

CLASSIC SCOTTISH SHORTBREAD

1⅓ cups butter (2 sticks plus 6 tablespoons), softened
1 cup superfine sugar
¾ teaspoon salt
1 teaspoon vanilla
3⅓ cups all-purpose flour

1. Heat oven to 275 degrees F. and spray a 9x13-inch baking pan with nonstick cooking spray or line with parchment paper.
2. Cream butter in a stand mixer fitted with the paddle attachment until light and fluffy—about 3 minutes. Add sugar and continue to cream until the sugar is completely incorporated. Add salt and vanilla and stir to combine.
3. Add flour to butter mixture and mix until dough comes together and is just combined. Press dough into prepared pan or shape on a parchment-lined baking sheet.
4. Score dough lengthwise into 9 strips and then cut crosswise into 36, 3-inch strips. Use fork tines to create a perforated pattern. Sprinkle with sanding sugar if desired.
5. Bake 60 to 75 minutes or until an even, pale golden color. Cool completely. Cut with a serrated knife.

DUNDEE BISCUITS

1½ cups all-purpose flour
¼ cup sugar
¼ cup quick-cooking oats
¼ cup butter
⅓ cup milk
1 large egg, separated
Sliced almonds

1. Heat oven to 400 degrees F.
2. In a medium bowl, combine flour, sugar, and oats. Cut in butter with a pastry blender until mixture resembles coarse crumbs.
3. In a small bowl, combine milk and egg yolk; stir into flour mixture.
4. On a lightly floured surface, roll dough out into ½-inch thickness. Cut biscuits using a 1½-inch round cutter. Place on baking sheet.
5. Brush with lightly beaten egg white and top with sliced almonds.
6. Bake 10 to 12 minutes or until lightly browned.
7. Transfer to wire racks to cool.

FRENCH TOAST

Half a loaf of bread
2 eggs, slightly beaten
½ cup milk
1 tablespoon sugar
¼ teaspoon salt
¼ teaspoon cinnamon
Butter or shortening to fry

1. Cut bread into 1½-inch slices, then cut slices in half diagonally.
2. In a shallow dish, mix eggs, milk, sugar, salt, and cinnamon. Dip bread into mixture.
3. Melt butter in a large skillet, then fry coated bread until golden brown on both sides.
4. Serve hot with toppings of your choice (butter, jam, syrup, etc.).

RHUBARB AND BLUEBERRY COMPOTE

1 pound rhubarb (peeled and cut into small chunks)
2 tablespoons water
2 tablespoons sugar
12 ounces frozen blueberries

1. Heat oven to 325 degrees F.
2. Cover the bottom of a large pan with one layer of rhubarb chunks.
3. Sprinkle water and sugar over rhubarb, then cover with blueberries.
4. Bake uncovered 40 minutes or until rhubarb is soft.
5. Stir compote and serve warm.

SCOTTISH CHOCOLATE TRIFLE

- 6 to 8 Belgian chocolate chip shortbread rounds
- 1 (14.5-ounce) can black or sweet cherries, with juice, drained
- 1 (1.5-ounce) package raspberry or strawberry gelatin
- 1⅔ cups prepared chocolate custard
- 1⅔ cups heavy cream
- 1 (6-ounce) package chocolate shortbread
- Decorations: candied cherries, sprinkles, grated chocolate, or chocolate curls

1. Break chocolate chip shortbread rounds into chunks and place in the bottom of trifle bowl. Top with half of the cherries. (You can slice the cherries if desired.)
2. Mix gelatin according to package instructions and pour over the broken shortbread and cherries until just covered. Allow to set in the fridge.
3. Pour chocolate custard over trifle to create the next layer. Whip the cream in a bowl until stiff peaks form. Carefully dollop or pipe cream on the top of the trifle.
4. Top with chocolate shortbread and remaining cherries.
5. If desired, decorate with grated chocolate, chocolate curls, or sprinkles. Serve immediately or place in refrigerator to chill.

SCOTTISH POTATO SCONES

1 pound boiled russet potatoes (see note)
2 tablespoons butter, softened
½ teaspoon kosher salt or sea salt
½ cup plus 1 tablespoon all-purpose flour, sifted

1. Peel boiled potatoes, then rice them into a large bowl. (You can mash them if desired, but the scones won't be as light or as dry.)
2. Add butter and add salt to taste. Then lightly mix in the sifted flour until it forms a dough. Turn dough onto a floured workspace and gently fold over until smooth.
3. Divide dough into 4 or 5 equal portions, roll into balls, and then flatten balls into disk shapes. Each disk should be about ¼-inch thick. Prick dough with a fork, then cut into quarters or sixths, whichever you prefer.
4. Heat a pan or griddle to medium-high heat. Cook scones until brown on each side. Remove to a clean dish towel, then cover with the other half to cool.

NOTE: Potatoes should be cooked in salted water, preferably with the skin still on, and weighed after cooking.

SCOTTISH TABLET

5½ tablespoons milk
4 tablespoons butter
2 cups caster sugar
⅔ cup sweetened condensed milk

1. Combine milk and butter in a deep, heavy-bottomed saucepan over medium heat and bring to a boil.
2. Remove from heat and quickly add sugar. Return to heat and stir until sugar has completely dissolved. Add condensed milk.
3. Return to a boil then reduce to a simmer. Stir constantly to prevent the mixture from sticking to the bottom of the pan.
4. Cook 10 to 15 minutes, or until golden in color.
5. Remove from heat and beat with a spoon until mixture thickens. Pour into a square pan or shallow baking tin lined with parchment paper.
6. Allow to set. Cut into squares to serve.

ALAN GABLES'S TARTAN TARTE TATIN

2½ rhubarb stalks, washed with ends trimmed
3½ tablespoons unsalted butter
½ cup caster sugar
small handful blueberries (fresh or frozen)
1 teaspoon vanilla sugar
1 package ready rolled puff pastry

1. Using a tarte tatin pan (or an ovenproof frying pan) as a template, cut lengths of rhubarb to fit inside to make a layered, lattice formation.
2. Once all rhubarb has been placed in the dish, quickly invert it onto a board. Set aside.
3. Melt butter over low heat in the pan. Add sugar and gently heat, about 5 minutes, until bubbling and sugar starts to caramelize. (It might look lumpy and pale.) Tip dish and swirl occasionally; don't use a wooden spoon.
4. Remove dish from heat and top with latticed rhubarb. Return to gentle heat and cook for 10 minutes, or until sugar has dissolved.
5. Top with blueberries and sprinkle with vanilla sugar. Set aside.
6. Unroll pastry dough and prick all over with a fork. Then

drape the pastry over the dish. Trim dough around dish to leave a ¾-inch overhang.

7. Tuck and fold the pastry under itself and into the pan.
8. Place pan on the middle shelf of oven and bake at 400 degrees F. for 25 minutes, until risen and golden.
9. Once baked, run a knife around the outside of the pastry and quickly invert onto a serving dish.
10. Serve hot, topped with ice cream.

ACKNOWLEDGMENTS

Thanks to my sanity-slash-plotting team of Heather Moore, Jen Johnson, and Hannah Groesbeck for keeping me in line, saving the story at least three times, and never calling my ranting, questions, or random quotes stupid. At least not to my face.

Thanks go out to *The Great British Baking Show*, as always, for giving me endless inspiration and fodder for Claire Walker.

Thanks to Lisa Mangum, Heidi Gordon, and Callie Hansen for being the three-dimensional fine-toothed comb required to properly coif this project into the perfect style. (See what I did there?)

Thanks to the Steamtown Train Museum in Scranton, PA, for being amazing and giving me the book I didn't know I needed on dining by rail. It's like they had it waiting for me!

Thanks to the Jacobite Steam Train for inspiration and insight.

Massive thanks to David Tennant for existing.

RESOURCES

Deary, Terry. *Dangerous Days on the Victorian Railways*. Weidenfeld & Nicolson, 2014.

Nelson, Kay Shaw. *The Scottish-Irish Pub and Hearth Cookbook*. Hippocrene Books, Inc., 1999.

Porterfield, James D. *Dining by Rail: The History and the Recipes of America's Golden Age of Railroad Cuisine*. St. Martin's Griffin, 1998.

Worsley, Lucy. *A Very British Murder: The Story of a National Obsession*. BBC Books, 2013.

DISCUSSION QUESTIONS

1. What plot twists and turns did you enjoy in the story?
2. Were you able to figure out who the killer or culprit was? Were you fooled by any of the red herrings in the story? Why or why not?
3. Did Claire grow or change in this book? How about in the series overall?
4. Was there a character other than Claire who grew or changed? How did they transform through the course of the book?
5. How did the setting of the steam train add or change the mystery aspect?
6. What clues came together to help Claire and Jonny finally solve the mystery?
7. Which detail of Alan's past surprised you most?
8. How did the dynamics between characters change as the book went on? How did that affect the mystery?
9. What do you think might have happened on the trip if there hadn't been the sudden appearance of a dead body?
10. Was there a specific passage, chapter, or page that you liked best?

ABOUT THE AUTHOR

Photo by Sarah Schroering

REBECCA CONNOLLY is the author of more than two dozen novels. She calls herself a Midwest girl, having lived in Ohio and Indiana. She's always been a bookworm, and her grandma would send her books almost every month so she would never run out. Book Fairs were her carnival, and libraries are her happy place. She received a master's degree from West Virginia University.

Visit Rebecca online at
Facebook: Rebecca.Connolly.Books
X: @authorrconnolly
Instagram: @author.rebecca.connolly
Pinterest: @writerbecks

Historical Novels by

REBECCA CONNOLLY

A Brilliant Night of Stars and Ice

"The narrative emphasizes hope, heroism, and faith."—*Compass Book Ratings*

Under the Cover of Mercy

"[A] fast-paced novel of faith and bravery."—*Booklist*

Hidden Yellow Stars

"I was one of the hidden children saved by the Belgian resistance. . . . This magnificent book is not to be missed."—Professor Shaul Harel, author of *A Child without a Shadow*

A Carol for Mrs. Dickens

"Fans of Dickens and his era will enjoy this quick and inspirational read."—*Booklist*

Enjoy More

CLAIRE WALKER —MYSTERIES—

AN UNEXPECTED ROMANCE.
A HAUNTING MYSTERY. PASTRIES TO DIE FOR.

INCLUDES 6 RECIPES

"Connolly . . . opens this new ro-mystery series, crafting a slow, charming, sweet fall and filling the case with details of baking, estate living, and reality TV filming."—*LIBRARY JOURNAL*

"[The] sweet romance and the details of participating in a competitive baking show will please romance fans, those who enjoy watching *The Great British Baking Show*, and readers of baking-framed cozies like those by Joanne Fluke."—*BOOKLIST*